Praise for

The Geography of You and Me

"Smith captures the romantic sparks that fly in
unusual situations and the way love can build
even when circumstances keep people apart.
If you like your romances with a bit of European
adventure, some New York glamour, and a lot
of honest heart, this one's for you."
—E. LOCKHART,
author of *The Boyfriend List* and *We Were Liars*

"*The Geography of You and Me* is a true, tender
long-distance love story guaranteed to strike a
resonant chord in hopeful romantics everywhere."
—MEGAN McCAFFERTY,
author of the Jessica Darling series

"Jennifer E. Smith represents the absolute best in
YA writing, and readers will carry this poignant love
story in their hearts long after the last sentence is read."
—SUSANE COLASANTI,
author of *When It Happens*

★ "The meet-cute master behind *The Statistical
Probability of Love at First Sight* and *This Is What
Happy Looks Like* delivers her best book yet, a
straightforward, old-fashioned swoon-fest that, in
another time, would be a film starring Audrey Hepburn."
—*Booklist* (starred review)

THE GEOGRAPHY OF YOU AND ME

JENNIFER E. SMITH

poppy

Little, Brown and Company
New York Boston

Also by Jennifer E. Smith:
This Is What Happy Looks Like
The Statistical Probability of Love at First Sight
The Storm Makers
You Are Here
The Comeback Season

Poppy

Hachette Book Group
1290 Avenue of the Americas, New York, NY 10104
Visit us at lb-teens.com

Poppy is an imprint of Little, Brown and Company.
The Poppy name and logo are trademarks of Hachette Book Group, Inc.

The publisher is not responsible for websites (or their content) that are not owned by the publisher.

First Paperback Edition: March 2015
First published in hardcover in April 2014 by Little, Brown and Company

Library of Congress Cataloging-in-Publication Data

Smith, Jennifer E., 1980–
The geography of you and me / Jennifer E. Smith. — First edition.
pages cm
"Poppy."
Summary: "Sparks fly when sixteen-year-old Lucy Patterson and seventeen-year-old Owen Buckley meet on an elevator rendered useless by a New York City blackout. Soon after, the two teenagers leave the city, but as they travel farther away from each other geographically, they stay connected emotionally, in this story set over the course of one year"— Provided by publisher.
ISBN 978-0-316-25477-9 (hc) — ISBN 978-0-316-25474-8 (e-book) — ISBN 978-0-316-25476-2 (pb)
[1. Love—Fiction. 2. Voyages and travels—Fiction. 3. Social classes—Fiction. 4. Electric power failures—Fiction. 5. New York (N.Y.)—Fiction.] I. Title.
PZ7.S65141Geo 2014 [Fic]—dc23 2013022845

10 9 8 7 6 5 4 3
RRD-C
Printed in the United States of America

To Allison, Erika, Brian, Melissa, Meg, and Joe—
for being such great company
during the real blackout

and this is the wonder that's keeping the stars apart
i carry your heart(i carry it in my heart)
— e.e. cummings

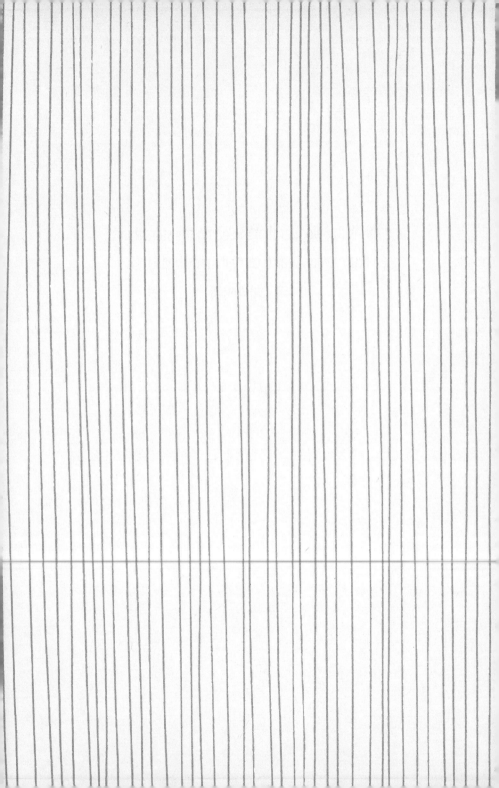

PART I

Here

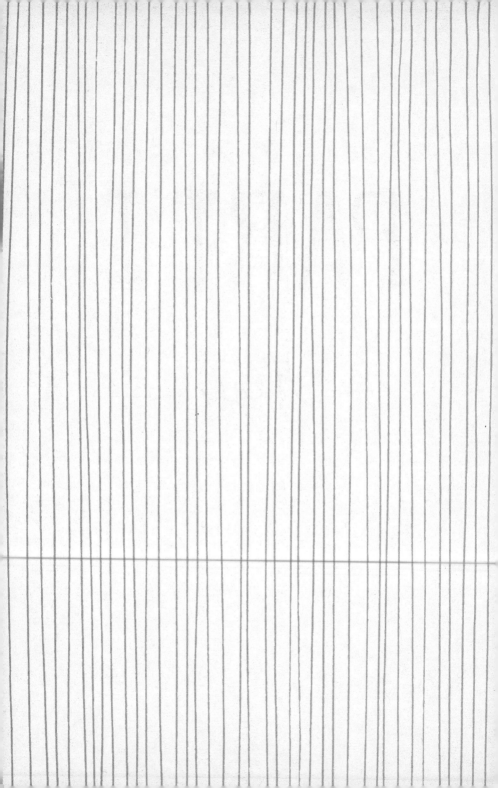

1

On the first day of September, the world went dark.

But from where she stood in the blackness, her back pressed against the brassy wall of an elevator, Lucy Patterson had no way of knowing the scope of it yet.

She couldn't have imagined, then, that it stretched beyond the building where she'd lived all her life, spilling out onto the streets, where the traffic lights had gone blank and the hum of the air conditioners had fallen quiet, leaving an eerie, pulsing silence. Already, there were people streaming out onto the long avenues that stretched the length of Manhattan, pushing their way toward home like salmon moving up a river. All over the island, car horns filled the air and windows were thrown open, and in thousands upon thousands of freezers, the ice cream began to melt.

The whole city had been snuffed out like a candle, but from the unlit cube of the elevator, Lucy couldn't possibly have known this.

Her first thought wasn't to worry about the violent jolt that had brought them up short between the tenth and eleventh floors, making the whole compartment rattle like a ride at an amusement park. And it wasn't a concern for their escape, because if there was anything that could be depended on in this world—far more, even, than her parents—it was the building's small army of doormen, who had never failed to greet her after school, or remind her to bring an umbrella when it was rainy, who were always happy to run upstairs and kill a spider or help unclog the shower drain.

Instead, what she felt was a kind of sinking regret over her rush to make this particular elevator, having dashed through the marble-floored lobby and caught the doors just before they could seal shut. If only she'd waited for the next one, she would've still been standing downstairs right now, speculating with George—who worked the afternoon shift—about the source of the power outage, rather than being stuck in this small square of space with someone she didn't even know.

The boy hadn't looked up when she'd slipped through the doors just a few minutes earlier, but instead kept his eyes trained on the burgundy carpet as they shut again with a bright *ding*. She'd stepped to the back of the elevator without acknowledging him, either, and in the silence that followed she could hear the low thump of music from his headphones as the back of his white-blond head bobbed, just slightly, his rhythm not quite there. She'd noticed him around before, but this was the first time it struck her how much he looked like a scarecrow, tall and lanky and loose-limbed, a study of lines and angles all jumbled together in the shape of a teenage boy.

He'd moved in just last month, and she'd watched that day from the coffee shop next door as he and his father carried a small collection of furniture back and forth across the gum-stained sidewalk. She'd known they were hiring a new superintendent, but she hadn't known he'd be bringing his son, too, much less a son who looked to be about her age. When she'd tried getting more information out of the doormen, all they could tell her was that they were somehow related to the building's owner.

She'd seen him a few more times after that—at the mailboxes or crossing the lobby or waiting for the bus—but even if she'd been the kind of girl inclined to walk up and introduce herself, there still was something vaguely unapproachable about him. Maybe it was the earbuds he always seemed to be wearing, or the fact that she'd never seen him talking to anyone before; maybe it was the way he slipped in and out of the building so quickly, like he was desperate not to be caught, or the faraway look in his eyes when she spotted him across the subway platform. Whatever the reason, it seemed to Lucy that the idea of ever meeting him—the idea of even saying something as harmless as *hello*—was unlikely for reasons she couldn't quite articulate.

When the elevator had wrenched to a stop, their eyes

met, and in spite of the situation, she'd found herself wondering—ridiculously—whether he recognized her, too. But then the lights above them had snapped off, and they were both left blinking into the darkness, the floor still quivering beneath them. There were a few metallic sounds from above—two loud clanks followed by a sharp bang— and then something seemed to settle, and except for the faint beat of his music, it was silent.

As her eyes adjusted, Lucy could see him frown and then pull out his earbuds. He glanced in her direction before turning to face the panel of buttons, jabbing at a few with his thumb. When they refused to light up, he finally hit the red emergency one, and they both cocked their heads, waiting for the speaker to crackle to life.

Nothing happened, so he punched it again, then once more. Finally, he lifted his shoulders in a shrug. "It must be the whole building," he said without turning around.

Lucy lowered her eyes, trying to avoid the little red arrow above the door, which was poised somewhere between the numbers 10 and 11. She was doing her best not to picture the empty elevator shaft below, or the thick cables stretched above them.

"I'm sure they're already working on it," she said, though she wasn't at all sure. She'd been in the elevator when it got stuck before, but never when the lights had gone out, too, and now her legs felt unsteady beneath her, her stomach wound tight. Already, the air seemed too warm and the space too small.

She cleared her throat. "George is just downstairs, so . . ."

The boy turned to face her, and though it was still too dark for details, she could see him more clearly with each minute that passed. She was reminded of a science experiment her class did in fifth grade, where the teacher dropped a mint into each of the students' cupped palms, then switched off the lights and told them to bite down hard, and a series of tiny sparks lit up the room. This was how he seemed to her now: his teeth flashing when he spoke, the whites of his eyes bright against the blackness.

"Yeah, but if it's the whole building, this could take a while," he said, slumping against the wall. "And my dad's not around this afternoon."

"My parents are away, too," Lucy told him, and she could just barely make out the expression on his face, an odd look in her direction.

"I meant 'cause he's the super," he said. "But he's just in Brooklyn, so I'm sure he'll be back soon."

"Do you think . . . ?" she began, then paused, not sure how to phrase the question. "Do you think we're okay till then?"

"I think we'll be fine," he said, his voice reassuring; then, with a hint of amusement, he added: "Unless, of course, you're afraid of the dark."

"I'm okay," she said, sliding down the wall until she was sitting on the floor, her elbows resting on her knees. She attempted a smile, which emerged a little wobbly. "I've heard monsters prefer closets to elevators."

"Then I think we're in the clear," he said, sitting down, too, his back against the opposite corner. He pulled his phone from his pocket, and in the dim light, his hair glowed green as he bent his head over it. "No signal."

"It's usually pretty iffy in here anyway," Lucy said, reaching for her own phone before realizing she'd left it upstairs. She'd only run down to grab the mail, a quick round-trip to the lobby and back, and now it felt like a particularly bad moment to find herself completely empty-handed.

"So," the boy said, tipping his head back against the wall. "Come here often?"

She laughed. "I've logged some time in this particular elevator, yes."

"I think you're about to log a lot more," he said with a rueful smile. "I'm Owen, by the way. I feel like we should probably introduce ourselves so I don't end up calling you Elevator Girl whenever I tell this story."

"I could live with Elevator Girl," she said. "But Lucy works, too. I'm in 24D."

He hesitated a moment, then gave a little shrug. "I'm in the basement."

"Right," she said, remembering too late, and she was glad for the darkness, which hid the flush in her cheeks. The building was like a small country in and of itself, and this was the currency; when you met someone new, you didn't just give your name but your apartment number as well, only she'd forgotten that the super always lived in the small two-bedroom flat in the basement, a floor Lucy had never visited.

"In case you're wondering why I'm on my way up," he said after a moment, "I've figured out that the view's a whole lot better on the roof."

"I thought nobody was allowed up there."

He slipped his phone back into his pocket and pulled out a single key, which he held flat in his palm. "That's true," he said with a broad grin. "Technically speaking."

"So you have friends in high places, huh?"

"Low places," he said, returning the key to his pocket. "The basement, remember?"

This time she laughed. "What's up there, anyway?"

"The sky."

"You've got keys to the sky?" she said, and he knitted his fingers together, lifting his arms above his head in a stretch.

"It's how I impress all the girls I meet in the elevator."

"Well, it's working," she said, amused. Watching him over the past weeks, studying him from afar, she'd imagined he must be shy and unapproachable. But sitting here now, the two of them grinning at each other through the dark, she realized she might have been wrong. He was funny and a little bit odd, which at the moment didn't seem like the worst kind of person to be stuck with.

"Although," she added, "I'd be a lot more impressed if you could get us out of here."

"I would, too," he said, shifting his gaze to scan the

ceiling. "You'd think the least they could do would be to pipe in some music."

"If they're planning to pipe in anything, hopefully it's some cool air."

"Yeah, this whole city's like a furnace," he said. "It doesn't feel like September."

"I know. Hard to believe school starts tomorrow."

"Yeah, for me, too," he said. "Assuming we ever get out of here."

"Where do you go?"

"Probably not the same place as you."

"Well, I hope not," she said with a grin. "Mine's all-girls."

"Then definitely not the same one," he said. "But I'd already figured that out anyway."

"What do you mean?"

"Well," he said, waving a hand around. "You live here."

Lucy raised her eyebrows. "In the elevator?"

"In this building," he said, making a face.

"So do you."

"I think it would be more accurate to say I live *under* this building," he joked. "But I'm betting you go to some fancy private school where everyone wears uniforms and worries about the difference between an A and an A-minus."

She swallowed hard, unsure what to say to this, since it was true.

Taking her silence as an admission, he tilted his head as if to say *I told you so*, then gave a little shrug. "I'm going to the one up on One Hundred and Twelfth that looks like a

8

bunker, where everyone goes through metal detectors and worries about the difference between a C and a C-minus."

"I'm sure it won't be that bad," she said, and his jaw went tight. Even through the darkness, something about his expression made him seem much older than he'd looked just moments before, bitter and cynical.

"The school or the city?"

"Doesn't sound like you're too thrilled about either."

He glanced down at his hands, which were resting in a knot on top of his knees. "It's just... this wasn't really the plan," he said. "But my dad got offered this job, and now here we are."

"It's not so bad," she told him. "Really. You'll find things to like about it."

He shook his head. "It's too crowded. You can't ever breathe here."

"I think you're confusing the city with this elevator."

The corner of his mouth twitched, but then he frowned again. "There are no open spaces."

"There's a whole park just a block away."

"You can't see the stars."

"There's always the planetarium," Lucy said, and in spite of himself, he laughed.

"Are you always so relentlessly optimistic, or just when it comes to New York?"

"I've lived here my whole life," she said with a shrug. "It's my home."

"Not mine."

"Doesn't mean you have to play the sullen-new-guy card."

"It's not a card," he said. "I *am* the sullen new guy."

"Just give it a chance, Bartleby."

"*Owen*," he said, looking indignant, and she laughed.

"I know," she told him. "But you're sounding just like Bartleby from the story." She waited to see if he knew it, then pushed on. "Herman Melville? Author of *Moby-Dick*?"

"I know *that*," he said. "Who's Bartleby?"

"A scrivener," she explained. "Sort of a clerk. But throughout the whole story, anytime someone asks him to do something, all he says is 'I would prefer not to.'"

He considered this a moment. "Yup," he said finally. "That pretty much sums up my feelings about New York."

Lucy nodded. "You would prefer not to," she said. "But that's just because it's new. Once you get to know it more, I have a feeling you'll like it here."

"Is this the part where you insist on taking me on a tour of the city, and we laugh and point at all the famous sights, and then I buy an *I♥NY* T-shirt and live happily ever after?"

"The T-shirt is optional," she told him.

For a long moment, they eyed each other across the cramped space, and then, finally, he shook his head. "Sorry," he said. "I know I'm being a jerk."

Lucy shrugged. "It's okay. We can just chalk it up to claustrophobia. Or lack of oxygen."

He smiled, but there was something strained about it. "It's just been a really tough summer. And I guess I'm not used to the idea of being here yet."

His eyes caught hers through the darkness, and the elevator felt suddenly smaller than it had just minutes before. Lucy thought of all the other times she'd been crammed in here over the years: with women in fur coats and men in expensive suits; with little white dogs on pink leashes and doormen wheeling heavy boxes on luggage carts. She'd once spilled an entire container of orange juice on the carpet right where Owen was sitting, which had made the whole place stink for days, and another time, when she was little, she'd drawn her name in green marker on the wall, much to her mother's dismay.

She'd read the last pages of her favorite books here, cried the whole way up and laughed the whole way down, made small talk to a thousand different neighbors on a thousand different days. She'd fought with her two older brothers, kicking and clawing, until the door *ding*ed open and they all walked out into the lobby like perfect angels. She'd ridden down to greet her dad when he arrived home from every single business trip, and had even once fallen asleep in the corner as she waited for her parents to come home from a charity auction.

And how many times had they all been stuffed in here together? Dad, with his newspaper folded under his arm, always standing near the door, ready to bolt; Mom, wearing a thin smile, seesawing between amusement and impatience with the rest of them; the twins, grinning as they elbowed each other; and Lucy, the youngest, tucked in a corner, always trailing behind the rest of the family like an ellipsis at the end of a sentence.

And now here she was, in a box that seemed too tiny to hold so many memories, with the walls pressing in all around her and nobody to come to her rescue. Her parents were in Paris, across the ocean, as usual, on the kind of trip that only ever included the two of them. And her brothers—the only friends she'd ever really had—were now thousands of miles away at college.

When they'd left a few weeks ago—Charlie heading off to Berkeley, and Ben to Stanford—Lucy couldn't help feeling suddenly orphaned. It wasn't unusual for her parents to be away; they'd always made a habit of flying off to snow-covered European cities or exotic tropical islands on their own. But being left behind was never that bad when there were three of them, and it was always her brothers— a twin pair of clowns, protectors, and friends—who had kept everything from unraveling.

Until now. She was used to being parentless, but being brotherless—and, thus, effectively friendless—was entirely new, and losing both of them at once seemed unfair. The whole family was now hopelessly scattered, and from where she sat—all alone in New York—Lucy felt it deeply just then, as if for the very first time: the bigness of the world, the sheer scope of it.

Across the elevator, Owen rested his head against the

wall. "It is what it is…" he murmured, letting the words trail off at the end.

"I hate that expression," Lucy said, a bit more forcefully than intended. "Nothing is what it is. Things are always changing. They can always get better."

He looked over, and she could see that he was smiling, even as he shook his head. "You're totally nuts," he said. "We're stuck in an elevator that's hot and stuffy and probably running out of air. We're hanging by a cord that's got to be smaller than my wrist. Your parents are who-knows-where, and my dad's in Coney Island. And if nobody's come to get us by now, there's a good chance they've forgotten about us entirely. So seriously, how are you still so positive?"

Lucy slid out from the wall, folding her legs beneath her and leaning forward. "How come your dad's in Coney Island?" she asked, ignoring his question.

"That's not the point."

"For the roller coasters?"

He shook his head.

"The hot dogs?" she asked. "The ocean?"

"Aren't you at all worried that nobody's coming to get us?"

"It won't help anything," she said. "Worrying."

"Exactly," he said. "It is what it is."

"Nope," she said. "Nothing is what it is."

"Fine," he said. "It's not what it isn't."

Lucy gave him a long look. "I have no idea what you're saying."

"Or maybe you'd just prefer not to," he said, sitting forward, and they both laughed. The darkness between them felt suddenly thin, flimsy as tissue paper and even less substantial. His eyes shone through the blackness as the silence stretched between them, and when he finally broke it, his voice was choked.

"He's in Coney Island because that's where he first met my mother," Owen said. "He bought flowers to leave on the boardwalk. He wanted to do it alone."

Lucy opened her mouth to say something—to ask a question, perhaps, or to tell him she was sorry, a word too small to mean anything at a moment like this—but the silence felt suddenly fragile, and she could think of nothing worthy enough to break it.

His head was bowed so that it was hard to make out the expression on his face, and she felt useless, sitting there without any idea of what to do. But then a faint knock sent her heart up into her throat, and his eyes found hers in the dark.

The sound came again, and Owen stood this time, moving over to the door and pressing his ear against it. He knocked back, and they both listened. Even from where she was still sitting numbly in the middle of the floor, Lucy could hear the muffled voices outside, followed by the scrape of something metal. After a moment, she rose to her feet, too, and without a word, without even looking at each other, they stood there like that, shoulder to shoulder, like a couple of astronauts at the end of a long journey, waiting for the doors to open so they could step out into a dazzling new world.

2

The day had started in darkness, too. Owen had woken before the sun was up, just as he had for the last forty-two mornings, jolted out of sleep with the feel of something heavy on his chest, a weight that pressed down on him like a fist. He blinked at the unfamiliar ceiling, the faint cracks that formed a sort of map, and the fly that roved between them, like an X marking some unknowable spot.

In the next room, he could hear the clink of a coffee mug, and he knew his father was awake, too. The last six weeks had turned them into bleary-eyed insomniacs, their days as shapeless as their nights, so that one simply bled into the other. It seemed fitting that they were living underground now; what better place for a couple of ghosts?

His new room was less than half the size of his old one back in their sprawling, sun-drenched house in rural Pennsylvania, where he'd been woken each morning by the sparrows just outside his window. Now he listened to a couple of pigeons squabbling against the narrow panel of glass near the ceiling, where the protective metal bars made what little light there was fall across his bed in slats.

When he emerged into the hallway that separated his room from his father's and led back to the small kitchen and sitting area, Owen caught a whiff of smoke, and the intensity of it, the vividness of the memory, almost took his knees out from under him. He followed the scent to the living room, where he found his father sitting on the couch, hunched over a mug that was serving as a make-shift ashtray.

"I didn't think you'd be up," he said, stabbing out the cigarette with a guilty expression. He ran a hand through his hair, which was just a shade or two darker than Owen's, then sat back and rubbed his eyes.

"I didn't really sleep," Owen admitted, collapsing into the rocking chair across from him. He closed his eyes and took a long, slow breath. He couldn't help himself; they'd been his mother's cigarettes, and the scent clenched at something inside him. There'd been eight left when she died, the crumpled pack recovered from the accident site and returned to them along with her wallet and keys and a few other odds and ends, and though his father didn't usually smoke, there were now only two. Owen could chart the bad days in this way, by the tang of smoke in the mornings, the best and worst reminder of her—one of the only ones left.

"You always hated these," Owen said, picking up the nearly empty box and spinning it in his hands. His father smiled faintly.

"Terrible habit—it drove me crazy," he agreed, then shook his head. "I always said it would kill her."

Owen lowered his eyes but couldn't help picturing the police report, the theory that she'd been distracted while trying to light a cigarette. They'd found the car upside down in a ditch. The box was ten yards away.

"I thought I'd head out to Brooklyn today," Dad said, a forced casualness to his voice, though Owen knew what that really meant, knew exactly where he was going and why. "You'll be okay on your own?"

Owen thought about asking whether he might like some company, but he already knew the answer. He'd seen the flowers resting on the kitchen counter last night, still wrapped in cellophane and already wilting. It was their anniversary; the day didn't belong to Owen. He ran a hand over the pack of cigarettes and nodded.

"We'll have dinner when I get back," Dad said, then picked up the ash-filled mug and padded out into the kitchen. "Anything you want."

"Great," Owen called, and then before he could think better of it, he slid one of the last two cigarettes from the pack, twirled it once between his fingers, and tucked it into his pocket without quite knowing why.

In the doorway to his bedroom, he paused. They'd been here nearly a month now, but the room was still lined with boxes, most of them half-open, the cardboard flaps spread out like wings. This sort of thing would have driven his mother crazy, and he couldn't help smiling as he imagined what her reaction would be, a mix of exasperation and bemusement. She'd always kept things so tidy at home, the counters sparkling and the floors dust-free, and Owen was suddenly glad she couldn't see this place, with its dim lighting and peeling paint, the mold that caked the spaces between bathroom tiles and the dingy appliances in the kitchen.

Whenever Owen used to complain about cleaning his room or having to do the dishes the moment they were finished with dinner, Mom would cuff him playfully on the head. "Our home is a reflection of who we are," she'd say in a singsong voice.

"Right," Owen would shoot back. "And I'm a mess."

"You are not," she'd say, laughing. "You're perfect."

"Perfectly messy," Dad would say.

She used to make them take off their shoes in the laundry room, only ever smoked on the back porch, and kept the pillows on the couches from getting too squashed. Dad said it had always been this way, from the moment they bought the house, the two of them thrilled to finally own something so permanent after so much time on the road.

They'd spent the previous two years traveling around in a rickety van with all their worldly belongings stashed in the back. They'd crisscrossed the country, camping out under the stars or sleeping curled in the backseat, whittling away their meager savings as they made their way across every state but Hawaii and Alaska. They'd seen Mount Rushmore and Grand Teton, driven up the California coast and gone fishing in the Florida Keys. They'd been to New Orleans and Bar Harbor and Mackinac Island, Charleston and Austin and Napa, traveling until they ran out of land, and money, too. It was only then that they returned to Pennsylvania, where they'd both grown up—and where it was time to grow up for a second time—and settled down for good.

But in spite of all the stories he'd heard of their years on the road, Owen had never been much of anywhere. His parents seemed to have gotten it out of their system by the time he came along, and they were content to be in one place. They had a house with a porch and a yard with an apple tree; there was a swingset around the side and a neighboring field of grazing horses. They had a round kitchen table just big enough for three, a door the perfect size for a wreath at Christmastime, and enough nooks and crannies for long and drawn-out games of hide-and-seek. There was nowhere else they ever wanted to be.

Until now.

Alone in his bedroom, Owen heard the front door fall shut, then waited a few minutes before grabbing his phone and wallet and heading out, too, jogging up the stairs from the basement to the lobby, which he passed through quickly, his head bent. It wasn't that he had anything against the residents of the building, but he didn't belong here, and neither did his father. Owen was just waiting for him to realize that, too.

All morning, he walked. This was his last day of freedom,

the last day he wouldn't be bound to show up for classes in a school that wasn't his, and he found himself pacing like a restless animal along the edge of the Hudson River. He left his earbuds on, drowning out the sounds of the city, and he kept moving in spite of the heat. For lunch, he bought a hot dog from a street vendor, then cut over to Central Park, where he sat watching the tourists with their cameras and their maps and their round, shiny eyes. He followed their gazes, trying his best to see what they saw, but all he could see were more people.

It wasn't until late afternoon that he made his way back to the corner of Seventy-Second and Broadway, to the ornate stone building that was now his home. He paused just inside the lobby, reluctant to go back downstairs, where there was nothing to do but sit alone for the next few hours and wait for his dad to return. Instead, he felt for the key in the pocket of his shorts.

He'd taken the master set from his dad's dresser during their first week here, a wildly uncharacteristic move for him. Owen had always been overly cautious, not prone to breaking rules, but after only a few days here, the claustrophobic feel of the place had become too much to take, and he found a locksmith to make a copy of the key that unlocked the door to the roof—the only peaceful place, it seemed, in this entire city.

As he stepped into the elevator, he was already imagining the vast, windblown quiet forty-two stories above, his music loud in his ears and his thoughts far away. He punched the button and stood waiting for the ground to lift beneath his feet, still lost in thought, and he hadn't even bothered to look up when someone caught the doors just before they could close.

But now, less than an hour later, he felt suddenly *too* aware of her, a presence beside him as prickly as the heat. As they listened to the sounds on the other side of the door, he glanced down, noticing that her right foot was only inches away from his left one, and he curled his toes and rocked back on his heels and looked away again. He realized he was holding his breath, and he wondered if she was, too.

Just before the door was pried open, he narrowed his eyes, expecting to be greeted by a sudden brightness. But instead, the faces peering down at them from the eleventh floor—which started halfway up the length of the elevator, a thick slab of concrete that bisected the doors—were mostly lost in shadows, and the only light came from a couple of flashlights, which were being pointed directly in their faces, causing them both to blink.

"Hi," Lucy said brightly, greeting them as if this was all very ordinary, as if they always met in this way: the doorman above them on his hands and knees, his face pale and moonlike in the dark, and beside him, a handyman sitting back on his heels and wiping at his forehead with a bandanna.

"You guys okay?" George asked, passing down a water bottle, which Owen grabbed from him and then handed to Lucy. She nodded as she untwisted the cap and took a long swig.

"It's a little toasty," she said, giving the bottle back to Owen. "But we're fine. Is the whole building out?"

The handyman snorted. "The whole city."

Owen and Lucy exchanged a look. "Seriously?" she asked, her eyes widening. "That can happen?"

"Apparently," George said. "It's chaos out there."

"Traffic lights and everything?" Owen asked, and the older man nodded, then clapped his hands, all business.

"Okay," he said. "Let's get you guys out of here."

Lucy went first, and when Owen tried to help her, she waved him away, hoisting herself up over the lip of the floor, then rising to her feet and brushing off her white dress. Owen followed much less gracefully, flopping onto the ledge like a fish run aground before hopping up. There was an emergency light at the far end of the hallway that cast a reddish glow, and it was a little bit cooler up there but not much; his palms were still sweaty and his T-shirt was still glued to his back.

"So when do they think we'll have power again?" he asked, trying to keep the nervous edge out of his voice. He couldn't help thinking of his father. No electricity meant no subways. No subways meant there was no way he could get back anytime soon. And in a situation like this, his absence would not go unnoticed.

"No idea," George said, stooping to help pack up the tools. The clanging metal rang out along the walls, interrupting the eerie silence. "The phone lines are all jammed and the Internet's down, too."

"No cell-phone reception, either," the handyman added. "It's impossible to get any kind of information."

"I heard it's the whole East Coast," George said. "That a power plant in Canada got struck by lightning."

The handyman rolled his eyes. "And I heard it was an alien invasion."

"I'm just telling you what they were saying on the radio," George muttered, standing up again. He put a hand on Lucy's shoulder, then looked from her to Owen. "So you guys are okay?"

They both nodded.

"Good," he said. "I've got to go door-to-door and make sure everyone's all right. You both have flashlights?"

"Yup," Lucy said. "Upstairs."

"Have you heard from my dad at all?" Owen asked as casually as he could manage. "He's—"

"Yeah, I know," George said. "He picked one hell of a day to beg off. I haven't heard from him, but I wouldn't be worried. Nobody's heard from anyone."

"He had to go out to Brooklyn," Owen said, trying to think of some kind of excuse, an explanation to follow this, but the handyman—who had been walking toward the stairwell—paused and turned back around.

"Subways are down," he said. "It's gonna be a long walk over the bridge...."

Owen felt another pang of anxiety, though he was no

longer sure if it was for the fact that his father wasn't here to help or the idea that he might already be crossing the length of Brooklyn to get home. It seemed far more likely that he was sitting on the darkened boardwalk, lost in memories and oblivious to the whims of the electrical grid. Even so, there was something odd about being separated like this, on opposite ends of the same city, a whole network of roads and rivers, bridges and trains between them, but still unable to make it across the miles.

"You two be careful," George called back to them as he stepped into the stairwell behind the handyman. "I'll be around if you need anything."

The heavy door slammed shut behind them, and Lucy and Owen were left alone in the quiet hallway. Their gazes both landed on the gaping black hole of the empty elevator, and Lucy gave a little shrug.

"I kind of thought it'd be cooler on the outside," she said, reaching back to twist her long brown hair into a loose ponytail, which quickly unraveled again.

Owen nodded. "And maybe a little brighter."

"Well, at least we have our freedom," she joked, and this made him smile.

"Right," he said. "You know what they say about the inside of a cell."

"What?"

He shrugged. "That it can drive a person mad."

"I think that's solitary confinement."

"Oh," he said. "I guess ours wasn't solitary."

"No," she said, shaking her head. "It definitely wasn't."

He leaned against the wall near the open elevator. "So what now?"

"I don't know," she said, glancing at her watch. "My parents are in Europe, and it's already late there. I'm sure they're out to dinner or at a party or something. They probably have no idea this is even happening...."

"I'm sure they do," Owen said. "If it's the whole city, this has got to be pretty big news. They let you stay home by yourself?"

"They travel way too much to worry about always finding someone," she explained. "It was usually me and my brothers, anyway."

"And now?"

"Just me," she said. "But it's not like I'm not old enough to be left alone."

"How old is that?"

"Almost seventeen."

"So sixteen," he said with a grin, and she rolled her eyes.

"Quite the math whiz. Why, how old are you?"

"Actually seventeen."

"So you're gonna be a senior?"

"If we have school tomorrow," he said, glancing around. "Which I sort of doubt."

"I'm sure it'll be fixed by then. How hard is it to flip a power switch?"

He laughed. "Quite the science whiz."

"Funny," she said, but the word was hollow. Her smile

fell as she regarded him, and Owen found himself straightening under her gaze.

"What?"

"You'll be okay on your own?"

"You think *I* need a babysitter?" he asked, but the joke landed heavily between them. He lifted his chin. "I'll be fine," he said. "And I'm sure my dad'll find a way to get back here soon. He's probably worried about the building."

"He's probably worried about *you*," Lucy said, and something tightened in Owen's chest, though he wasn't sure why. "Just be careful, okay?"

He nodded. "I will."

"If you need a flashlight, I think we might have extras."

"I'm fine," he said as they started walking down the hall. "But thanks."

"It's only gonna get darker," she warned him, waving a hand around. "You'll need—"

"I'm fine," he said again.

When he opened the door to the stairwell, the sealed-in heat came at them in a fog of stale air. From somewhere above, they could hear muddled voices, and then the slamming of a door, the sound of it crashing down flight after flight until it reached them.

They stepped inside, where the little white emergency lights along the edges of the stairs gave off a faint glow, and for the first time, Owen could see her face clearly: the freckles scattered across the bridge of her nose, and the deep brown of her eyes, so dark they almost looked black. She climbed the first step so that she was even with him, their eyes level, and they stood there for a long moment without saying anything. Above her, there was the seemingly endless spiral of stairs leading up to the twenty-fourth floor. Behind him, there was the long descent to his empty apartment in the basement.

"Well," she said eventually, her eyes shining in the reflection of the lights. "Thanks for making the time pass, Elevator Boy."

"Yeah," he said. "We'll have to do it again the next time there's a massive citywide blackout."

"Deal," she said, then turned to begin walking, her sandals loud against the concrete steps. Owen watched her go; her white sundress made her look like a ghost, like something out of a dream, and he waited until she'd disappeared around the corner before he began to walk himself, moving slowly from one step to the next.

Two flights down, he paused to listen to her footsteps above him, which were growing fainter as she climbed away, and he thought again of the dismal apartment below, and the chaotic city outside, the sense of possibility in a night like this, where everything was new and unwritten, the whole world gone dark like some great and terrible magic trick. He stood very still, one hand on the railing, breathing in the warm air and listening, and then, before he could think better of it, he spun around and went flying back up the stairs.

He made it only three flights before he had to pause, breathing hard, and when he lifted his head again, she was there on the landing, peering down at him.

"What's wrong?" she asked. "Are you okay?"

"I'm fine," he said, smiling up at her. "I just changed my mind about the flashlight."

Upstairs, they spilled out into the darkened hallway—identical to the one thirteen floors below—both out of breath. Lucy had taken her sandals off somewhere around the eighteenth floor, and she let them dangle now from one hand as she used the other to feel her way along the wall, aware of Owen a few paces behind her, his footsteps light on the carpet. At the door to 24D, she fished the keys from the pocket of her dress, then fumbled with the lock as he leaned against the wall beside her, squinting.

"It's not easy in the dark," he said, but she didn't respond. She'd been opening this door for nearly sixteen years. She knew the incremental movements by heart: the way the key stuck so that you had to jiggle it to the left and the noisy click of the bolt as it finally turned. She could have done this blindfolded. She could have done it in her sleep.

It wasn't the dark. It was him.

As the lock finally gave and the door swung open, Lucy

hesitated. She realized she'd never had a boy in her apartment before. At least not like this. Never alone. And certainly never in the dark.

There had always been friends of her brothers around, cleaning out the refrigerator and playing music so loud it thumped through the walls. But Lucy's school was all-girls, so she'd never really had any guy friends of her own.

Of course, she'd never really had very many girl friends, either.

Last year, while making a rare and mandatory appearance as a chaperone at the winter formal, her mother had noticed that after a few obligatory dances, Lucy had disappeared into the hallway with a book. After that, she'd suddenly started paying attention to her daughter's lack of a social life. If Lucy wasn't hanging out with her brothers, she was usually just wandering the city by herself, neither of which apparently was a productive use of her time. And so she'd begrudgingly agreed to attend a basketball game, where a junior named Bernie, who went to their brother school, approached her at the snack booth to say that he liked her skirt. It was the exact same plaid skirt that every single other girl at the game was wearing, but he seemed nice enough, and she had nobody else to sit with, so she let him buy her popcorn.

They started meeting behind the Metropolitan Museum of Art every day after school, doing their homework together just long enough to maintain the illusion that they weren't only there to make out. But never once had he invited her over to his Fifth Avenue apartment, and never once had she considered inviting him back to hers. Theirs was a relationship built on neutral ground and impartial geography: park benches and stone fountains and picnic blankets. Bringing him into her home would have given the relationship a weight that it was never meant to bear, and it seemed to Lucy that there was no faster way to sink something. Especially something that would so easily sink on its own just two short months later, when Bernie met a different girl in a different plaid skirt at a different game.

But this was a unique situation, an emergency of sorts, and that changed everything. An ordinary afternoon had given way to an evening that felt hazy around the edges, tinged with recklessness and a kind of unfamiliar abandon. This was the first time she'd been left entirely on her own—no parents, no brothers, nobody at all. And now here she was, swinging the door wide open, a boy she barely knew waiting at her back.

From the front hallway, she could see all the way down past the kitchen and into the living room, where at this time of dusk, the windows were usually beginning to reflect the many lights of the city, a seemingly endless grid of yellow squares. But now it was empty, just a pale blue rectangle at the end of a long black corridor.

Behind her, Owen cleared his throat. He was still standing just outside the door, apparently unsure whether or not he was being invited inside.

"So did you want to just grab the flashlight for me, or…?"

"No," Lucy said, stepping aside. "Come on in."

The fading light from the windows didn't reach this far back into the apartment, so Lucy kept her hands outstretched as she moved tentatively into the kitchen. Owen had wandered into the living room, and she heard a scrape followed by a thud as he tripped over something.

"I'm okay," he called out cheerfully.

"I'm so relieved," she yelled back as she reached the pantry. On the bottom shelf, she found the enormous blue crate that held all the misfit items that never seemed to belong anywhere else. It was the one disorganized place in the whole apartment, a treasure trove of broken umbrellas and sunglasses and an assortment of pens from various hotels around the world. She rummaged through the debris until she found a single flashlight, and when she clicked it on, she was glad to discover that it worked.

Stepping out of the pantry, she swung the beam around the kitchen so that the light made shapes that lingered across the backs of her eyelids. In the living room, she found Owen standing at the window, his hands braced on the sill. When he twisted to face her, the cone of light fell directly across his face, and she lowered it again as he blinked.

"It's so strange out there," he said, jabbing his thumb behind him. "It seems so quiet without all the lights."

Lucy moved to the window beside him, her nose inches from the glass. The sky was a deepening blue, and the checkerboard of windows, which were usually filled with glowing scenes of family dinners and flickering TVs, looked hunched and forsaken tonight. From where Lucy and Owen were standing, they could see dozens of buildings stretched across Seventy-Second Street, all of them made up of hundreds of windows, and behind them, thousands of people hidden deep within the folds of their own separate homes. It always made Lucy feel small, standing here on the edge of something so vast, but tonight was the first time it felt a little bit lonely, too, and she was suddenly grateful for Owen's company.

"There was only one flashlight," she said, and he glanced down at it. She waited for him to make some kind of joke about being afraid of the dark, and when he didn't, when he simply remained silent, she added, "So maybe we should just stick together."

He turned back to the window and nodded. "Okay," he agreed. "But it's already getting warm in here. Want to go for a walk before it's too dark?"

"Outside?"

"Well, this *is* a pretty big apartment, but..."

"I just meant...I mean, do you think it's safe?"

"This is your city," he said with a smile. "You tell me."

"I guess it's probably fine," she said. "And it wouldn't hurt to pick up some supplies."

"Supplies?"

"Yeah, like water and stuff. I don't know. Isn't that what you're supposed to do in these types of situations?"

He dug around in his pocket and pulled out a few crumpled bills. "You can get as much water as you'd like," he said. "I think a night like this calls for some ice cream."

She rolled her eyes. "It'll just melt," she said, but he was undeterred.

"All the more reason to rescue it from such a sad fate..."

Before they left, they checked their cell phones, but neither had any reception, and Owen's was nearly out of battery. Lucy used what little power was left on her laptop, which had been sitting unplugged on her bed all day, to try to send an e-mail to her parents, telling them everything was fine, but there was no connection. Not that it probably mattered anyway; it was six hours later there, and if they weren't still at some stuffy party, they were likely asleep.

Downstairs, Lucy and Owen burst out of the blazing heat of the stairwell into the lobby, which was nearly as humid. They almost ran over a beleaguered-looking nanny, who was paused with one hand on a stroller, steeling herself for the climb. A few other people were milling around near the mailroom, but it seemed as if most of the residents were either upstairs in their apartments or else still trying to find their way back home.

The handyman who'd helped rescue them was sitting at the front desk, his arm propped on his toolbox as he listened to a handheld radio, and he waved when he saw them. "How were the stairs?"

"Better than the elevator," Owen said. "Any news?"

"No power until tomorrow at the earliest," he reported,

his mustache twitching. "They're saying it goes all the way down to Delaware and all the way up into Canada." He paused for a moment, then shook his head. "It must be quite a sight from up in space."

"We're going to pick up a few things," Lucy said. "You need anything?"

The man was in the middle of requesting a six-pack of beer—which Lucy was about to tell him would be tricky to procure, given that they were both well under twenty-one—when Owen tapped her on the arm.

"Look," he said, and she turned toward the front doors of the building, which faced out across Broadway. But instead of the usual herds of yellow taxis and black town cars and long city buses, she was shocked to see that the entire road was choked with people, the whole massive crowd moving uptown with a kind of plodding resolve.

Together, she and Owen stood in the doorway, their eyes wide as they watched the sea of bodies move past. Many of them were barefoot, their shoes tucked like footballs under their arms, and others had wrapped their shirts around their heads to try to keep cool. They wore suits and ties and dresses, and they carried briefcases and laptops, all of them taking part in the world's strangest commute. There were no traffic lights to guide them, and no police in sight, though somewhere up the road, Lucy could see the faint throb of blue and red, unnaturally bright in the darkening sky.

"This is unbelievable," she breathed, shaking her head.

On the corner, one of the bars was jammed with people, many of them spilling out onto the sidewalks. Whether they'd given up on their way home or simply wandered outside to join in the camaraderie, there was a festive air to the gathering. High above them, perched on their balconies, people were using magazines for fans as they watched the scene unfolding below. Others hung out of their open windows, the apartments all dark behind them. It was like the whole city had been turned inside out.

"Come on," Owen said, and she followed him out to the corner, where a guy wearing a dusty construction vest was helping a man in a pin-striped suit direct traffic, holding up the throngs of people to let a few cars slip through the intersection, then motioning for those on foot to continue their long treks homeward.

Lucy and Owen kept to the sidewalk, and when they reached the little bodega on Seventy-Fourth Street, which sold everything from cans of soda and toilet paper to dog food and lottery tickets, she grabbed his arm and dragged him inside. There were only a few bottles of water left, and they lined them up in a row on the counter before going back to grab a lighter and some candles, plus extra batteries for the flashlight.

When Lucy pushed some money toward the man behind the register, he gave her what seemed like an unlikely amount of change.

"I don't think..." she began, but he flashed her a toothy smile.

"Blackout discount," he said matter-of-factly.

"Who knew?" Owen said with a laugh. "Think that applies to any of the ice-cream shops, too?"

The man nodded as he packed their items into two plastic bags. "I heard the place on Seventy-Seventh is giving it away for free. It's all melting anyhow."

Owen turned to Lucy. "I think I like this city better in the dark."

Outside, they stood for a moment with the plastic bags hooked around their fingers. The last streaks of pink had been erased from the sky over the Hudson, and an inky black had settled over the street. As they walked uptown to join the line for free ice cream, there was still a feeling of celebration to the evening. The price of beer at the bar next door was plummeting as the kegs grew warmer, and on the other side of Broadway, a restaurant was serving a makeshift dinner by candlelight. A few kids ran past with purple glow sticks, and two mounted policemen steered their wary-eyed horses through the crowds, surveying the scene from above.

As the line inched forward, Lucy glanced over at Owen, who was looking around with a dazed expression.

"You'd think there'd be looting or something," he said. "In a place like this, you'd think it'd be mayhem. But it's just a big party."

"I told you it's not so bad here," Lucy said. "Give it a chance."

"Okay," he said with a little smile. "As long as you promise every night will be like this."

"What," she asked, "dark?"

"That's the thing," he said, looking up. "It's not that dark. Not really."

She followed his gaze to where the sliver of moon hung above the shadowy outline of the buildings, a thin curve of white against a navy sky that was dotted with stars. In all her years here, Lucy had never seen anything like it: a million points of light, all of them usually drowned out by the brilliant electricity of the city, the billboards and streetlights, the lasers and sirens, the fluorescent lamps and the neon bulbs, and the great white noise of it all, which left no room for anything else to break through.

But tonight, the world had gone quiet. There was nothing but the black canopy of the sky and the wash of stars above, burning so bright that Lucy found she couldn't look away.

"He was right," she murmured. "This must be quite a sight from up in space."

Owen didn't answer for a moment, and when he finally did, his voice was hushed. "I don't know," he said. "I think it's even better from down here."

By the time they made it back up all the flights of stairs—red-faced and panting and holding their sides—the apartment was like an oven, and there was nothing to do but collapse onto the cool tiles of the kitchen floor. There was no cure for this kind of heat, no fans and no air-conditioning and no breeze from the window, and even the ceramic tiles grew warm beneath them as they lay there in silence, still breathing hard.

Eventually, Owen sat up and reached for one of the water bottles, handing another over to Lucy, who was sprawled out beside the refrigerator, her white dress pooled all around her. She wiped at her forehead with the back of her hand, then propped herself up on her elbows to take a sip.

"That's it," she said when she was done.

Owen lay back again. "What is?"

"I'm never going downstairs again."

"Until the elevator's fixed…"

"Maybe not even then," she said. "That elevator and I

go way back, but after tonight, I'm not sure I can ever trust it again."

"Poor old elevator."

"Poor old me."

There was a ceiling fan above them, and Owen stared at the outline of the blades through the dark for so long that he could almost imagine it spinning. His whole body was spiky with heat, even his eyelids, which felt heavy and thick. He reached absently for the flashlight on the floor between them, then clicked it on, shining it around the kitchen like a spotlight: circling the sink and zigzagging across the cabinets.

"There's pretty much nothing in there. My mom doesn't cook," Lucy said, following the beam with her gaze. "None of us really do."

"That's too bad," he said. "You've got a great kitchen."

"Do you?"

"Have a great kitchen?"

"No," she said, lying back again so that their heads were inches apart, their bodies fanned out in opposite directions. "Do you cook?"

"Yup," he said. "And I clean, too. I'm a regular Renaissance man."

He flicked the light over the dishwasher, then the oven, and finally up to the refrigerator, which was covered with postcards, each one pinned by a brightly colored magnet. He sat up to take a closer look, focusing the light so he could read the names scrawled over them: Florence, Cape Town, Prague, Barcelona, Cannes, Saint Petersburg.

"Wow," he said. "Have you been to all these places?"

Lucy laughed. "Do you think I'm sending myself postcards?"

"No," he said, his face burning. "I just figured—"

"They're from my parents. They go to amazing places, and I get a piece of cardboard," she explained with a shrug. "It's kind of a tradition. They always bring one of my brothers a magnet and the other a snow globe. Apparently I asked for a postcard once when I was little, and I guess it sort of stuck."

He scooted closer to the refrigerator, holding the flashlight in his fist. "So where are they now?"

"Paris," she said. "They go there all the time."

"They don't ever take you?" he asked without turning around, and her voice behind him was quiet when she answered.

"No."

"Oh," he said, sitting back on his heels. "Well, who needs Paris when you live in New York, right?"

This made her smile. "I guess so," she said, then pointed at the fridge. "I haven't gotten one from this trip yet. That's actually why I was downstairs before. I was checking the mail."

There was a note of sadness in the words, and Owen cast around for something to say in response, something to fill the quiet of the kitchen. He glanced again at the mosaic of photographs. "Postcards are overrated anyway."

"Oh yeah?" she asked, raising her eyebrows.

"Yeah, I mean, what's the worst thing you can say to someone who isn't on some beautiful beach with you?"

Lucy shrugged.

" 'Wish you were here.' " He rapped his knuckles against a scene from Greece, which was hanging near the bottom. "I mean, come on. If they really wished you were there, they'd have invited you in the first place, right? It's kind of mean, if you really think about it. It should say: 'Greece: Where nobody's all that upset you're not here.' "

There was a long pause, and as the silence lengthened, he realized his mistake. He'd only been joking, but it had come out sounding harsh and somehow too specific, and he was gripped now with a sudden fear that he'd managed to make things worse.

But to his relief, she began to laugh. " 'Rome: Where it's so beautiful, we've pretty much forgotten about you,' " she said, sitting up. Her arms were looped around her bare legs, and her mouth was twisted with the humor of it. " 'Sydney: Where you're really missing out.' "

"Exactly," Owen said. "That's a lot more honest anyway."

"I guess you're right," she said, her face growing serious again.

"But I bet your parents really do wish you were there."

"Yeah," she said, but her voice was hollow. "I bet."

He switched off the flashlight, then pivoted so that his

back was against the refrigerator, the postcards fluttering above his head, and he thought of the notes his mother used to leave for him around the house, little yellow Post-its scrawled with blue ink, reminders to clean his room or to heat up the casserole she'd made. Sometimes she left them before running out to do errands, or going to dinner with Dad, but other times she wouldn't be far, just out in the backyard, weeding the garden. It didn't matter whether she'd see him again in two minutes or two hours or two days; the notes always ended the same way: *Thinking of you.*

"I have an idea," he said, and Lucy let her head fall to one side so she could look at him, her eyes dark and searching. He reached into his pocket and held out the keys to the roof. "It'll be a hike," he told her. "But I think it'll be worth it."

They loaded a backpack with water and snacks, candles and a blanket, and then Owen led them back toward the stairwell, flashlight held before him like a sword. The hallway was still quiet, and he wondered what he'd be doing now if his father were home. He would probably just be waiting while his father went door-to-door through the building, pretending as best he could at this new role of caretaker, as Owen sat alone in the basement, pretending not to notice that his dad could hardly even take care of himself these days.

They started up the stairs at a brisk pace, but their footsteps soon slowed, and by the time they passed the thirty-fifth floor, they were walking side by side, hauling themselves up on opposite railings, one sweaty hand at a time. When they finally reached the metal door at the top, Owen gave it a push, but it didn't budge.

"A lot of the time, they leave it unlocked," he explained. "Which is why I don't feel too bad about the key."

"Aha," she said. "So you're not as much of a badass as you would first appear."

He laughed. "I'm not a badass at all. I'm just a guy with a key."

When he unlocked the door, they stumbled out onto the darkened roof, their eyes focused on the ground as they picked their way across the tar-covered surface.

"Over there," Owen said, pointing at the southwest corner, and Lucy walked over to the ledge that ran along the perimeter, where she stood looking out.

"Wow," she breathed, rising onto her tiptoes. Owen dropped the backpack before joining her, positioning himself a few inches away. The wind lifted her hair from her shoulders, and he caught the scent of something sweet; it smelled like flowers, like springtime, and it made him a little dizzy.

They were quiet as they took in the unfamiliar view, the island that was usually lit up like a Christmas tree now nothing but shadows. The skyscrapers were silhouettes against a sky the color of a bruise, and only the spotlight from a single helicopter swung back and forth like a pendulum as it drifted across the skyline.

Together, they leaned against the granite wall, invisible

souls in an invisible city, peering down over forty-two stories of sheer height and breathless altitude.

"I can't believe I've never been up here," she murmured without taking her eyes off the ghostly buildings. "I always say the best way to see the city is from the ground up, but this place is amazing. It's—"

"A million miles above the rest of the world," he said, shifting to face her more fully.

"A million miles *away* from the world," she said. "Which is even better."

"You're definitely living in the wrong city, then."

"Not really," she said, shaking her head. "There are so many ways to be alone here, even when you're surrounded by this many people."

Owen frowned. "Sounds lonely."

She turned to him with a smile, but there was something steely about it. "There's a difference between loneliness and solitude."

He was about to say more but was reminded of the postcards just downstairs, dozens of monuments to one or the other—loneliness or solitude—depending on how you looked at them.

"Then I guess you've come to the right place," he said, watching her fingers drum an unconscious rhythm on the rough stone of the ledge. "Even though you're not technically alone at the moment."

"No, that's true," she said, fixing her gaze on him again, and this time the smile was real.

They spread the picnic blanket on the uneven surface of the roof, then spilled out the contents of the backpack. The sun was long gone, but it was still warm out, even up here, where the wind made it difficult to light the candles. After a while, they gave up and dined in the dark instead, sharing an assortment of cookies and crackers and fruit, and Lucy's eyes kept straying back up to the sky between bites, as if she couldn't trust the unfamiliar stars to stay put.

When they were full, they dragged the blanket over to the wall so that they could lean against it, sitting side by side, their heads tilted back, their shoulders nearly touching.

"If you could go anywhere in the world, where would it be?" Lucy asked, and Owen felt a flash of recognition; it was a question that was always on his mind, and the first thing he usually wondered about other people, even if he never got around to asking.

"Everywhere," he said, and she laughed, the sound light and musical.

"That's not an answer."

"Sure it is," he said, because it was true, possibly the truest thing about him. Sometimes it seemed as if his whole life was an exercise in waiting; not waiting to leave, exactly, but simply waiting to go. He felt like one of those fish that had the capacity to grow in unimaginable ways if only the tank were big enough. But his tank had always been small, and as much as he loved his home—as much as he loved his family—he'd always felt himself bumping up against the edges of his own life.

New York City wasn't the answer. What Owen wanted was something wider, something vaster; he had applications ready for six different colleges that ranged up and down the West Coast, from San Diego all the way to Washington, and he couldn't wait for the day when he could take off to start a new life out there, crossing through states heavy with vowels beneath skies flat as paper, through the impossible bulk of jagged mountains, all the way to the silvery ocean.

For as long as he could remember, he'd felt the pull of the road, an itinerant streak that chimed from somewhere deep inside him, perhaps inherited from his once-restless parents. One day, he hoped to find their kind of peace, too—a home that was nothing special until they'd deemed it so—but that would come later, and for now there were thousands of places he burned to see, and next year would just be the start of it.

He could feel Lucy's eyes on him, and when he turned to face her, she dipped her chin. "Okay, then," she said matter-of-factly. "Everywhere."

"What about you?" he asked, and she considered this a moment.

"Somewhere."

He grinned. "How is that a better answer than 'everywhere'?"

"It's more specific," she said, as if this should be obvious.

"I guess that's true." He looked down at his folded hands. "You know, I've never really been anywhere. New York, obviously. And Pennsylvania. We went to the Delaware shore once when I was little. And crossed through New Jersey a few times. That's what? Four states." He shook his head and smiled ruefully. "Pitiful, huh?"

"What about next year?" she asked. "College seems like a pretty good excuse to get out of here."

"It is," he agreed. "I'm looking at a lot of places out west. California, Oregon, Washington..."

She raised her eyebrows. "Those are all really far."

"Yeah," he said. "That's kind of the point. They've all got pretty good science programs, too."

"Ah," she said. "So you *are* a science whiz."

He shrugged. "Whiz might be taking it a bit far."

"What about your dad?"

"What about him?" Owen asked, but he knew what she meant, and he felt something go cold in his chest at the thought. There were so many parts of this—this lonely next chapter—that he dreaded now, most of them having to do with his mother: that she wouldn't be there to watch him walk across the stage at graduation, or to help him pack, or to make the bed in his new dorm room the way she always did at home. But the worst of it was actually this: that, after dropping off his only son, his dad would have to come back to this miserable basement apartment on his own.

That was the part that knocked the wind out of him every single time.

He swallowed hard and raised his eyes to meet Lucy's.

"Won't he miss having you nearby?" she asked, and he forced himself to shrug.

"He'll come visit," he said with as much confidence as he could muster. He felt beside him, where there was a small piece of gravel, and then used it to scratch absently at the black surface of the roof. "What about you?"

"Will *I* miss having you nearby?" she asked with a grin, and he smiled in spite of himself.

"No," he said. "Tell me where you've been."

"Well, New York, of course," she said, holding out a hand to tick off her fingers as she counted. "Connecticut, New Jersey, Rhode Island, Massachusetts, Pennsylvania, Florida. I was hoping to get to California when my brothers left for school a few weeks ago, but they ended up just driving out together. My cousin's getting married there in a few months, though, so I guess I'll be able to add it to the list then."

"Pretty good list," he said with a little nod.

"Oh, and London," she said, her face brightening. "Almost forgot about that. Just twice, though. It's where my mom's from, so..." She shrugged. "But that's it for me. Not all that impressive, either."

He sighed. "When my parents graduated from high school, they bought a van and saw the whole country. Two years on the road. They went everywhere."

"I'm more interested in going abroad," she said, her voice unmistakably wistful. "I want to see all the places on those postcards. Especially Paris."

"Why Paris?"

"I don't know," she said. "All those beautiful buildings and cathedrals..."

"You mean all those postcards."

"Yeah," she admitted. "All those postcards. They're very selling."

"What do you want to see most?"

"Notre Dame," she said without hesitation.

"Why?" he asked, expecting to hear something about the architecture or the history or at least the gargoyles, but he was wrong.

"Because," she said. "It's the very center of Paris."

"It is?"

She nodded. "There's a little plaque with a star in front of it that marks the spot: Point Zero. And if you jump on it and make a wish, it means you'll get a chance to go back there again someday. There's something kind of magical about that, don't you think?"

"It'd be nice if every place came with that kind of guarantee." He leaned over to draw an X between them with the piece of gravel, then rubbed it out with the heel of his hand and replaced it with a crooked star.

"Does that mean we're in the exact center of New York?" she asked, nodding at it, and he felt momentarily unsteady beneath her gaze.

"I think," he said quietly, "that we're in the exact center of the whole world."

She held out a flattened palm, and it took a moment for him to realize that she was asking for the rock, not his hand. He passed it over, and she drew a circle around the edges of the star, then scratched the words *Point Zero* along the outside.

"There," she said. "Now it's official."

"See? No need for Paris."

"Not for tonight, anyway," she said, handing back the stone. "But I'd still like to go."

"How come they never took you along?"

She shrugged. "I don't know. I guess it's hard to travel with three kids. My brothers are awesome, but they're twins, and when we were little, they were complete nightmares. The first time we went to London, I remember them running up and down the aisles of the plane, locking themselves in the bathroom." There was a hint of a smile on her face, but then she shook her head. "That's not really it, though. The thing is, I think my parents just really like traveling alone together."

"Alone together," Owen said. "Oxymoron."

"You're an oxymoron," she said, rolling her eyes. "But really, it's always been their thing. It's partly his job, but they also just really love it. Some people shop. Some people fish. My parents travel."

"What does he do?"

"He works for this British bank. They met in London,

but he's had jobs in all these other places, too, Sydney and Cape Town and Rio. When my brothers were born, he took a job in the New York office, since he's from here, and I think the plan was to settle down, but that part never really took. Instead, they were always just jetting off and leaving us with the nanny."

"Sounds glamorous."

"For them," she said. "But I would have loved to go, too. I still would." She swept a hand through the air, scattering a few mosquitoes. "Sometimes I think they liked their lives a whole lot better before they had kids."

Owen thought of his own parents, putting down roots the moment they found out they were pregnant. "It's probably not that it was better," he said. "Just different. My parents did the same thing, settling down when I came along, and they were happy." He paused, blinking fast. "We were all happy."

Lucy was sitting with her arms resting on her knees, and when she turned to look at him, her leg bumped against his. Right then, he had a sudden urge to inch closer to her, to close the space between them, and the force of it surprised him; it felt like a very long time since he'd wanted anything at all.

"I'm sorry," she said, reaching over to put a hand over his. "About your mom."

The warmth of her palm cracked at something inside him, that hard shell of hurt that had formed over his heart like a coat of ice. She was watching him intently, her eyes seeking his, but he couldn't bring himself to look at her. Because the numbness was the only thing keeping him going, the only thing preventing him from falling to pieces in front of his dad, who was falling to pieces enough for both of them.

He turned his eyes back to the sky. "They look almost fake," he said. "Don't they?"

Lucy followed his gaze. "The stars?" she asked, but he didn't answer. He was thinking of the ones on the ceiling of his bedroom back home, little pieces of plastic that glowed green in the dark. His mother had put them up when he was little, when Owen first became obsessed with the sky, spending summer nights on his back in the front yard, staring up at the scattering of lights until his eyes burned. They bought him a telescope, and they bought him binoculars; they even bought him a globe that showed all the constellations. But, in the end, the only way to convince him to go to bed were those glowing plastic stars, which his mother tacked up on the ceiling herself.

"They're not in the right places," Owen had said that first night, his eyes pinned above him as he climbed into bed.

"Sure they are," she told him. "It's just that these are very rare constellations."

He frowned up at them. "What are they called?"

"Well," she'd said, scooting in next to him and pointing at the ceiling. "That's Owen Major."

He let his head fall to the side, so that it was resting on

her shoulder, and in the dark, his voice was hushed. "Is there an Owen Minor?"

"Sure," she said. "Right over there. And that's Buckley's Belt."

"Like Orion's Belt?"

"Even better," she said. "Because you can always see it. Every single night."

Now, beside him on the roof, he could feel Lucy smiling. "They don't look fake at all," she said. "They look real. Really real. They might be the realest thing I've ever seen."

Owen smiled, too, letting his eyes fall shut, but he could still see them, glowing bright against the backs of his eyelids. And for the first time in weeks, he felt all lit up inside, even on this darkest of nights.

5

When she woke, everything was blurry. As soon as she opened her eyes, Lucy brought an arm up over her face to block out the blazing sunlight. But several seconds passed before she remembered where she was—high up on the roof beneath a whitewashed sky—and several more went by before she realized she was alone.

She rubbed her eyes, then propped herself up on her elbows, staring at the blanket beside her, where just last night Owen had fallen asleep, and which was now only an Owen-shaped indent, like a plaid flannel snow angel.

They hadn't planned to sleep up here, but as the night had deepened and their voices had grown softer, slowed by the heat and the weight of the past hours, they found themselves lying side by side, their eyes fixed on the stars as they talked.

Owen had fallen asleep first, his head tipping to one side so that his hair fell over his eyes, and he looked peaceful in a way he hadn't when he was awake. His hair smelled faintly of lemons from the cleaning solution on the floor of the kitchen, and Lucy listened to him breathe, watching the shallow rise and fall of his chest.

Being there like that, so close to him, she had to remind herself that this wasn't real. It wasn't a date but an accident. It wasn't romantic, only practical. They were just two people trying to make it through the night, and it didn't mean anything beyond that.

After all, hours didn't necessarily add up in that way. Time didn't automatically amount to anything. There was only so much you could ask from a single night.

Still, Lucy hadn't expected him to disappear completely. It was true that they'd made no plans for the morning, no promises for the next day. They'd shared nothing more than a blanket and some food and a little bit of light. But somehow, it had seemed like more than that—at least to her. And now, as she glanced around the roof—empty except for a few pigeons milling about on the far side—she couldn't help feeling wounded by his absence.

She rose to her feet, still squinting from the brightness of the morning, and shuffled over to the ledge. In the daylight, the city looked entirely different. The sky to the east was splashed with orange, and below it, Central Park was stretched out, a vast and manicured swath of wilderness interrupted only by the occasional pond, like dabs of blue-gray paint on a palette. Lucy stood with the breeze on her face, wondering whether the city had power again. It was impossible to tell from this high up.

Downstairs, when she pushed open the door to her apartment, the answer quickly became clear. She held her breath against the wall of heat that greeted her—so dense it almost felt like something she could touch—and moved down the sweltering hallway and into the kitchen, where she stood staring at the place they'd been lying just last night, their heads close so that their bodies formed a kind of steeple.

On one of the gray tiles, something thin and white stood out even in the dim lighting, and when she stooped to pick it up, Lucy was surprised to find a cigarette. She wrinkled her nose as she examined it, trying to square this new fact—that Owen was a smoker—with her memory of the night before. Once again, she felt jolted by the realization that she didn't actually know him at all, and that those long hours together seemed to have lost something in the light of day.

She was about to toss the cigarette into the trash when something made her stop. It was all that was left of this night. So instead, she grabbed her wallet from the kitchen counter, unzipping the little pocket that held all the coins, and slipped it inside.

On the refrigerator, there was a small piece of paper with the number of her parents' hotel in Paris. By now, Lucy guessed they must have heard what had happened. She lifted the portable phone from its cradle on the wall, ready to dial the long string of numbers, but there was only silence on the line—no power meant no charge, which meant no dial tone—and so she hung up again with a sigh.

The water wasn't working, either. When she twisted the faucet, there was only a slow dribble that quickly petered out altogether. Without electricity, there was no way to pump the water up to the twenty-fourth floor. So she wiped at her forehead with the back of her arm and stood with a hand on either side of the sink, trying to figure out what to do next.

There was a stillness to the apartment that she usually enjoyed when everyone was gone. But now, without even the hum of the appliances, the huge vaulted rooms felt strangely foreign, like it was someone else's home entirely.

Lucy had never minded being alone. She was plenty used to it, with parents who traveled so much and brothers who weren't usually around. Unlike Lucy, who participated in absolutely no school-related activities, they had played basketball and lacrosse and were involved in student government; they led clubs and volunteered on weekends and had even joined a band last year, though it was a largely earsplitting affair that fell more into the category of noise than music.

Lucy, on the other hand, had always drifted along unseen at her school; she had a knack for making herself invisible that had always felt like a kind of superpower, something that belonged only to her. Being on her own had never been a burden. Instead of weighing her down, it buoyed her up; when she was alone, she was lighter. When she was by herself, she felt untethered and free.

But this morning, she was left with an uneasy feeling as she paced the empty apartment. A few years ago, on their first weekend without any supervision whatsoever, her brothers had turned to each other with matching grins the moment the door fell shut behind their parents.

"What should we do first?" Charlie had asked, and Ben pretended to think about this, tapping his finger against his chin.

"Well, we should probably eat a sensible breakfast."

"Definitely," Charlie agreed, laughing as he grabbed a frozen pizza from the freezer, and after that, it had become a tradition. Pizza for breakfast. Just because they could.

Now Lucy stood in front of the freezer, the last of the cool air leaking out, and ran a hand over the damp and wilting box of the frozen pizza she'd bought in preparation for her first time entirely on her own. After a moment, she closed it again with a sigh, frowning at the calendar on the door. It was the first day of school, but the city was still stuck, dark and gridlocked, and she was certain it would be postponed. This knowledge was neither welcome nor disappointing; it only meant that the countdown to the end of her junior year—to the end of high school, really— would begin tomorrow instead of today.

Lucy had always enjoyed her classes and endured her classmates, and these two things canceled each other out, resulting in a generally neutral attitude toward the whole endeavor. She'd been at the St. Andrews School since kindergarten, and it was always exactly the same: the same girls and the same uniforms. The same dramas and fights and scandals. The same catty conversations and ruthless jostling and mystifying objectives. Every year was like a rerun of the same boring show, everyone else moving fast all around her, a blur of people and plans and conversations, while Lucy remained alone in the middle of it all, standing absolutely still.

She wandered into her bedroom and stood in front of the open closet, where her plaid skirt and white blouse hung, pressed and ready to wear. But instead, with some amount of relief, she grabbed a pair of red shorts and a T-shirt, suddenly in desperate need of a walk.

The now familiar temperature of the stairwell stung her eyes, and she wound her way down the steps again, passing neighbors too tired and sweaty to do more than raise a hand in greeting. They all wore the heat like a kind of weight, and Lucy, too, couldn't help feeling like something inside her was wilting.

With each flight, the red numbers flashed by on the gray doors, but it wasn't until somewhere around the sixteenth floor that she realized she was no longer sure of her destination. Her intention had been to spend the rest of the morning wandering the neighborhood, but by the time she passed the tenth floor, she understood she wasn't headed outside after all, and she was all the way down to the eighth floor before realizing she was actually on her way to the basement.

She was going to see Owen.

But when she stepped out into the lobby—which needed to be crossed to reach the door in the mailroom that led downstairs—she was greeted by Darrell, one of the newer doormen, who was sitting at the front desk, drenched in sweat.

"I feel like it's only fair to warn you," he said, mopping his forehead with a paper towel, "that it's hotter than hell out there."

Lucy paused halfway between the elevator and the front desk. "Can't be worse than my apartment," she said, stealing a glance at the mailroom.

"I don't know," Darrell was saying. "I walked in from the Bronx, and—"

Lucy turned back to him with wide eyes. "You did?"

"Well, halfway," he admitted. "The subway's still down, and the buses were all packed, but I hitched a ride on the back of a fruit truck for part of it."

"So everything's still a mess, then," she said, and something about the tone in her voice made Darrell's expression soften.

"It's not as bad as all that," he said with an encouraging smile. "I heard they got power back upstate, and Boston, too."

Through the mailroom, she could see the far door swing open, and she caught her breath, surprised by the sudden quickness of her heart. But it was only the handyman from last night, who waved as he turned the corner.

Lucy sighed. "Hopefully we're next," she said, and Darrell nodded.

"Where're you off to now?"

"Nowhere," she said, a bit too quickly, and he laughed.

"Sounds nice," he told her. "Be sure to send me a postcard."

Once again, something seized inside her chest, and she hesitated a moment, looking from the lobby doors back to the mailroom, hoping that Owen might come loping out. It would be so much better to run into him here. She was terrified of knocking on his door only to find that he didn't want to see her. Even now, she could imagine the painful awkwardness of such an exchange, his face going red as he made some sort of excuse because he was too polite to tell her as much.

After all, he was the one who'd left this morning.

Lucy was normally a firm believer that things worked out for the best, and she usually had no problem being optimistic, but now she felt her legs go weak as she stood weighing her next move, her cheeks pink at the thought of showing up unannounced. Something about Owen had thrown her off, twisting her into uncertain knots, and so before she could do anything she might regret, she headed for the revolving doors that led to the street.

Outside, it was clear that last night's celebration had officially ended, and all that was left was the hangover. The streets, which had seemed like one big party just hours before, were now full of sweaty and miserable-looking people, everyone fanning themselves with day-old newspapers.

As she walked, Lucy saw a few kids chasing each other along the sidewalk, but otherwise, everyone seemed listless and beaten down by the weather. There were police officers stationed at the major intersections to direct traffic, but it was a haphazard affair, slow and grinding. All the energy seemed to have been sapped right out of the city.

She pressed her way up the street, heading in no particular direction, as she had a thousand times before. The ice-cream shop from last night was now closed, along with most of the other stores, which were all shuttered and silent. A few blocks farther uptown, she passed by her school, an imposing stone building, where a handwritten sign on the door announced that classes would begin tomorrow as long as the power was back, though there was no way to know if the note had been written yesterday or today.

Finally, having covered most of the neighborhood, and with nowhere else to go, she made her way back home again. As she climbed the stairs, she considered heading back up to the roof, in case Owen was there, and the thought propelled her up the next six flights before she reconsidered it for the same reason she'd walked away earlier.

She'd lived in this city her whole life, had gotten lost countless times at night, survived two muggings, and once broken her arm while climbing the rocks in Central Park.

But it was finally Owen—who wasn't scary in the least; who had, in fact, been nothing but nice to her—who had somehow managed to turn her into a coward.

Back in the apartment, she closed all the blinds and tried to nap on the couch, but the heat was oppressive and stifling. Wide-awake and miserable, she paged through her well-worn copy of *The Catcher in the Rye*—the ultimate guide to losing yourself in New York City—but the words swam in front of her, blurry as everything else from the heat. Finally, she gave up and returned to the kitchen floor, which was only marginally cooler. As the late afternoon began to sink into darkness, the kitchen grew dimmer and she pressed her bare arms and legs on the tiles and tried not to think about the fact that this was where they'd been lying just last night.

She wondered if there was a word for loneliness that wasn't quite so general. Because that wasn't it, exactly; it wasn't that she was feeling lonesome or empty or forlorn. It was more particular than that, like the blanket on the roof this morning: Here in the kitchen, there was an Owen-shaped indent.

She drifted to sleep there, her cheek pressed against the tiles, and when she woke, it was once again to a blur of light. Only this time, it was coming from the bulb in the ceiling fixture, which was blaring down on her, harsh and unnatural and much too bright.

She sat up so fast she felt dizzy, spinning around to see

that it was back now, all of it, the blinking green lights on the microwave clock, the red numbers on the answering machine, the churning of the overhead fan, and beyond the doorway, the lamps that had flickered on across the rest of the apartment.

All of the clocks were wrong, so she had no idea what time it was, but she shot to her feet and hurried from room to room, greeting each appliance like an old friend. Even the air-conditioning had powered back up, and the stagnant air felt cooler already, all of it conspiring to make the apartment seem recognizable again.

In her room, Lucy plugged in her computer and her phone, and while she waited for them to charge, she dashed over to the bathroom to test the water, which trickled out slowly but enough for her to splash her face. She looked around, feeling giddy, wondering what to do first: take a shower or try to contact her parents or just simply sit in front of the fan, now suddenly a luxury.

But on her way out of the bathroom, she paused in front of the living room windows, where the blinds were still drawn. She walked over and tugged on the cord, pulling hand over hand as the skyline revealed itself inches at a time, all lit up in a brilliant patchwork of glowing windows, a checkered ode to the power of electricity.

Lucy stood there for a long moment, taking it in, the city once again warm and bright as it was in her memory of it. But when she glanced up, she was surprised to feel an ache in her chest. High above the buildings, the sky had shifted, and there was now only a deep, unsettling darkness, as if last night's version of the skyline had been turned upside down. And the stars, every last one of them, had disappeared.

Owen was standing in the middle of Broadway when the lights came back.

The plastic bag he was carrying had just split open as he crossed the street, and the three lukewarm water bottles he'd finally found at a hot dog cart near the park had gone rolling toward the curb. As he scrambled to collect them, he glanced sideways down the darkened alley of the avenue, and it was just as he straightened up again that it happened.

It was as if someone had flipped a switch. Just like that, the city was plugged in again. Owen stood there, blinking, as the street lamps came to life, the windows and signs along Broadway all switching on just after them, once again bathing the street in an artificial glow.

There was an almost reverential pause as everyone stared, slack-jawed, and then the heat-weary crowd stirred into action again and a great cheer went up. People whooped and clapped as if discovering rain after a long drought, and even the police officers who stood stern-faced at the corner couldn't help grinning, their eyes sweeping over the restored reds and greens of the traffic lights.

A few people ran past Owen, eager to get home, and a man with a dog tucked under his arm did a little jig on the corner. Everyone wore the same expression, halfway between relief and amazement, and all of them were squinting; in just over twenty-four hours, they'd become unaccustomed to the brightness of their own city, and, faced with it now in all its intensity, they cupped their hands over their eyes as if staring into the sun.

Owen tucked the water bottles into the crook of his arm, letting the crowd surge around him, and he thought about what Lucy had said the night before, about how you can be surrounded by so many people here but still entirely on your own.

He saw the truth in it now, but it felt lonelier than what he'd imagined, and he lifted his gaze to the building on the corner of Broadway and Seventy-Second, wishing he was someone different, the kind of guy who would run up twenty-four flights of stairs just to see her again, even for a minute.

He hadn't meant to abandon her this morning. But when he'd woken up with the sun on his face and Lucy curled beside him, her eyelids fluttering in sleep, he was gripped by a sudden worry about his dad, who might well have returned by then to an empty apartment with no idea where his son could have disappeared to on such a muddled and hectic night.

His plan was to run downstairs, check the apartment, leave a note if Dad wasn't there yet, and then climb the forty-two stories back up to the roof before Lucy woke up. Even as he clamored down the long flight of steps, he was already thinking of that space on the blanket, where he'd lie down again and wait for her eyes to open so they could start the day together.

But when he made it down to the basement, it was to find his dad slumped in the front hallway of the apartment, clammy and shivering in spite of the heat. There was a fine sheen of sweat across his forehead, and his eyes were bright and feverish.

Owen's heart was already thumping hard as he slid to the floor. "Dad?" he said, his voice full of panic, shaking him a little. "Are you okay?"

His father had nodded and attempted a feeble smile. "Just a little tired," he said, his tongue too thick in his mouth. "I walked...."

"You walked? All that way?"

He swallowed, as though steeling himself to speak, then changed his mind and simply nodded instead.

"It's okay," Owen said, repeating the words dumbly as he tried to figure out what to do. "It's okay. I'm here."

Dad muttered something else, but his words were slurred, and his face had a grayish tinge to it. He must have walked all night, all the way from the very end of Brooklyn; he was clearly dehydrated, and he probably had heat exhaustion, too, if not worse. Owen's thoughts were slow and hazy. There was no water pressure, no way to cool him off. He felt frantic as he looked around the apartment without knowing what exactly he was looking for; something to help, something to make this better.

"Look, Dad," Owen said, stooping so that they were at eye level. "I'm going to get you to bed, then go out for some water, okay?"

"Okay," he whispered through cracked lips.

"I'll be right back," Owen assured him. "You're okay now." He sat back on his heels, shaking his head. "I can't believe you walked all that way."

"To get back home."

Owen tilted his head toward the ceiling, trying to swallow the lump in his throat. But all he could think was: *This isn't home.*

"Okay," he said after a moment, snaking a hand under Dad's arm and around his back. "On the count of three."

Once he managed to get his father up and into his bedroom, bearing most of his weight as they shuffled along, he helped lower him down on top of the sheets, and then promised he'd be back, grabbing the keys and heading for the lobby. He thought of asking one of the doormen for help, but after his dad had disappeared yesterday in the middle of one of the biggest crises the city had seen in years, he decided it would be better not to draw any more attention to themselves.

He slipped through the lobby, then went sprinting around the corner to the same bodega from last night, but they were out of water, and so were the next two shops he tried. His heart was hammering in his chest as he thought of his father. He didn't know much about heat exhaustion other than the importance of water, and as he moved from store to store with no luck, he could feel a widening panic inside him. Finally, he found a pretzel cart with only two bottles left, and he practically threw a five-dollar bill at the man before taking off down the street at a jog.

All day, he watched over his father. He sat in a chair beside the bed, keeping a damp washcloth pressed to his forehead and fanning the stuffy air with an old issue of *Sports Illustrated*. Dad only woke once, and when he did, Owen helped him take a few sips of water. But he fell asleep again almost immediately, and there was nothing to do but sit there, looking on helplessly. It wasn't until midafternoon that the color slowly began to return to his cheeks, and Owen finally allowed himself to sit back with a sigh, realizing for the first time how tense he'd been all day.

When dusk crept in through the window, dipping the room in shades of blue, Owen had decided it was safe to venture outside again for more water, and he circled the neighborhood for what felt like forever before stumbling across a hot dog vendor who was charging ten bucks apiece.

Now he stood across the street from their building, juggling the bottles in his arms and watching the giant clock above a department store, which had just come back to life along with everything else, the slow ticking completely at odds with the urgency he felt as he waited for the signal to cross.

The lobby was still unbearably hot, but there were a few people standing around the front desk, and Owen bent his head and hurried toward the mailroom, hoping to go unnoticed, eager to return to his father. But just before he could disappear through the door, he was pulled up short by the sound of his name.

"Owen Buckley!"

His first thought, strangely, was of Lucy. That something might have happened to her today—that he shouldn't have left her on the roof, that he should have come back for her, like he'd meant to—and his chest flooded with fear. But when he swiveled to look, he realized it wasn't that at all, and his shoulders slumped.

Striding toward him was Sam Coleman, his father's second cousin and the owner of the building, the one who had given him the job here.

The only time Owen had ever seen him was at his mother's funeral, where after the ceremony, in the midst of all the handshakes and kisses, the hugs and condolences, he'd noticed a man handing his father a business card. Dad had taken it with numb fingers, nodding mechanically, and Owen watched as he slipped it into the pocket of his suit. It wasn't until a few weeks later that he brought it up.

"I don't know if you met my cousin Sam at the..." he trailed off, unable to say the word *funeral*. In the days leading up to it and in the days that had followed, he'd somehow managed to avoid it altogether, talking around it, the word a black hole that had opened up in the very center of their lives.

Owen shook his head. They were sitting at the kitchen table, an untouched casserole dish between them, one of dozens that were stacked like bricks in the fridge.

"He offered me a job. In New York," Dad said, raising his eyes from the table, where a column of light from the window spotlighted a thin layer of dust. Already, the house no longer felt like the same one they'd lived in just ten days before.

"New York City?"

Dad nodded. "He owns a few buildings there," he explained. "He wants me to manage one of them."

"Why?" Owen asked, and Dad was silent for a moment. The question wasn't a necessary one. He'd been out of work for almost a year now, a contractor in a town where there was nothing new to be built. He'd picked up work as a handyman here and there, enough to keep them going, but it wasn't permanent. He'd needed a job long before the accident, and he still needed one now.

"Because," Dad said quietly. "Because I'm not sure we can stay here."

It wasn't the answer Owen had been looking for; it wasn't even a response to the right question. He didn't know whether his father meant for financial reasons or emotional ones, whether he'd given this a lot of thought or was just saying it out loud for the first time now, and he wasn't sure how he felt about it yet himself.

But even so, he understood.

"Let's go out west, then," he said, sitting forward at

the table. "Let's just get in the car and drive, like you and Mom used to do."

Dad's eyes flashed with pain at the memory, and he shook his head. "This isn't just some lark, O," he said. "We have to be logical about this. There's no work for me here. If we sell the house—" He paused, his voice cracking at this, then pushed on. "We'll have the money for whatever's next. But who knows how fast that'll happen, and for now he's offering us an apartment with the job. And I just can't..."

"...stay here," Owen had finished. He breathed out, then raised his eyes to meet his dad's. "I know," he said finally. "Me neither."

It was true. Too much had changed. His mother was gone, and the house didn't feel like theirs anymore. Even his two best friends were different. At the funeral, Owen had watched the pair of them—who had said all the right things and been nothing but supportive—begin to laugh helplessly when one tripped over nothing at all, his arms windmilling before he managed to right himself again. They were trying their best to hold it together, their laughter threatening to bubble over, and from across the lawn, Owen just stood there—alone and apart, solemn and heartbroken and hopelessly, endlessly, miserably sad— and it was then that he felt the first pinpricks of doubt that things would ever be normal again.

It had always been the three of them: Owen, Casey, and Josh: a steadfast team, a solid unit. They'd grown up playing hide-and-seek and then tag, soccer and then football; they'd studied together a thousand times and found a thousand ways to avoid studying at all; they'd talked about girls and sports and their futures; they'd teased each other mercilessly and had been there for one another in the most surprising of ways. But in that moment, everything was different. They were over there, and he was over here, the space between them already too big to cross.

And as it turned out, Owen and his dad left town before he even had a chance to try, his best friends becoming just two more items on the list of things they left behind.

Now his knees felt unsteady as he watched Sam approach him from the other side of the lobby. He was short and dark and broad-shouldered, the opposite of Owen and his dad in every way, and he offered a hand when he was close enough, which Owen shook warily.

"Nice to see you again," he said, though they hadn't actually met before. "Quite a night, huh?" He didn't wait for a response. "I've been doing the rounds today, checking on all my buildings. Obviously, this thing has caused a lot of hiccups. Any chance your dad's around?"

Owen opened his mouth, then closed it again, unsure what to say. But it didn't matter anyway. Sam barreled on without giving him a chance.

"Because I gotta tell you, I've got a boatload of problems here, too many for the doormen to be handling on their own." He reached out and put a beefy hand on Owen's thin shoulder. "Listen, I know you guys are going through a rough time, but the whole reason to hire a building manager

75

is so there's someone to manage the building, you know? And on a day like this, it doesn't look too good when he's nowhere to be found."

"I think maybe he called in—"

"Sick?" Sam said with raised eyebrows. "No."

Owen shook his head. "Then it was a vacation day...."

"After only a couple of weeks?" Sam asked, then flashed a smile that came off as more of a leer. "I don't think so. No way I'd have cleared that even if he'd bothered asking. Which he didn't."

"I'm really sorry...."

Sam waved this away. "Is he back now, or is he still sipping mai tais on the beach?"

Owen glanced over at George, who was now at the front desk and who gave him a helpless shrug.

"He's back," he said through gritted teeth. "But he's not feeling well."

"Well, give him a message for me, will you?" Sam leaned in a little closer. "Tell him the water's back but not the pressure. And since he's already on fairly thin ice," he said, demonstrating with his thumb and index finger, only the tiniest sliver of space between the two, "he might want to see about fixing it tonight. Okay?"

There was nothing to do but nod. Sam gave him a little pat on the shoulder before turning to walk back over to the desk, and as soon as he did, Owen hurried through the mailroom and down the stairs, biting back his anger at Sam and his frustration at Dad.

It was impossible to know what he'd been thinking, simply taking off for the day without asking after only a few weeks on the job. It was stupid and completely shortsighted.

But when he opened the door to the apartment, his eyes fell on the kitchen counter, where he'd seen the bouquet of flowers just a couple of nights before, and something about the memory made him feel like crying.

He thought about what Sam had said. There was no way his father would have gotten the day off even if he'd asked.

But Owen understood why he had to go.

He went out there for Mom; to stand in the place where they'd first met, the rough wood of the boardwalk beneath their feet and the salty smell of the ocean at their backs. He'd gone to relive that day. And he'd gone to say good-bye.

He'd gone there for her.

And then he'd walked all the way back for *him*.

From down the hall, Owen heard Dad call his name, his voice hoarse. In the bedroom, he was sitting up now, propped against a couple of pillows. When he saw Owen, he reached over and switched on the bedside lamp with a grin.

"Ta-da," he said. "Electricity."

For a moment, Owen thought of not telling him about Sam, of letting the night pass without fixing the water pumps. He knew what it would mean—they'd have to leave the building. They'd probably even leave New York.

The two of them could drive out west, find some place better suited for them, a place with more sky and fewer people. Maybe they'd even retrace the route his parents had taken all those years ago. Maybe, in that way, Owen would be able to say good-bye, too.

But standing there in the doorway, he knew he couldn't do it. He had to give this a chance, if only for his dad. It was what his mom would have wanted. And it was the right thing to do.

Besides, after last night, Owen wasn't so sure he was ready to leave New York behind anyway. At least not yet.

Instead, they would haul the heavy red toolbox into the utilities room, where Dad would sit on the cool concrete floor with a glass of water and show Owen what to do. Together, they would figure out a way to make it work. They would figure out a way to make *this* work.

Owen crossed the threshold of the room, stepping into the pool of light from the lamp, and handed over one of the water bottles.

"So," he said, his voice bright. "Now that we've got electricity, think you're up to conjuring some water, too?"

7

For the next two days, Lucy got herself out of bed and went to school. She sat through her classes and tolerated her classmates. She looked for Owen each morning and then again each afternoon. And when she didn't see him, she returned to her apartment, trying not to be disappointed, and ate dinner alone.

Then, on the third day, George appeared at the door to help carry her suitcase downstairs and hail her a cab to the airport.

Just before midnight on the day the lights came back, her parents had finally gotten through to her. Lucy had been asleep already, and when she reached for her phone and saw a jumble of numbers too long to be local, she picked it up.

It was morning in Paris, and her parents were on two separate extensions, wide-awake and talking over each other.

"Lucy," her dad kept saying. "Luce, are you okay?"

"I'm fine," she said groggily, sitting up in bed. "Just sleepy."

"We've been trying and trying," Mom said, her usually clipped accent softened by worry. "You gave us such a fright."

"I couldn't get through," Lucy explained, fully awake now. "The circuits were all busy. But it's fine. I'm okay."

"Listen," Dad said, his voice brisk and businesslike. "We want to hear all about it. But first, you should know that I called the airline...."

Lucy waited for them to say they were coming home early, that they'd fought tooth and nail to get a flight back. She'd heard on the news earlier that the airports were all overrun with stranded travelers who had been stuck there since the power went out, living on pretzels and sleeping at the gates, and that it would take days for the schedules to return to normal. But her father must have figured something out, must surely know the type of people who could help, or at least the type of people who knew other people, and Lucy felt a sudden rush of gratitude for her parents, who must have been trying to get home to her this whole time.

"...and I've got you on a flight to London on Friday," Dad was saying, and Lucy's mouth fell open as she pressed the phone closer to her ear. "I know you've got school that day, but how much do they actually cover in the first week anyway, right?"

"London?" she said, her voice cracking.

"Yes, London," Dad said impatiently, as if this were a ridiculous question. "Your mother and I are going tomorrow, and you'll meet us there on Friday."

Lucy was torn between the impulse to simply agree—in case they might change their minds—and the urge to ask a thousand more questions. "Uh, why...?"

"We want to see you, darling," her mother said. "We want to be sure you're all right."

"I'm fine," she said again. "I just—"

"Coming home was out of the question," Dad said, once again businesslike. "So we'd like you to meet us there."

Lucy felt like laughing. On the scale of worldwide emergencies, nothing could have given her a truer sense for where the blackout ranked: not urgent enough for her parents to interrupt a trip but just alarming enough for them to buy her a plane ticket.

The details were discussed and the rest of the plans arranged. Lucy would miss two days of school, but she'd be getting a cultural experience, which seemed like justification enough. She thought of her earlier trips over, once when she was five and once when she was eight. The first time had been during Christmas; they'd visited her grandmother in the stately town house where her mother had grown up, and all toured the city together: the ornate parliament buildings and the giant clock that towered over them, Oxford Street with its garlands and wreaths, and St. Paul's Cathedral, where Lucy had sung carols, her voice loud and warbling beside her mother's more melodic one.

They went again three years later, just after her grand-mother had passed away, a more somber trip that was spent mostly in the living room of the old town house, nodding politely to black-clad strangers and playing cards on the floor with her brothers.

Still, she had loved it there. It was the thing that—even more than the postcards—had sparked her obsession with travel. When she was little, she'd believed the whole world—or at least all its cities—would look exactly like New York: tall and jagged and imposing. She had no other basis for comparison, and it seemed only logical that a city was a city, just as a farm was a farm, and a mountain was a mountain. But London was completely different from what she'd imagined; it was regal and charming, stately and enchanting, and she'd fallen under its spell from the moment she arrived.

So she was excited to be going back now. It wasn't Paris and it wasn't Cape Town. It wasn't Sydney or Rio. And it wasn't anywhere new.

But it was definitely Somewhere.

And there was nobody she wanted to tell more than Owen. But she still hadn't been able to bring herself to knock on the door of the basement apartment. And as often as she'd lingered in the lobby, making small talk with the doormen, she still hadn't run into him again.

Even now, as she waited on the curb while George tried to flag down a cab, she couldn't help glancing back toward the lobby one last time, hoping he might appear. But there was no sign of him, and there hadn't been in three days.

It was almost as if she'd made him up entirely.

At the airport, she sat at the gate and watched out the window as the planes took off, trying to decide whether it was nerves or excitement that was making her stomach churn. This was what she'd wanted, of course, but it wasn't how she'd pictured it happening: being sent rather than invited, summoned rather than whisked away.

On the plane, she sank low in her seat, looking out the window while the other passengers boarded. Her thoughts drifted to Owen again, the way his eyes had flashed when he spoke about traveling the country, and she was so focused on this, so lost in the memory of him, that when someone sat down heavily beside her and she turned to find that it wasn't him—that it was, instead, an old Englishman with red cheeks and whiskers in his nose—she was more surprised than it made sense to be.

She slept the whole way across the Atlantic, the night passing as the ocean slipped by beneath the plane, and when she woke, it was to discover that they'd caught up with the morning, the light streaming through the oval windows all up and down the length of the plane. She rubbed her eyes and squinted out at the clouds that tumbled over the city, and the fine mist of rain that clung to the plane as they landed.

There was a car waiting for her just outside the arrivals

area, and she sat in the backseat and tried to keep her bleary eyes open as it glided through the rainy London streets. She realized how much she'd forgotten in the last eight years; it was half a lifetime ago that she was here, and only now did she recall the quirky details of the place: the colorful doors and the painted signs on the pubs, the roundabouts and the lampposts, the buildings that stood shoulder to shoulder along the winding streets.

The town house had long ago been sold, so her parents now stayed at the Ritz whenever they were in the city. Lucy couldn't help staring as they pulled up to the grand old building wreathed in lights, and a bellhop appeared out of nowhere to help her with her suitcase. When she told the man at the front desk that she was looking for her parents, he gave her the room number, and then pointed to the doorway behind her.

"The lift is just around the corner," he said, and Lucy smiled all the way up to the sixth floor, wondering if there would be much difference to getting stuck in a lift instead of an elevator.

Upstairs, she knocked on the door to her parents' room. When it opened, they were both standing there as if they'd been waiting; her mother, tall and willowy, her hair dark as Lucy's, and her father, sandy-haired and enormous, with glasses and a haircut that made him look every inch as serious as he was. They were both generally reserved, not prone to huge amounts of affection, but before the door had even closed, Lucy found herself folded into a hug, tucked between the two of them in a way that felt so safe, so overwhelming, and most of all so surprising that she began to cry without meaning to.

"We're so sorry," Mom said, letting go and looking at her with concern. "If we'd known..."

"No, it's fine," Lucy said, wiping her eyes. "It really wasn't a big deal. I don't know why I'm crying. I'm just... I guess I'm just happy to see you."

"We're happy to see you, too," Dad said, bringing her suitcase in from the hallway and then closing the door. "Because of—well, because of some scheduling things, we couldn't get back. But we felt terrible that you were all alone through an ordeal like that, and we just really wanted to see you."

Lucy felt a little dazed by all the attention. "I'm fine," she said for what felt like the thousandth time as Mom guided her over to the bed, where they sat together on the edge, knees touching.

"So what was it like?" Dad asked as he pulled out the desk chair. Once seated, he crossed his legs and gave her a long look, the kind she'd seen him give lawyers and bankers when they'd come for dinner; it was a look that meant she had his full concentration, and it wasn't one she was used to seeing.

"It was dark," she said, and Mom laughed. "I was actually in the elevator when it happened."

"We heard," Dad said. "The boys told us."

Lucy had called her brothers the very next day, first

Charlie and then Ben, and she'd told them about climbing out of the elevator and walking up and down the stairwells; she'd told them about the doormen running around with flashlights and the masses of people moving through the streets; she'd told them about the free ice cream and the stars overhead and the heat. But she hadn't told them about Owen. Part of it was self-preservation—she knew Ben would tease her endlessly and Charlie would get overprotective—but part of it was instinct, too. It would have been like blowing out the candles on a birthday cake and then immediately announcing what you'd wished for; logical or not, saying it out loud made it seem less likely to come true.

"Was it awful?" Mom was asking, her eyes wide with worry.

"It wasn't so bad," Lucy said with a smile, hoping they didn't notice the pink that crept into her cheeks. "We were only in there for, like, half an hour." She paused, realizing for the first time that it was true—it couldn't have been more than thirty minutes. How had it felt like so much more? "The worst part was the heat," she continued. "*That* was pretty horrible."

They both nodded, like they wanted to hear more, but she thought she noticed Dad sneak a glance at his watch, and Mom's foot had started to bob in the way it did sometimes when guests at their dinner parties were still there even after the coffee cups had been cleared.

"You should have seen it, though," Lucy pressed on.

"The whole skyline just blinked out. And all the streets were completely full of people. It was unbelievable."

This time, Dad didn't bother to disguise it when he looked at his watch, and Mom cleared her throat. "Listen, darling," she said. "We want to hear a lot more about all this at dinner tonight, but we figured you'd want to nap, so we thought we'd head out for a little while."

"Oh," Lucy said. "Where?"

Dad looked up, his face a picture of confusion. "What do you mean?"

"I mean," Lucy said, raising her eyebrows, "where are you planning to go?"

"We made some plans before we knew you'd be here, too," Mom said, giving Dad a sideways glance. "I'm getting my hair done, and your father has . . . a meeting."

Lucy turned back to him, but he seemed suddenly interested in his shoes. "Well, where is it? Maybe I'll tag along, go explore a new neighborhood . . ."

He coughed, his face reddening. "We just assumed you'd be tired."

"I slept on the plane," she said, and they exchanged a look. "Okay, seriously," she said, glancing from one to the other. "What's going on?"

"Nothing," Dad started to say, but Mom rolled her eyes. "Let's just tell her now."

"Tell me what?" Lucy asked, suddenly anxious.

Dad was playing with his wedding ring, a nervous habit of his. "We were going to wait for dinner. . . ."

"Listen," Mom said, taking one of Lucy's hands in hers. "You know how much I miss it over here."

Lucy nodded, frowning.

"And you know that we'd always planned to live abroad again once the three of you were off to university, right?"

This was true. Ever since she was little, Mom had spoken dreamily of returning to London. She'd never really been at home in New York, where she found the summers too hot and the people too rude, the garbage too visible and the culture too limited. It had only ever been a matter of time before they moved back to London, where they'd first met all those years ago, and Lucy and her brothers had always known this. But they'd promised it wouldn't be until all three kids had left for college. Now, however, Mom was giving Lucy a pleading look—whether for understanding or forgiveness, she didn't know.

"Well," she was saying, her voice a bit too bright, "an opportunity has come up a little early."

"They called me about an open position in the UK office," Dad jumped in, his eyes shining behind his glasses. "I'd heard rumors about it, but it's very, very high level, so I didn't think I'd have a shot...."

"But it looks like he might," Mom finished, looking at him proudly. "And it won't be long now until we find out for sure."

"Right," Dad said. "Just a few more meetings today, and then we'll see...."

Lucy stared at him. "So we'd be moving to London?"

"Yes," Dad said, beaming.

"Next year?"

Mom shook her head. "Next month."

"Next month?" Lucy asked, reeling a bit. She could feel that her voice had risen an octave and her eyes had gone wide, but she couldn't help it. *Next month*, she thought, astonished by the nearness of it.

"It wouldn't be—" Dad began, but Lucy cut him off.

"What about the apartment?"

"Well, we'd keep it, of course," he said. "In case we wanted to go back for the summer, or if the boys ended up with internships there…"

Lucy stared at him. "What about school?"

"I've looked into it," Mom said with a hint of a smile, "and it seems they have those over here as well. And since you've never exactly *loved* your old school…"

She was right, of course, but Lucy still wasn't sure what to say. After sixteen whole years in New York, it almost didn't matter what she loved and what she didn't; the city was a part of her, and she a part of it. The idea that she could be living in London in just a few short weeks struck her as wildly unimaginable. She opened her mouth, then closed it again, blinking at them.

"I know this is a lot of information all at once," Mom said gently, her brow furrowed as she looked over at Dad. He leaned forward, steepling his hands together.

"And it's not for sure yet," he said. "Though I'm hoping we'll have something to celebrate soon…"

"London," Lucy repeated, and Mom smiled encouragingly.

"You love it here."

"I love New York, too."

Dad waved this away. "We've done New York," he said. "It's time for a change, don't you think?"

"I don't know," Lucy said, fumbling for the words. "I—"

"Why don't we pick this up over dinner later?" Dad suggested, clapping his hands on his knees and then standing up. "You can take a nap while Mom gets her hair done, then you two can meet up and do some shopping or something."

"I'm not—" Lucy was about to say *tired*, but there didn't seem to be a point. Dad stood there smoothing his tie, while Mom rose to grab her purse. "That sounds fine."

They left in a flurry of noise—reminders that if she needed anything, Lucy could call the front desk, and that she should feel free to order room service if she was hungry; they gave her some cash and promised they'd see her soon; they told her not to think too much about what they'd discussed until they all knew more—and then they were gone, and Lucy was alone again.

London, she thought, the word sinking inside her.

She waited only a few minutes before grabbing her bag and heading out the door, too restless to stay put. As she walked, her mind spun furiously, and she found herself gawking at everything she passed, the white columned buildings and the striped crosswalks, the pharmacies and fruit shops, the cafés and pubs: the whole world suddenly seen through a whole new lens.

Everything was so different here, which had—only hours before—been precisely the point. But now it felt foreign and strange, the unusual street names and the squat buildings; the shops were unfamiliar, and the traffic was heading in the wrong direction, and it was only the first week of September, but everyone was already wearing winter coats.

Lucy wasn't sure where she was exactly, but she kept moving anyway, too anxious to do anything but walk. A low fog hung over the streets, making everything damp and silvery, and she tugged the sleeves of her hoodie over her hands and pushed on.

It wasn't until she found herself approaching Piccadilly Circus—the huge electric signs burning through the mist—that she paused. It was the very first thing that reminded her of New York, and she stood there in the middle of the sidewalk, thinking of Times Square, the panic loosening its grip on her. She took a deep breath as she scanned the plaza. There were huddles of tourists peering in windows, brightly colored billboards, a few pigeons poking around near a fountain, and of course, the enormous stone buildings that formed a kind of cavern all around her.

It was beautiful, in a way. In its own way. And she thought it again—*London*—only this time, there was something lighter about it, a word like a sigh, like a possibility.

Just as she was about to turn back for the hotel, she spotted a small souvenir shop up ahead, the windows filled with little red buses and teacups with pictures of the queen. She walked over to take a closer look, drawn by the display of postcards just outside the door, and she spun the rack so that the images whizzed by in a blur of color: Buckingham Palace and Westminster Abbey, Big Ben and a series of red phone booths.

Finally, she came to an aerial shot, the city spread out from a distance, the River Thames woven through it like a gray ribbon, and there, written on top of it all in bold blue letters, were the words: *Wish You Were Here.*

Inside the shop, she slid a five-pound note across the counter.

"I'll take this," she said, waving the postcard. "And a stamp as well."

The clerk, a young woman with purple hair and a nose ring, rolled her eyes when she saw it. "Wish you were here," she said, snapping her gum. "Right."

Lucy only smiled. "Can I borrow a pen, too?"

After writing her note, she walked back out into the street. The fog was starting to lift now, the sun coming through unevenly. Lucy clutched the postcard in one hand, running a thumb along its edges as she looked around for a mailbox. She was halfway back to the hotel when she finally spotted one, and she realized why it had taken her so long. She'd been searching for the familiar blue. But here, the mailboxes—like the buses and phone booths—were a brilliant shade of red.

For a moment, she stood holding the little piece of cardboard over the open mouth of the chute. She was thinking about the mailroom back home in her apartment building, the wall of brass squares etched with numbers, and just beside them, the door leading down to the basement. But what she was really imagining was Owen—his blond head bent over the postcard, smiling as he read the words—and in spite of herself, she realized she was smiling, too.

Just as the sun broke through the clouds, she let go.

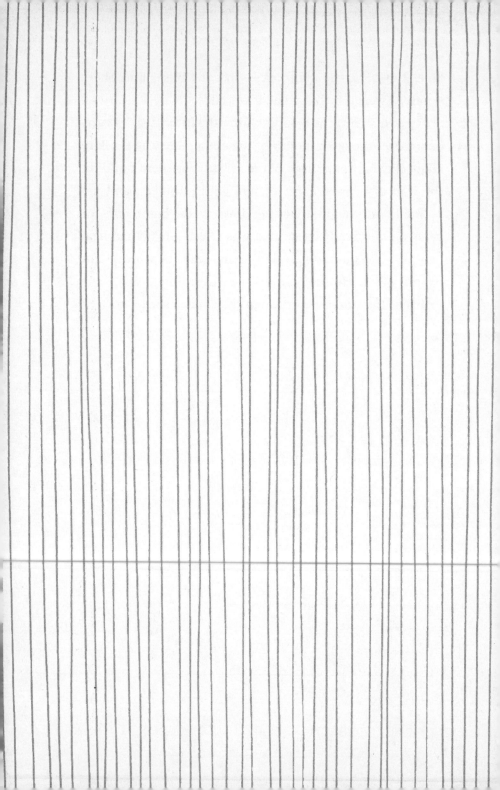

On Sunday, Owen and his father took the subway down to Times Square.

"A day out to celebrate surviving your first week of school," Dad said cheerfully as they emerged from belowground, finding themselves immediately surrounded by a sea of tourists, their faces all hidden by maps or cameras.

"Surviving being the operative word there," Owen said under his breath, though it was apparently still loud enough to make Dad roll his eyes.

"It can't be that bad," he said, tilting his head back to take in the blinking signs all around them. There were huge television screens and tickers with scrolling stock quotes, billboards and advertisements all lit up so that even in the middle of the day, the whole strange, electric landscape gave off a whitish glare.

"Actually, it is," Owen said without looking at him. A crowd of tourists brushed past, bumping into him, and he was shoved forward a step.

"You've got to stop acting like such a country mouse," Dad said, clapping him on the back. "You're a New Yorker now."

"Hardly," Owen said quietly, but if Dad heard him this time, he didn't say anything. Instead, he looked left and then right before stepping forward.

"This way," he said, starting to walk down Broadway with all the confidence of a man headed in the right direction.

"Where are we going?"

"Wherever," he said, his voice bright. "We're seeing the sights. Taking it all in. Enjoying the city. Getting to know the place. Making the best of it."

They paused at an intersection to let a red tour bus pass, and Owen jabbed a thumb at it. "You should really be working for them."

"I might just get the chance," Dad said, but to Owen's relief, he was still smiling.

Ever since the night the power came back, he'd gone about his superintendent duties with a quiet doggedness that was unlike him. Even when he'd been unemployed for all those months, he'd still started each morning by proclaiming that this might be the day, the one where everything turned around. He was a believer in fresh starts and second chances, and even in the throes of his grief this summer—a fog of sadness so thick he couldn't seem to see around it—he'd still been heartened by the idea of a new job. He'd wanted to get back to work. It didn't matter whether it was building houses or fixing clogged drains; work had always been a tonic. But this week, it had seemed like just another burden.

It wasn't hard to guess what had happened. Owen had no doubt that Sam Coleman had been in touch, and he hated to think of that boxy little man yelling at his father, warning him in the same way he'd warned Owen. They'd managed to get the water pumps working that night, the two of them crouched on the floor of the utilities room until late, his father holding a flashlight while Owen worked the wrench with gritted teeth, following instructions as best he could. But he knew enough to know that wouldn't be the end of it, and watching his father now—his face alight with the reflected glow of the billboards all around them— he understood not everything would be so easily fixable.

"What should we do first?" Dad asked as the light turned green and they were swept across the street by a tide of people.

Owen shrugged. "Whatever you want."

"Oh, come on," he said, looking around. "We could go see a show?"

"Um..."

"Or a play?"

Owen made a face.

"Fine," Dad said with an exaggerated groan. "Then you pick something."

He was about to refuse. He was about to point out that this whole excursion wasn't his idea. He was about to suggest simply going home. But they were approaching an enormous gift shop, the whole window filled with green foam crowns shaped like the Statue of Liberty, Big Apple pens and pencils and paperweights, Yankees jerseys, and *I ♥ NY* shirts like the ones he'd grumbled about to Lucy.

"Let's check this place out," he said, veering to the right, and though Dad gave him a mystified look, he followed without comment.

Inside, the shop was crowded, and while Dad wandered over to check out a display of old subway tokens, Owen slipped by a family trying on matching T-shirts and wove his way over to the enormous racks of postcards.

Every day this week, he'd looked for Lucy. Every day, he'd thought about knocking on the door of her apartment. At first, because he wanted to apologize for leaving the roof that morning. And then later, simply because he was anxious to see her again. But something kept stopping him. He couldn't let go of the worry that the night hadn't meant the same thing to her. For him, it had been a kind of oasis—not just the elevator, and not just the roof, but the simple fact of being with her. And as soon as he'd seen the gift shop, he was right back there again, lying on the floor of her kitchen and talking about faraway places.

As he flipped through the postcards, he came across one where a series of bright pink letters spelled out the words *Wish You Were Here* in a banner across the Manhattan skyline. He felt a strange electricity go through him at the sight of it. They'd laughed together at the slogan that night, at the halfheartedness of the words, but standing there, he couldn't remember why he'd found them so ridiculous only days ago.

Wish you were here, he thought, closing his eyes for a moment.

When he opened them again, there was a clerk standing in front of him, an older man with unruly sideburns and a bored expression. "Can I help you?" he asked, not sounding particularly excited about the prospect.

"I'll take this," Owen said, surprising even himself. "And can I get a stamp, too?"

From across a sea of miniature yellow cabs and red apples, he could see his father wandering back in his direction. Before he could think better of it, he reached for a pen shaped like the Empire State Building and scrawled a few words across the back of the postcard, then grabbed the stamp, slid a couple of dollars across the counter, and thanked the clerk.

"Find anything?" Dad asked as he joined him at the counter, but Owen only shook his head.

"This stuff's for tourists," he said with a shrug. "We live here."

Though he tried to hide it, Owen could see the grin that crept onto his dad's face, which remained there all the way out of the shop and into the street. They turned back down Broadway, moving toward the lights like a couple of moths, but just before the next intersection, Owen hesitated, letting Dad—who didn't even seem to notice—move on without him. There was a blue mailbox beside a lamp-post near the edge of the sidewalk, and before he could think better of it, he stepped over to it, opened the chute, and let the postcard go sailing away from him.

Later, they took the subway back home, tired and sun-burned. As they walked the last few blocks, Owen noticed for the first time an edge of coolness in the air, an early hint of the shifting season. His first thought was of home—not so much the house in Pennsylvania as his mother—and his second, of course, was to recall that it didn't exist any-more. At least not the way he remembered it.

Beside him, Dad seemed lost in thought, too, but when Owen looked over, he offered a smile "Not a bad day, huh?" he said. "Maybe we should do something tonight, too. Go see a musical or something?" He laughed at the expression on Owen's face. "I'm only kidding. Maybe just a movie...or hey, what about the planetarium? That's probably more up your alley...."

As they walked up to the revolving doors, Owen was momentarily lost for words. He didn't know whether to be cautious or hopeful. Every night since they'd been here, Dad had simply disappeared into his room after dinner. He'd always been a morning person, so going to bed early wasn't unusual, but ever since the accident, it seemed that all he did was sleep, like it was some sort of drug and he couldn't get enough of it. All this week, it had been even worse, worn down as he was by the lingering effects of the heat exhaus-tion, and Owen had assumed tonight would be no different.

But now it seemed possible he was starting to wake up again.

As they swung through the doors—Dad first, followed by Owen in the next compartment—he readied his response. "That sounds great," he would say, as they spilled out onto the other side. "I'd really like that."

But when he stepped out of the carousel and into the lobby, he stumbled straight into Dad, who was standing stock-still in front of the doors. Owen looked around him to see the broad back of Sam Coleman, who was leaning on the desk and talking to a man in a blue shirt with a cap that read EMK Plumbing.

For a moment, Owen considered bolting. He thought about shoving his father through the doorway to the mail-room and straight downstairs, where they could order a pizza and turn on a movie and act like none of it had happened: the accident or the move or the blackout, the trip to Coney Island and the sad and weary aftermath.

But instead, he simply watched as Dad squared his shoulders and lifted his chin. "Everything okay there, Sam?" he called out, and both men turned in their direction.

Sam smiled—a smile that felt like its opposite—and the plumber lowered his clipboard. "That him?" he asked, and Sam nodded, stepping forward.

"Hey there, Buckleys," he said, all friendliness and teeth. "How's it going?"

"Fine," Dad said shortly. "What's happening?"

Sam's eyebrows shot up, like he was surprised Dad

wasn't in the mood for chitchat. "You have a real knack for picking your days off," he said with a short laugh. "We had a little issue with the pipes this afternoon." He turned to Owen. "Hope you don't get seasick, 'cause you practically need a boat to get around down there."

"We've got it sorted out now," the plumber said, scanning his clipboard. "It'll be just fine."

Sam nodded. "Yup," he said. "He's got it sorted out now. But what I'd like to know is why he found the valve still loose on the pump."

Owen had been standing there listening with clenched fists, but now his heart plummeted. He cast a wild glance in Dad's direction and saw that his face had drained of color. But he didn't move a muscle; he stood entirely still, his eyes fixed on Sam.

"I guess I must not have tightened it up enough," he said, his words slow and measured.

"Well, somebody sure didn't," the plumber chimed in, looking up. "That wasn't real smart."

"No, it wasn't," Sam said. "Not real cheap, either."

The plumber shook his head and gave a low whistle.

Owen stepped forward. "Listen," he said, but Dad held up a hand, and he was pulled up short, falling abruptly silent.

"It's my fault," Dad said to Sam, who bobbed his head.

"You bet it is," he agreed, the false smile wiped from his face. "And look, I know you're family, and I know you're going through a rough patch here, but I can't have this kind of sloppy work in one of my buildings, especially not after what happened the other day."

Dad said nothing, but he kept his back very straight as he listened.

"I don't feel good about this, Patrick," Sam was saying. "I don't feel good about it at all. But I've got to find someone I can rely on."

"I understand," Dad said, his voice tight.

Sam rubbed at the back of his neck, his eyes cutting over to Owen. "You can take your time getting out of the apartment, okay? Take all the time you need."

"That's good of you," Dad said. "But we'll be out by the end of the week."

"Okay," Sam said.

"Okay," Dad said.

"Okay," the plumber said, tearing off a bill and handing it over to Sam.

Owen was still staring dumbly at the scene before him, but when Dad began to cross the lobby, heading for the basement door, he snapped back, hurrying after him.

Dad said nothing as they walked down the stairs, nothing as he led them through the concrete hallways, ducking his head below the pipes that ran across the ceiling like a maze. It wasn't until they were inside the apartment with the door closed behind them that he let out a long breath, his shoulders slumping. He leaned against the wall, the same place where he'd been huddled when he'd come back from Coney Island the other night, visibly shaken.

Owen was the first to speak. "It's my fault," he said. "I was the one who didn't close the valve all the way."

Dad smiled wearily. "I was the one who should have reminded you."

"You were sick."

"Doesn't matter," he said. "You couldn't possibly know how to do something like that. It was my job and my responsibility. So it's my fault."

"Yeah, but—"

"Hey," he said, looking up sharply. "It's fine. We're going to be fine."

Owen said nothing, only watched as Dad pushed himself off the wall, walking over to the kitchen, where he opened one of the drawers and pulled out the box of cigarettes. He held it for a moment, just looking at it, then opened the lid with great care. But when he saw there was only one left, he set it gently back in the drawer.

He glanced over at Owen, who was hovering in the doorway, and his face was entirely expressionless. "I'm gonna go lie down for a bit," he said. "We'll figure it out later, okay? Wake me when you're ready for dinner...."

Owen nodded, then retreated back down the hallway to his own room, where he sifted through an overgrown pile of laundry, fishing out the pair of shorts he'd been wearing a week ago, the day the lights had gone out. He reached into one pocket, then the other, then turned each one inside out. But the cigarette—his mother's cigarette—was no longer there.

Sitting on the edge of the bed, he felt a great weariness wash over him, and rather than fight it, he let it carry him out to sea. He curled up and closed his eyes, and he knew then that he wouldn't wake his father later, that he'd let him sleep, and that he'd sleep, too, and with any luck, tomorrow would be better.

In the morning, when the column of sun reached in through his tiny window, he hauled himself out of bed and back down the hallway, where he found his dad bent over a map at the kitchen counter. It was faded and curling at the corners, and there were small rips along the seams.

"How old is that thing?" Owen asked, stifling a yawn.

"Older than you," Dad said without looking up. He was tracing a finger along a thread of highway, and when Owen leaned in, he could see the direction it was moving: west.

"Was California even a state then?" he joked, and Dad shot him a look, but there was something good-natured about it, something almost joyful, and Owen sensed that some curtain had been lifted since last night, some weight they'd both been carrying.

"I was thinking we might take a little drive."

"Oh yeah?"

"Yeah," he said with a grin. "I was thinking we'd head out on the road, see how far we get."

Owen tried to hide his smile but failed completely. "That sounds like a pretty good plan."

"You'd be fine with it then?" Dad asked. "Not staying here, not going back?"

"Yes," he said with a decisive nod, and the word echoed through his head: *Yes, yes, yes.* His chest felt light and expansive, his heart lifting at the thought, and it seemed so sensible, so obvious—that they would go west, that they would move forward, because where else was there to go?—that it almost felt like a trick, like at any moment, Dad might tell him it was all some terrible joke.

But he didn't. Instead, he folded up the map, giving Owen a searching look. "You'd be missing some school...."

"I'll survive," Owen said, nodding at the map. "You can use that thing to teach me geography."

"Seriously," he said. "I don't want you falling behind because of this."

"I have enough credits to graduate now, if I wanted to," Owen said. "And I can do my applications on the road. It won't be a problem. Really."

Dad smiled, but it didn't make it all the way up to his eyes, which remained solemn. "So we're doing this."

Owen nodded. "We're doing this."

"Okay," Dad said, and he lifted his coffee mug, nudging another toward Owen. They raised them at the same time, the clink of the ceramic ringing out through the drab kitchen and along the halls of the little apartment.

Owen floated through the school day in a haze, day-dreaming about the road ahead of them. They could end up in Chicago or Colorado or California. It didn't matter. It would be a new start. Not in the dungeon of some great city castle but out west, where there were more mountains than people and where the skies were lousy with stars.

After school, he walked home with his head still buzzing, his thoughts several time zones away. He crossed the lobby and hurried through the mailroom, eager to get downstairs and see what other plans his dad might have come up with while he was at school, pausing only to unlock the little cubby that belonged to the basement apartment. He threw the two catalogs and the envelope full of coupons directly into the bin, and was just about to slam the door when he noticed something in the back.

Even before he reached for it, he knew what it was. He had no idea where it was from, or what it would say, but he knew it was from her. He just knew.

The scene on the front was an overhead view of the city of London, and he stared at it, stunned that she could be an ocean away without him even knowing. He was still puzzling over this as he flipped it over, and his heart began to beat quick as a hummingbird.

There, on the back of the postcard, were the exact same words he'd written just yesterday.

I actually do.

He blinked at it, stunned, and he felt his mouth stretch into a slow smile.

She'd sent him a postcard, too, and with the very same

message he'd sent her. It seemed impossible, yet here it was, and as he stood there gaping at it, his mouth hanging open, he sensed someone in the doorway.

"It's because of what it says on the front," she said, and it took Owen a moment to wrench his eyes from the message in his hand. When he finally looked up, there she was, leaning on the handle of her suitcase, her cheeks flushed and her eyes bright. "The whole 'wish you were here' thing." She shook her head, and a few strands came loose from her ponytail. "It's stupid. I didn't expect—I didn't think I'd be here when you got it...."

"No," he said, holding it up like an idiot. "It's great. Really. Thank you."

"I'm just getting back, actually," she said, pointing at the bag. "My parents flew me over there a few days after the blackout."

"I looked for you," he said, then shook his head, wishing he could think of something better to say, wishing his mind would keep up with his heart, which was thundering in his chest. "I guess that's why."

She nodded. "Guess so."

"Listen, I'm sorry about—about the roof that day," he said in a rush. "I was coming back, but then—"

"No, it's fine," she said. "I wasn't expecting—"

"It was just that my dad—"

"It's okay," she said as their words crossed like swords in the air between them.

Owen glanced down at the postcard, the small blocky

letters on the back. Then he flipped it over again, and the words went tumbling around in his head: *wish you were here.*

He had. And he did. And now he was leaving.

He raised his eyes to meet hers, pulling in a breath. "There's actually something—" he began, but once again, she had started to speak as well.

"I need to tell you something," she was saying, and he nodded. Her mouth twisted to one side. "I think," she said, then paused and began again. "I think we're probably moving."

Owen stared at her. "You are?"

"It's still not completely for sure, but it looks that way, yeah."

"Where?"

"To London, actually. My parents are still over there, working out the details."

"Wow," he said, shaking his head back and forth. "That's . . . wow."

"I know," she said. "It's crazy. And really fast."

"How fast?"

"Next month, probably," she said, and he must have looked surprised, because she hurried on. "But we'd be keeping the apartment here, and my dad promised we could still come back for the summer, or at least some of it. So maybe . . ."

Owen forced a smile. "Yeah," he said. "Maybe."

Lucy sighed. "I'm still not sure how I feel about all this."

He nodded numbly; he wasn't sure why this news should be hitting him so hard—why he should be feeling left behind—when he was leaving, too. "Well," he said, "it's a lot closer to Paris."

"And Rome."

"And Prague."

She grinned. "So you're saying I shouldn't play the sullen-new-girl card."

"Not at all," he said, twisting the postcard around in his hands like a pinwheel. "You can complain to me anytime you want."

"I might just take you up on that," she said, and he took a deep breath, trying to work up to his own news, to explain that he would be leaving, too, that they'd been brought together again only to go pinballing off in opposite directions.

But he couldn't find the words. And so instead, they just stood there, regarding each other silently, the room suddenly as quiet as the elevator had been, as comfortable as the kitchen floor, as remote as the roof. Because that's what happened when you were with someone like that: the world shrank to just the right size. It molded itself to fit only the two of you, and nothing more.

Eventually, a woman with a baby on her hip inched her way around Lucy's suitcase, scraping her key against the lock of her mailbox, and they stepped aside to give her room. When she left, the spell had been broken.

"So," Lucy said, turning her suitcase around so that

it was facing the other direction. "I should probably go unpack." She nodded at the postcard he was still clutching. "I know it's kind of cheesy...."

"No, it's great," Owen said, and a laugh escaped him. "Actually, you should keep an eye on your mailbox, too."

She tilted her head, eyeing him like she didn't quite believe it. "Really?"

"Really."

"Okay, then," she said with a smile.

He nodded. "Okay, then."

He watched as she wheeled the suitcase back through the lobby and over to the elevators, the place where they'd first met. As soon as she punched the button, the door opened with a bright *ding*, but just as she was about to step inside, he called out to her.

"Lucy," he said, and she whirled around, looking at him expectantly. Behind her, the doors eased shut again, and he jogged over with no plan at all, no words in mind, no brilliant speech, no idea at all what he might possibly say next. But something urgent had bubbled up inside him at the sight of her walking away, something desperate and true.

"If you're about to suggest the stairs instead..." she said, teasing him, but he only shook his head.

"I was just going to say..." He trailed off, looking at her helplessly. He wanted to tell her that he was leaving, too, even sooner than she was, and that this might be goodbye. He wanted to say *let's keep in touch* or *I hope we'll see each other again* or *I'll miss you*. But none of it seemed quite right. Instead, he just stood there, tongue-tied and faltering, unable to say anything at all.

But it didn't matter. After a moment, she leaned forward and put a hand on his shoulder, and then, to his surprise, she rose onto her tiptoes and kissed him. His eyes widened as their lips met, and the nearness of her made the world go blurry, until all at once, it wasn't; all at once, it came into focus again, and the clearest thing of all—the truest thing of all—was the girl right in front of him. And so he closed his eyes and kissed her back.

Too soon, she broke away, and when she stepped back again, he could see that she was smiling. "Don't worry," she said, just before stepping into the open elevator. "I'll send you a postcard."

PART II

There

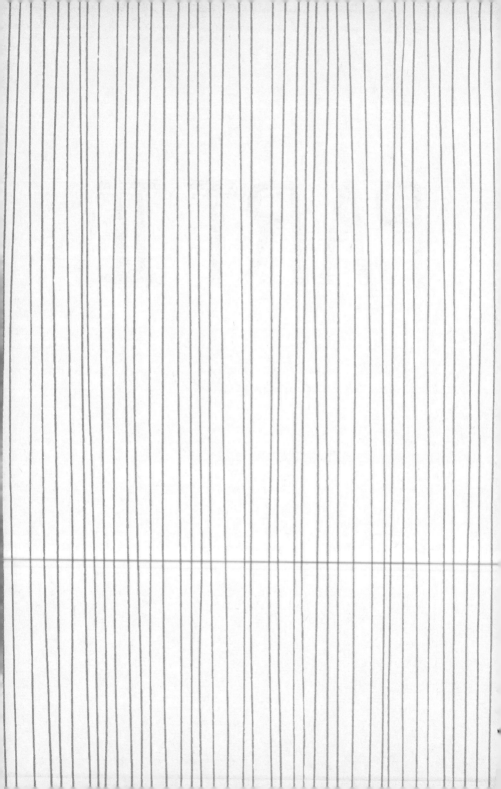

There was only one square of pizza left on the table between them, and it was no great prize. The cheese had lost its battle with gravity, slumping off to one side, and the whole thing was shiny with grease. But still Owen refused to give in, his eyes watering as he stared down his father, whose face was twisted in concentration. A few more seconds went by, and finally—half gasping and half laughing— Dad closed his eyes and then opened them again.

"Ha," Owen said, reaching for the slice, which he flopped onto his plate. He blinked a few times himself. "I don't think you've ever beat me. You need a new game."

Dad sat back in his chair and rubbed his eyes. "How about arm wrestling?"

"Not fair," Owen said around a mouthful of pizza. Even though it had been months, his dad's arms were still muscular from working construction sites. Owen's were alarmingly scrawny by comparison.

Dad grinned. "Then maybe we need a third game to decide what game we play to decide on things."

"The pizza would be cold by the time we figured it out."

"Maybe that would be an improvement," he joked, letting his eyes rove around the room, which was filled with checkered tablecloths and lit by dozens of lopsided candles in wax-covered jars. Out the large windows that ran the length of the restaurant, the streets of Chicago were dusky and gray, the sidewalks still slick with rain from an afternoon shower.

Owen finished the slice and licked his fingers, following Dad's gaze to a table in the corner just beneath a vintage poster advertising romantic Italian getaways.

"Is that where you sat?" he asked. "With Mom?"

Dad nodded. "Looks the same."

"I bet she got the last piece, too," Owen teased, trying to pull him back, and for once it worked. Dad laughed, turning around again.

"You don't think I could beat my own wife in a staring contest?"

Owen shook his head. "I do not."

"Then you'd be correct," he said with a smile.

Afterward, they walked out into the chilly Chicago night, pulling up their collars against the wind coming off the lake. They'd been here since early afternoon, wandering around Michigan Avenue, their heads tipped back to take in the jagged skyline until it started to rain, and they'd huddled beneath some scaffolding to wait it out, eating bags of warm popcorn and watching the world grow soggy.

It had been this way in the other cities, too, first Philadelphia, then Columbus and Indianapolis. They'd arrive in the afternoon and set off together through the city streets until night fell and they left the lights behind them, finding some remote motel on the outskirts that would better suit their meager budget.

Tonight would only be their fourth since leaving New York, but it felt to Owen like it had been much longer. They were taking their time, inching their way across the country with only the concern over finding a school to propel them forward, though even that felt somewhat insubstantial. Owen had always been way ahead of his class, especially in math and science, and they both knew a couple of weeks wouldn't make a difference in the long run.

But it wasn't just the pace that made them feel suspended, like they were doing little more than drifting. It was the odd feeling that they'd been set loose into the world with nothing—and no one—left to reel them back again.

Owen now understood that the words on all those side-view mirrors were wrong. Objects behind them were *not* closer than they appeared. Not at all. So far, they'd put eight hundred miles between them and New York, but it might as well have been eight million.

They walked back toward the car in silence, crossing over the brackish waters of the Chicago River beneath glassy buildings that threw back the city's lights. They were still a few blocks away when they passed a gift shop, the windows crowded with the usual tokens—specific to Chicago but still somehow generic all the same—and before Owen even had a chance to pause, Dad wheeled around with a broad grin.

"Let me guess...."

Owen bristled. "I'll just be a minute," he said, but Dad held up both hands in defense.

"By all means," he said. "Take your time, Romeo."

"It's not like that," Owen insisted, pulling open the door of the shop, but as he made his way over to the display of postcards, he realized he wasn't so sure. Pretty much everything else in his rearview mirror had disappeared at this point. But somehow Lucy remained, the one sturdy thing in all that quicksand.

He thought of her now as he flipped through the display of postcards: the chipped nail polish on her toes, the way her hair fell across her shoulders, the funny little slope of her nose, which seemed to catch the freckles before they could slide off.

He'd only seen her once more before he left, just two short days after their run-in by the mailboxes. After a morning spent packing—squeezing what they could into their ancient red Honda and then lugging the rest out to the curb—Dad went out to take care of some last-minute things with Sam, who didn't seem particularly heart-broken about their quick departure. He'd already lined up a new building manager, who would be moving into the basement just as soon as they cleared out.

But for the moment, it was still theirs, and as Owen stood alone amid the remaining boxes, he glanced at the microwave clock for what felt like the millionth time that day. When he saw that it was after three, he hurried up to the lobby.

He didn't have to wait long. He sat on the bench between the two elevators, ignoring Darrell's inquiring looks from behind the front desk, and when she came whirling through the revolving doors in her school uniform, he shot to his feet.

"Hey," she said, drawing out the word long and slow, a look of confusion in her eyes as she approached him. There was a streak of blue pen near the collar of her white blouse, and he was momentarily distracted by it.

"Hey," he said, forcing his eyes up to hers.

She shifted her backpack from one shoulder to the other. "What's up?"

"Nothing," he said, then shook his head. "Well... something."

She raised her eyebrows.

"So... it's not just you."

"What's not?" she asked with a frown.

"I'm actually moving, too," he said, and she hesitated a moment, then let out a short laugh. But when she saw that he wasn't kidding, her mouth snapped back into a straight line.

"Seriously?" she asked, her eyebrows raised.

He nodded. "Seriously."

They stood there for a long time as he explained everything—about Sam and the water pipes, about their house in Pennsylvania that was still for sale, about wanting to move forward instead of backward. At some point—he couldn't be sure when—they both sat down on the bench, while on either side of them, the elevators scissored open and closed, making the people inside appear and then disappear over and over again.

After a while, Lucy reached for her backpack, which was slouched at her feet, then pulled out a pen and a scrap of notebook paper, holding them out for him.

"I don't know where we'll end up," he said, but she shook her head.

"Just give me your e-mail address."

"I don't have a smartphone," he said, digging in his pocket to show her. "I have a very, very dumb phone. In fact, it's kind of an idiot."

"Well, then there's always your computer," she said, handing him the pen and paper anyway. "Or, you know... postcards."

He couldn't tell if she was joking, but he smiled at this anyway. "Who doesn't like getting a piece of cardboard in the mail?"

She laughed, then motioned at the mailroom behind her. "You know where to find me."

"And if you go to London?"

"I'll e-mail you my new address."

"And hopefully I'll get it."

"Right," she said. "Otherwise I'll just keep sending e-mails into the void and hope maybe your dumb phone gets a little bit smarter."

"Doubtful," he said, as he scribbled his address onto the scrap of paper. He'd never been much for instant communication or social networking. It was true that he'd need his computer for college applications, and he'd probably have to get in touch with his old guidance counselor by e-mail at some point, but beyond that, he couldn't imagine being particularly plugged in on this trip.

He'd never really had a reason to keep in touch with anyone before. Everyone he knew had always lived within shouting distance. But it was starting to become clear that this wasn't a big strength of his, this whole communication thing. In the weeks since they left Pennsylvania, Casey and Josh had e-mailed him several times, but Owen hadn't been able to bring himself to write back. And since there were no other places to find him online, no additional outposts in the endless maze of the Internet, that was pretty much it for them: radio silence—the line gone well and truly dead. He'd never been on Twitter and was one of the last people he knew who had managed to avoid Facebook. He was a firm believer in having more friends in real life than online, though he didn't have very many of either at the moment.

Even so, when he handed back the paper, his heart beat fast at the thought that he might hear from Lucy. She folded it carefully, then tucked it into the front pocket of her bag with a smile, the kind of perfectly ordinary smile he suspected would take a very long time to forget.

So far on the trip, none of the motels they'd stayed at had any sort of Internet access, except for one that was charging way too much for it, so he'd checked his e-mail for the first time only yesterday, in a sandwich shop in Indianapolis that doubled as an Internet café. While his dad stood in line to get a couple of subs, Owen sat hunched beside a guy looking up instructions for how to make guacamole. There was only one e-mail from Lucy, who had written to say that they would no longer be going to London. Apparently, her father had missed out on the job there but was offered a different position instead. So they were now moving to Edinburgh.

I'm looking forward to wearing a kilt and learning to play the bagpipes, she wrote. *My very, very English mother is having a heart attack, but I think it'll be a nice change of scenery. And I'm excited to finally be Somewhere. I hope your Somewhere is living up to expectations, too. Hope to hear from you soon. Otherwise, will send word when I have my new address. And in the meantime, I'll be sure to give your regards to the Loch Ness Monster.*

Now, in the cramped souvenir shop in Chicago, Owen grabbed a photo of Lake Michigan—sweeping out from the skyline in a brilliant and seemingly endless blue—and thought for a moment before scrawling a few words on the back: *Wish Nessie were here.*

When he looked up, he was surprised to find that Dad was right beside him. Owen, lost in his own head, hadn't even heard him come in, and his first instinct was to cup a hand around the postcard. But it was too late.

"Who's Nessie?" Dad asked, looking genuinely puzzled, and Owen swallowed back a laugh.

"Don't worry about it," he said, slipping the postcard into his pocket. "You don't know her."

They walked over to the checkout together, where a girl with a pierced nose and a streak of pink in her hair was beaming at them for no particular reason.

"And how are you today?" she asked while punching a few things into a computer. "You must be traveling."

"We are," Dad said, smiling back.

"Where are you off to?"

Owen handed her a few crumpled bills. "Out west somewhere."

"Awesome," she said, bobbing her head. "I'm from California. Can't get more west than that."

"Not in this country, anyway," Dad agreed. "Where in California?"

"Lake Tahoe," she said. "So it barely counts. It's just over the Nevada border. But it's a great place. Mountains. Trees. The lake, obviously." She held up Owen's postcard before sliding it into a plastic bag. "This lake here might be a lot bigger, but the color doesn't even compare. Tahoe is so blue it looks fake."

Dad gave Owen a sideways glance. "It sounds pretty nice."

"It is," she said. "You should check it out."

"Hey, do you have any postcard stamps?" Owen asked, realizing he'd used his last one in Indiana.

"I think so," she said, opening the register and lifting the little tray of bills. She dug around with a frown, and then the too-bright smile returned to her face. "Got 'em," she said, holding up a little packet. "How many do you need?"

"Just one," Owen mumbled, but Dad clapped him on the back.

"Oh, let's not kid ourselves, son," he said cheerfully. "I think you're going to need more than one."

Owen felt his cheeks burn. "I'll take ten," he said, unable to look up.

"Great," said the clerk. "U.S. or international?"

"U.S.," he said, but as soon as he did, a little flash of realization went through him. Soon, he remembered, he would need international stamps. Soon, she'd be an ocean away.

When they finished paying, they started for the car in silence. Owen was grateful for this, his mind still busy with the idea that he'd soon need a special stamp just to send Lucy a postcard. It was a small thing, he knew. In fact, there were few things smaller. But something about it felt big all the same.

If you were to draw a map of the two of them, of where they started out and where they would both end up, the lines would be shooting away from each other like magnets spun around on their poles. And it occurred to Owen that there was something deeply flawed about this, that there should be circles or angles or turns, anything that might make it possible for the two lines to meet again. Instead, they were both headed in the exact opposite directions. The map was as good as a door swinging shut. And the geography of the thing—the geography of *them*—was completely and hopelessly wrong.

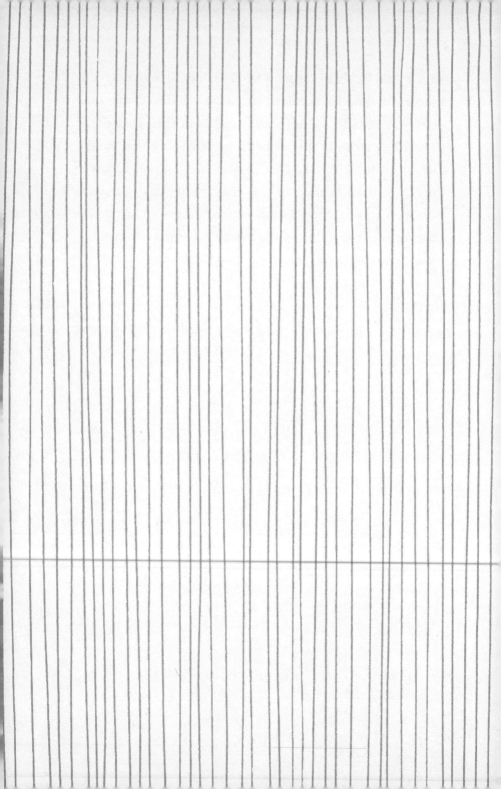

10

During breakfast on her fourth morning in Edinburgh, just before the start of the fourth day at her new school, a postcard came spinning across the table in Lucy's direction. She lowered her spoon, watching as it bumped up against her glass of orange juice and came to a stop, the light glinting off the photo: a cornflower-blue lake surrounded by a ring of mountains, like teeth around a yawning mouth.

"That got stuck in a catalog from yesterday's mail," Dad said, sitting down across the table. Mom looked up from her newspaper—the *Herald Scotland*, which was only a placeholder until she managed to sort out her subscription to the *New York Times*—and her eyes landed on the postcard.

"It seems your daughter has fallen for a traveling salesman," she said to Dad, who was too busy with his copy of *The Guardian* to respond.

"He's just a friend," Lucy said a bit too quickly, sliding the postcard toward the edge of the table and then lifting the corner to take a quick peek, like a poker player guarding his cards.

"Well, I think it's romantic," Mom said. "Nobody writes each other anymore. It's all just e-mails and faxes."

Dad glanced up. "Nobody faxes anymore, either."

"Another lost art," Mom said with an exaggerated sigh, and he winked at her.

"I'll fax you anytime."

Lucy groaned. "Please stop."

But it was true. There were never any e-mails from him. No letters, either. It was always, always the postcards—several a week, when he was still on the road, places she could track on a map as he'd moved steadily west—but lately there'd hardly even been any of those. Now that Owen and his father were planning to stay in Lake Tahoe—as he'd written to tell her a couple of weeks ago—Lucy understood that the postcard gimmick had probably run its course. She also realized that any mail from him might be slower in coming now that she was all the way in Scotland, almost five thousand miles from the little lake town that straddled the border between California and Nevada. But she'd hoped they'd at least move the conversation over to e-mail. She never imagined the whole thing might just taper off entirely.

This was the first she'd heard from him in more than a week, in spite of the three e-mails she'd sent, filled with questions about his new home in Tahoe and updates about their move to Edinburgh. She realized he was probably busy with a new school and a new house and a new life, but she was surprised by how fiercely she wanted to know about it all, and how difficult it was to wait and wait amid such crashing silence.

Maybe, she told herself, he just wasn't much of a correspondent. After all, her brothers were in California, too, and though they had a pretty questionable grasp of the time difference—especially Charlie, who'd called more than once in the middle of the night—even they managed to e-mail every couple of days. She supposed it was possible that Owen still didn't have wireless access, but that seemed like a thin excuse, even to her. Maybe he just wasn't a big fan of e-mail. It made sense; even his postcards were never very long. Or maybe he was simply a guy who was at his best in person. (That she suspected she was at her best from a distance was something she was trying not to think too hard about.)

While her parents finished their breakfast, Lucy flipped over the long-awaited card, which read simply:

Loch Ness = 745 feet deep
Lake Tahoe = 1,644 feet deep
Your new monster pal would love it here. I bet you
would, too.

Before leaving for school, she slipped the note into the pocket of her blazer. When she stepped outside the bright red door of the town house, she was met by a wind far too cold and damp for any October she knew, and she felt a small shiver go through her. She shoved her hands deep in her pockets and ran her thumb along the rough edges of the postcard, which was somehow reassuring.

It was nearly eight by now, but all along the crescent of stone buildings that neighbored theirs, the street lamps were still on, burning little pockets of light into the morning haze. When they first found out they'd be moving to Edinburgh, this was just one of the many things her parents had seemed to find discouraging.

"I heard there are only five or six hours of daylight in the winter," Mom said, looking miserable. "They might as well be sending us to Siberia."

"It won't be as bad as all that," Dad had told her, but Lucy could tell from the set of his mouth that he was only trying to make the best of it. She'd overheard them arguing after he lost out on the position in London. As a consolation prize, they'd offered him some big job in the Edinburgh office, and he'd accepted out of an odd sense of duty, as well as the hope that it might soon lead to better things.

"Scotland?" Mom kept repeating as if she couldn't quite believe it, and Lucy tried hard not to laugh at her accent, which had grown softer after all these years in New York, but which was now suddenly as crisp and precise as if she were speaking to the queen.

"I've heard it's nice," Dad said weakly, and Mom wrinkled her nose.

"I went once when I was Lucy's age."

"And?" he asked, looking hopeful.

"And the whole city smelled like stew."

"Stew?"

"Stew," Mom confirmed.

Now that they were here, Lucy could sort of see what she meant. There was definitely something heavy in the air, something vaguely soupy, but she only ever caught a whiff of it from time to time, when the winds shifted and the scent of the North Sea—full of salt and brine—drifted inland. She didn't mind it, though. And she didn't mind the darkness, either. Just as sunshine and clear skies suited beach towns, the constant rain and perpetual clouds suited Edinburgh, with its stone buildings and churches, its uneven cobblestone streets and the enormous castle that sat high above it all. There was something utterly romantic about it, as if you'd fallen straight into a fairy tale.

Once she reached Princes Street, Lucy waited for the bus beneath the gaze of the castle, a fortress of stone perched on a cliff above the gardens that separated the old section of the city from the new one. When the bus arrived, she was lucky to find a seat, shouldering in between two women in woolly jackets who proceeded to talk around her in nearly indecipherable accents. On her first day, Lucy had brought along her old copy of *The Catcher in the Rye*, clinging to that small piece of New York as she rode through the unfamiliar city. But halfway there, she lowered it to watch the buildings whip past the windows, and she hadn't picked it up since. There was too much to see.

Her school was all the way across town, tucked just behind a huge rounded hill that rose between the city and the sea. The sun had climbed higher now, pushing through the fog so that the world had turned from gray to gold, and when the bus hissed to a stop across the street from the school, Lucy stepped off behind a cluster of younger students, all of them chattering away as they hurried through the gate.

She wasn't sure exactly what she'd been expecting when she first arrived. She'd been kidding about the kilts and bagpipes in her e-mail to Owen, but there was still a little part of her that half expected to be greeted by a bunch of red-bearded, plaid-wearing, whiskey-swigging classmates. As it turned out, though, Scottish schools weren't all that different from American ones—at least not in any of the ways that were important. The uniforms were worse—knee-length skirts and boxy blazers—and the accents of her teachers forced her to pay close attention, straining to find something recognizable inside all those rolling *r*'s and twisted vowels. But the students were pretty much the same. The boys played rugby instead of football, and everyone talked about sneaking their parents' whiskey instead of their parents' beer on the weekends, but these were all small things.

The only real difference—the only big difference—was Lucy herself.

She realized it on the very first day, when she managed to get lost. The headmaster had walked her to registration and left her with a faint photocopy of a school map, which she'd promptly misplaced. So after the bell rang for first period and the halls emptied out with impossible speed, she was left standing there with no clue where to go and no one to ask for help. It wasn't until she wandered around the corner that she found someone.

He was standing at his locker, leisurely reaching for his books, in no particular hurry despite the empty halls, and Lucy knew right away that she would have absolutely avoided someone like him back home. He was tall and broad-shouldered with dark hair and an angular jaw, too handsome to seem approachable. But it was more than that. There was something completely effortless about him, a casual confidence that was unnerving, even from a distance, even without having met him yet.

He was the type of guy who couldn't ever be invisible, even if he tried.

"Hey," she said, walking up to him. "Can you help me find my math class?"

He turned to face her, his mouth twisted up at the corners. "Maths," he said, drawing out the *s*.

"Math," Lucy repeated with a frown. "It's not my best subject, but I'm pretty sure I know the difference between one and two."

This time, he laughed. "Here we call it *maths*," he told her, reaching for the schedule in her hand and scanning the page. "And you're on the wrong floor."

"Ah," she said, her cheeks burning. "Thanks."

"No bother," he said, clearly amused, then shut his locker door. "See you later."

"Yeah," she said. "Maybe in histories. Or sciences."

He squinted at her, but when he realized she was only joking, his face broke into a grin. "Or lunches," he said, raising his eyebrows as he walked away.

Standing there alone in the hallway, she couldn't help smiling. For the first time in her life, she realized there was no hope of blending in. Here, she was the one who was different. She was the one with the accent. The new girl. The object of curiosity. And to her surprise, she found she didn't mind. Maybe this was why Owen had been so desperate to travel, why she'd longed for it herself without ever really knowing why. It wasn't just that you got to be somewhere else entirely. It was that you got to be some*one* else entirely, too.

Now, as she made her way through the huddles of students—many of them flashing unnervingly friendly smiles in her direction—she saw him standing at her locker. Already, in such a short amount of time, this had become a habit of sorts. Later on her first day, just after fourth period, he'd found her wandering again, and this time he escorted her to class. When the bell rang at the end, she was surprised to once again find him waiting just outside the door.

"It would be an awful shame if you got lost and missed lunch," he said with that blinding smile of his, and Lucy let herself be led to the dining hall. She waited for him to introduce himself, and when he didn't, she finally stuck out her hand a little awkwardly.

"I'm Lucy, by the way," she said, and his eyes shone with laughter as he regarded her outstretched hand.

"I know," he said, taking it in his and giving it an exaggerated shake.

"How?"

"Everyone knows," he said. "We don't get a lot of new kids here. Especially not Yanks."

"Oh," she said, her cheeks hot. "And you are...?"

"Liam."

In the cafeteria, he guided her through the lunch line, identifying the various trays of mush. "Neeps and tatties," he said, picking up a spoon and piling some on her plate, and when she gave him a mystified look, he smiled. "Turnips and potatoes."

She sat with him and his rugby friends, who peppered her with questions about New York. They wanted to know if she'd been to the top of the Empire State Building and if everyone in America had a swimming pool and whether she'd ever ridden in a yellow taxi. She felt like a visitor from some alien planet, but there was a warmth to their curiosity, a sense of genuine interest, and for once in her life, she didn't seem to be wilting under such unwavering attention: instead, to her surprise, she was glowing.

Afterward, Liam walked her to her next class, and just like that, it became a routine. She was grateful for the company, and more flattered than she cared to admit, even to herself. She'd seen the way other girls looked at Liam, had heard the stories of some of the plays he'd made on the rugby pitch, had watched the effect his easy smile had on teachers and students alike. But still, each time she saw him there, waiting outside one of her classrooms, she felt a pang of guilt, too.

It was ridiculous; she knew this. In four days here, she'd already spent more time with Liam than she'd ever spent with Owen. He hardly even wrote anymore, and it wasn't like they'd made any sort of promises to each other. So why did she feel like some small but essential part of her had been left behind in New York?

This morning, Liam was waiting at her locker again, but even as their eyes met and he lifted a hand, she couldn't bring herself to wave. Instead, she felt around in her pocket for the postcard, tracing the edges, a portable reminder of Owen.

"I have an idea," Liam said as soon as she was close enough. "Do you have plans this afternoon?"

Lucy shook her head.

"You probably haven't gone up Arthur's Seat yet, right?"

"Arthur's what?"

"Seat," he said, his eyes bright. "The hills just over

there. It's really famous, and there's a great view up top. Want to go after school?"

Lucy glanced down at her loafers. "I'm not sure I'm dressed for a hike."

"Don't worry," he said, flashing a grin. "It's really more of a walk."

After school, Liam led the way through winding streets lined with little shops that sat beneath the hunched green hills, until the roads opened up into a sloping park, and they picked up a trail that went up, up, up as far as she could see.

It was, as advertised, mostly just a walk at first, and they talked about their families and their homes and their siblings.

"Will your brothers come visit, or will you go back and see them?" Liam asked. "Must be a bit odd, being so far apart. My brother moved to London last year, and the way my mum's been acting, you'd think it was China."

Lucy smiled, keeping her eyes trained on the gravelly trail. "My cousin's getting married in San Francisco over Christmas break, so we'll all see each other then," she told him. "But I bet they'll come over here for the summer, too. They'd never miss a chance to do some traveling on my parents' dime."

"You mean 10p," he said.

"Huh?"

He glanced back with a grin. "Ten pence. No dimes over here."

It wasn't long before the path grew steeper, and they were soon too winded to continue talking. Lucy's lungs strained in the sea-heavy air, and her feet slipped on the dirt as the afternoon began to ease into evening.

"Won't it be too dark on the way down?" she asked, squinting up at Liam, who was a few strides ahead.

"Don't worry," he said. "I know the way."

They trudged on, both of them breathing hard, and Lucy was reminded of all those walks up and down the stairwell during the blackout. An image of Owen flashed in her mind, tall and gangly, lurching up the stairs with all the grace of a broomstick. When she looked up, she saw Liam powering ahead, sturdy-legged and strong-backed, and she felt a tug inside her, something wrenching and bleak.

A few other hikers passed them on their way down, but it felt to Lucy like they were the only ones still winding their way up, and her mouth was dry and chalky, her chest burning as they pushed on. She knew the city was unfolding at her back, and she wanted to turn and look, but she was afraid to lose momentum—or worse, lose Liam.

Finally, they rounded one last bend, and though she could see that there was still room to climb, Liam stopped at a flat outcropping, a sort of makeshift lookout point, and waved his arm out over the edge with a little flourish. For a moment, she couldn't look; instead, she bent over with her hands on her knees and struggled to catch her breath. Liam had hardly broken a sweat, and briefly, fleetingly, she decided that she hated him. What was he thinking? It was nearly dark now, and he'd dragged her up some stupid mountain on a lark. She'd never in her life felt more like a city kid, and she was suddenly certain that she didn't belong here. She was built for rooftops, not mountains.

But then she turned around, and there it was, the city of Edinburgh: spread before her in shades of purple and gold, all spires and turrets and glittering lights. Lucy walked up to the edge of the overlook, her eyes wide and her chest tight. In the distance, the castle glowed a faint white, and a scattering of other monuments pierced the evening sky.

"It's beautiful," she murmured, and Liam stepped up beside her. He was so close that she could hear a small rattle in his throat when he breathed, could feel the heat rising off him, but in spite of this, her thoughts were still five thousand miles away, in another place with another boy, and the unfairness of this lodged itself in her chest and made her feel like crying.

Because what was she supposed to do now? There was no point in waiting for someone who hadn't asked, and there was no point in wishing for something that would never happen. They were like a couple of asteroids that had collided, she and Owen, briefly sparking before ricocheting off again, a little chipped, maybe even a little scarred, but with miles and miles still to go. How long could a single night really be expected to last? How far could you stretch such a small collection of minutes? He was just a boy on a roof. She was just a girl in an elevator. Maybe that was the end of it.

Beside her, she could feel Liam smiling as the sky went a notch darker and the lights a notch brighter. "It looks like a painting, doesn't it?" he asked, and the words stirred something inside her. She let out a long breath, then shook her head.

"It looks," she said, "like a postcard."

11

For Thanksgiving, they bought a chicken instead of a turkey.

"There's no way we could eat that much," Dad said as he wheeled their cart through the freezing-cold aisles of the grocery store. And then, as if they needed reminding, he added: "There are only two of us."

Owen gave in to this, and to store-bought stuffing, too, but he insisted they make all the sides, even turnips.

"I hate turnips," Dad said with a groan.

"So do I," Owen said, dropping them into the cart. "But they were her favorite."

"Maybe we should start some new traditions of our own."

"Fine with me," said Owen, "as long as chicken isn't one of them."

Dad sighed as he steered the cart toward the checkout. "Next year will be better."

Owen said nothing; he couldn't think of a response.

They spent the morning preparing mashed potatoes

and turnips and cranberry sauce in the cramped kitchen of their rental apartment, a small two-bedroom place with thin walls and a hissing radiator. The smell of the chicken in the oven was overpowered by the scent of salsa from the Mexican restaurant downstairs. They'd been here almost two months now, and Owen had grown used to the way everything from the carpets to the couches always smelled a little spicy. Even his clothes had a kick to them that deodorant couldn't quite mask.

"If all else fails," he joked as he stirred one of the pots, "we can always grab some tacos."

"Come on now," Dad said. "I used to do a lot of the cooking, too."

Owen snorted, and Dad couldn't help laughing.

"Fine," he said. "But I microwaved with the best of them."

"You still do," Owen conceded. "It's quite a skill."

When they sat down to dinner, there was an awkward pause. Mom had always been the one to say grace, and now, in the guttering light of a single candle, the two of them looked at each other over bowls of steaming food and a chicken that was slightly too brown. And for the first time all day—the first time in weeks, really—Dad's face sagged and his eyes went murky.

Finally, Owen cleared his throat. They'd never been much of a prayers-before-dinner family, but this day was a special one, a time for reflection, and Owen had always loved the simple act of holding his mother's hand while he listened to her count the reasons she was happy. Now he reached over and laid his palm over his father's.

"I'm thankful that we're here together," he said, his voice gruff. He wanted to say more, but most of what was in his heart were things that he wished, rather than things he was thankful for: that Dad would find a job that lasted more than a week, that someone would buy the house in Pennsylvania, that their apartment wasn't so cold, and mostly, mostly, that his mom was here with them, too.

After a moment, he glanced up at Dad, whose eyes were closed.

"And I'm thankful for this chicken," he concluded, "who sacrificed his life to save a turkey."

Dad shook his head long and slow, but Owen could see that he was smiling, too.

"Amen to that," he said, picking up a fork.

After dinner, Dad offered to do the dishes, and Owen didn't argue.

"I'm gonna head out for a little bit," he said, pulling on a coat, and Dad nodded.

"Don't stay out too late," he said. "I want to get an early start tomorrow." Then, just before the door fell shut, he added: "Tell Paisley I say hello."

Outside, it had started to snow, the flakes slow and heavy. Before coming here, Owen had never experienced this kind of weather. Back in Pennsylvania, the snow came in patches, icy and slick, and had hardly settled on the ground before turning gray and slushy. But out here, on the edge of this great blue lake, it fell thickly and steadily, blanketing the world in white and muffling everything it touched.

The streets were quiet tonight. Everyone was bundled into their homes, the lights on in the windows as they finished off the last of the turkey. Owen's boots made deep footprints as he trudged through the town, which looked like the set of an old western, full of saloon-like bars and art galleries with elaborate wood-paneled doors. This was a ski town in the winter and a vacation spot in the summer, a place so filled with tourists that it never felt quite real. Everything was seasonal and everyone was just passing through. It was a place of transition, and at the moment, that suited Owen just fine.

When he reached the old diner that was shaped like a train car, he wandered around to the side, waiting beneath the towering pines, which formed a kind of umbrella against the snow. Most evenings, he'd be back there in the narrow kitchen, elbow-deep in dirty dishes, his eyes burning from the soap and grease, his fingers clammy inside the damp rubber gloves. But he was off tonight for the holiday.

Through the windows, he could see that a surprising number of people had taken advantage of the turkey special tonight. He sat down on the wooden steps, but they were too cold, and so he stood again, pacing out front until he heard the door creak open behind him.

"Hey, you," Paisley said from where she stood a few steps above him. She'd thrown her coat over her shoulders without zipping it, and her cheeks were rosy from the heat of the kitchen. Owen felt his heart quicken at the sight of her. She was probably the most beautiful girl he'd ever seen, and certainly the most beautiful he'd ever kissed. She had pale blue eyes and impossibly long blond hair, and when she got worked up about something—the amount of pollution in Lake Tahoe or the plight of the red wolf or the various problems in Africa (anywhere in Africa)—she would absentmindedly braid it, never failing to look surprised later when she discovered what she'd done.

She didn't go to his school. Paisley's mother and her long-time boyfriend—a guy named Rick who owned the diner and always smelled faintly of pot—had chosen to homeschool her, which tended to happen around which shifts were quietest. But Paisley didn't seem to mind. Owen had met her there during his first week in town, when he'd taken his dad for a milk shake to cheer him up after another luckless day of job searches. There'd been a notice for a dishwasher on the bulletin board near the door, and while Dad was paying the bill, Owen stood with his hands in his pockets, reading the description.

"It's not particularly glamorous," Paisley had said over his shoulder, and when he whipped around, he was momentarily lost for words. She flashed him a dazzling smile. "But it comes with a lot of free burgers. If you're into that sort of thing."

They only needed someone a few days a week, and Owen had applied without telling Dad. At that point, they were both still holding out hope that he'd find a job on a construction site, but in the meantime, Owen knew he would take anything, and the thought of his father wearing those rubber gloves and scouring pans at a sink for minimum wage made something go sour in the back of his throat.

When he finally got around to telling him, after a full week of work, Dad had only sighed, looking resigned. "That's great," he said. "But the money is yours, okay?"

Owen had agreed, but he always snuck most of it into his father's wallet anyway. If he noticed, Dad didn't say anything, and that was just fine with Owen. It wasn't really about the money, anyway. He liked the distraction of the job, having something to do after school. He liked getting a paycheck, and he liked the free food. He even liked humming along to the radio in the steamy kitchen as he scrubbed at the flakes of dry ketchup that covered the plates like ink blots.

But mostly, he liked seeing Paisley.

She would flit in and out of the kitchen, teasing him for trying to do his homework while he worked, his textbook propped up near the sink, dotted with flecks of water so that after a while the pages became stiff and wrinkled.

"Always science," she noted one day, her legs dangling from the counter, where she sat eating an apple and watching him.

Owen had shrugged. "It's interesting."

"Which part?"

He used his forearm to wipe some soap from his cheek. "I like astronomy best."

"Like horoscopes and stuff?" she asked, raising her eyebrows.

"No, that's astrology."

"So what's your sign?"

"I have no idea," he said. "That's not—"

She grinned. "We should find out."

"Astrology is totally different," he said, glancing up to see if she was embarrassed by the mistake, but that was something he hadn't known about her yet: There was nothing in the world that embarrassed Paisley.

"I have a book about this stuff," she said. "You should come over tonight and we'll look you up."

"I have one, too," he teased, pointing a soapy glove at his textbook. "And mine has actual facts."

"Facts are so much less interesting," she said as she slid off the counter. He was about to ask "than what?" when she turned around and winked at him. "I'll see you tonight."

Now she stood on the top step with the light from the diner windows forming a kind of halo behind her, and he waited while she zipped her coat. When she was finished, she hopped down the steps and into the powdery snow.

"Happy Thanksgiving," he said, and she rolled her eyes.

"Happy Day the Pilgrims Screwed Over the Indians."

"I'm pretty sure it was the day they all came together and had a nice meal."

"Oh right," she said, leaning in to give him a quick kiss. "They screwed them over later."

"They're all set in there?" he asked, as she pulled on her mittens. "Did you get some turkey?"

"*Tofurkey*," she corrected, but when she realized he was kidding, she took his hand. "Let's get out of here."

They walked through the hushed streets in the direction of the lake. The beaches were mostly closed this time of year, but they often snuck out behind the private homes to sit on the piers and look out over the frozen water. Tonight, they found a darkened house and made their way around the back, watching the snow settle and disappear on the icy surface. The lake was so deep that it never fully froze, only turned cold and still, while the snow-capped mountains stood guard all around it.

"So how'd it go?" Paisley asked as they sat huddled together.

"It was okay, actually. He's in pretty good spirits, considering."

"Still no luck on the job front?"

Owen shook his head. "And now we're in the off-season."

"For construction maybe. But there's plenty of other work during ski season around here."

"Apparently not," Owen said, reaching up to brush the snow out of his hair. His fingers were going numb and his face was stiff with cold, but there was something about being out in the arctic mountain air that made his heart swell and his lungs expand. He thought of the way New

York City had been the opposite, how it had made him feel claustrophobic with its leaning buildings and swampy temperatures. How it had felt like the whole world was shrinking all around him.

Except on the roof.

Except when he was with Lucy.

For a moment, he allowed himself to think of her. It had been five weeks since her last e-mail. It hadn't been a good-bye, exactly—nothing as dramatic as that. There was no signing off, no grand farewell, no bitter questions about why he'd stopped writing. One day there was an e-mail from her, completely and utterly normal, and then, just like that, they stopped, their correspondence ending the same way this whole thing had started: all at once.

But it wasn't her fault. One day, not long after he'd mailed his second postcard from Tahoe, she'd sent him an e-mail about how much she was loving Edinburgh, how she'd visited the castle and seen the city from the top of a mountain called Arthur's Seat. After reading it, he walked down to one of the many gift shops in town and flipped through the various postcard options. He'd already sent her two: the first, a photo of the lake at sunset with news that they would be staying here; the second, the same lake in shades of green and blue, with a joke about the Loch Ness Monster. But now, as he looked through the rest, he realized they were all the same: the lake under a pink sky, under an orange sky, under a sky so clear that the water was like glass. After a while, the repetition of the display started to hurt his eyes as he flipped through the many options, and he realized there was nothing new here to show Lucy, and that maybe the sending of postcards had come to an end.

But back at the apartment, he couldn't bring himself to respond to her e-mail. A rhythm had been established where a postcard from him sparked an e-mail from her and vice versa. His were always lighthearted notes from the places they'd visited, scrawled in the limited space on the back of the cards, whereas hers tended to be longer and slightly rambling, unrestricted by the confines of paper. But sitting there with the cursor blinking at him, he wasn't sure what to say. There was something too immediate about an e-mail, the idea that she might get it in mere moments, that just one click of the mouse would make it appear on her screen in an instant, like magic. He realized how much he preferred the safety of a letter, the physicality of it, the distance it had to cross on its way from here to there, which felt honest and somehow more real.

That week, he sat down at his computer every single morning, fully intending to e-mail her. But the days passed without him producing so much as a draft. He kept half expecting her to write again, something new that might inspire a response from him, but nothing ever came, and he started to worry that maybe she'd moved on. After all, here in Tahoe, he had a new school and a new life, and he knew that five thousand miles away, she must be busy with her own version of these things, too.

Then, a week after her last e-mail, he met Paisley.

She sat beside him now, rubbing her mittened hands together. The moon hovered low over the lake, and when Owen blew out, his breath hung in the air.

"So he's still talking about moving on, then?" she asked, and he nodded, feeling guilty, though he knew she was used to this: Tahoe was a revolving door of a town, and for someone like Paisley, who had lived here forever, this was simply a way of life: the coming and the going, the hellos and good-byes. Still, he knew it couldn't be easy for her.

"Unless he miraculously gets a job in the next couple weeks," he said. "Or unless the house sells."

"Any bites?" she asked hopefully, but he shook his head. This was the worst part of it, knowing that the house— their house—was just sitting out there, completely empty, the answer to all their problems, if only someone would buy it. But it wasn't just about the money. To the Buckleys, it was so much more than just a house; it was a dream home, a monument, a shrine. And they couldn't understand why nobody else could see that, too. It was hard not to take it personally.

"We just decided to go down to San Francisco for the weekend, actually," he told Paisley. "To see if we like it."

She raised her eyebrows. "And if you do?"

"I think," he said with a little shrug, "there's a decent chance we'll be down there for good pretty soon. Probably by Christmas, so I can pick up at a new school right after the break."

She nodded, her expression hard to read. "You've never been before, right?"

Owen shook his head.

"You know my dad lives around there," she said. "So I usually go down in the summers. It's one of my favorite places in the world." She fixed her pale eyes on his, studying him for a moment. "I bet you'll love it, too."

She sounded so resigned that Owen put a mittened hand over hers. "It's not for sure," he said, but she only shrugged.

"You'll love it," she repeated, blinking away the thick flakes of snow. "Everyone leaves their heart in San Francisco."

Owen was fairly certain that he and his dad had both left their hearts back in Pennsylvania, but he didn't say this. He and Paisley had spent long stretches of time discussing things like oil spills and wars in the Middle East, but he always found himself stumbling over all those things that were closer to home: *My mother is dead, my father is sad, I once met this girl...*

He lifted his shoulders. "We'll see what happens."

"I guess it would probably be easier for your dad to find a job in a city," she said, and he could almost feel her floundering under the weight of the conversation. They didn't ever really do this sort of thing, he and Paisley. They went skiing and snowshoeing; they snuck into movies and drank frozen cans of beer behind the diner; they hiked the trails and went fishing on the Truckee River, and at night they borrowed people's piers to laugh and joke and talk about issues that didn't matter to either one of them in any sort of immediate way.

Being with her always made him feel light as air, which was exactly what he'd needed these past weeks. But this— this was heavy.

"It feels like you only just got here," she continued, her gaze fixed on the lake. "There's still so much we haven't done." She paused for a second, but when she turned back to him, he was relieved to see the hint of a smile. "I mean, look at all those piers out there. We've probably only checked off, like, three percent of them. Which means there are still thousands waiting for us to leave our mark."

"Oh yeah?" he said. "What's that?"

She hopped to her feet, stepping carefully away, then gestured with a little flourish at the heart-shaped patch of wood where she'd been sitting.

"Way more incriminating than fingerprints," she said, and he couldn't help laughing. When he stood up to join her, she doubled over in a fit of giggles at the narrow out-line he'd left on the dock, and he circled his arms around her waist and pretended to throw her into the icy lake until they both lost their balance, skidding into a graceless, sprawling heap. Only after their laughter had finally sub-sided did he lean forward, touching his cold nose to hers, and kiss her.

"There's a lot I'll miss about this place," he said later, as he helped her up, "if we end up going."

"The lake?" she asked, brushing the snow off her jacket. He shook his head. "You."

Together, they left the water behind, walking back toward town on stiff legs and frozen feet. The snow had mostly stopped, but the path back up to the road was covered in at least a foot of powder, and they clasped their mittened hands together as they stumbled through it.

"So what should we see this weekend?" he asked. "Alcatraz? Pier Thirty-Nine?"

She rolled her eyes, as he'd known she would. "You can't just go to all the tourist traps. There's this great vintage place in the Haight...."

When they reached the diner, Owen leaned in to kiss her again. "Happy Thanksgiving," he said, but she pulled away with a dizzying smile.

"Can we please stop celebrating a day where we slaughter innocent turkeys?"

"If it makes you feel any better, my dad and I had a chicken instead."

She shook her head. "Still awful."

"Still delicious," Owen said, kissing her for real this time.

When they broke apart, she turned and headed up to the back door of the diner. "Have a good trip," she called out, her voice trailing behind her, and Owen waved, though she couldn't see him. "But not too good..."

"I'll bring you back an Alcatraz snow globe."

"Very funny," she said, just before the door slammed shut behind her.

As he walked home, the snow crunching beneath his boots, Owen tried to imagine San Francisco. But the only thing he knew, the only thing he managed to call to mind, was the Golden Gate Bridge, the familiar red arches surrounded by fog. It was hard to know where the image came from, but even now, in the darkness of the mountains—the air so cold it stung his face, the snow so white it practically glowed—that was all he could see: the great red bridge against a square patch of bluish sky.

It wasn't until he was home in bed, halfway to sleep, that he realized why he couldn't see anything beyond the edges.

He was imagining a postcard.

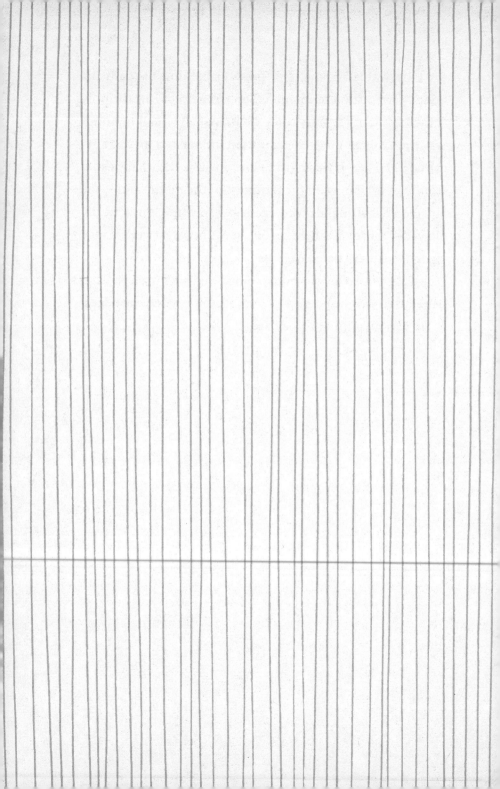

12

December was already six days old, and this was the first time that Lucy had seen it in daylight. Every morning she rode the bus in the dark, the sun rising around half past eight, when she was already inside the brick school building, and then setting again around three thirty, just as she burst out the doors and into the early dusk.

But today was Saturday, and though the light only broke through the clouds in thin patches, and though she was wearing a hooded sweatshirt underneath her coat, compared to the past few weeks, it still felt a bit like being at the beach, and she closed her eyes and tipped her head back to soak it in.

When the crowd around her began to cheer, her eyes flickered open again, and she squinted at the figures on the pitch, trying to make sense of it all. A girl from school named Imogen, who had an uncle who lived in Chicago, kept leaning over to explain the rules of rugby by way of football terminology: a try was like a touchdown, a fly-half was like a quarterback, a ruck was like a tackle. Lucy didn't have the heart to explain to her that she didn't know much about football, either.

The boys on the pitch were all wearing shorts, though it was the middle of winter, and their legs were pink blurs as they sprinted up and down the field, pausing to kick the ball at mystifying moments, hoisting each other in the air to try to catch a wild throw, forming knot-like scrums that were all kicking and shoving and never seemed to accomplish anything. The girls from school—friends of hers, she supposed, if you were using the term fairly broadly—sat on either side of her, their eyes darting back and forth, riveted by the game and apparently immune to the cold. Lucy did her best to keep her eyes pinned to Liam, but she kept losing him amid all the other boys in striped jerseys.

When the game ended, he came jogging over, and Lucy could feel the girls around her practically vibrating with the excitement of it all. He was a year older than them, a sixth year, and the rumor was that he had a good shot of making the Scotland Under-18 rugby squad, which was a training ground for the national team. When Lucy had asked him about this early on, he'd only shrugged.

"Sounds like a long shot to me," he said, but she could see the way he glowed, and she knew it must be true.

Now she walked over to the edge of the pitch to meet him. His cheeks were ruddy and he was covered in mud, from his knees to his shirt to his face, which was positively freckled with it. He jokingly held out his arms for a bear hug, and Lucy laughed and ducked away.

"It's hard to tell from your shirt that you guys won," she said.

"Those other lads came off a lot worse," he said, jabbing a finger over his shoulder. "So what did you think?"

"It's kind of confusing," she said. "And pretty rough."

"That's why the Americans leave it to us," he said, thumping his chest with a grin. Around them, the bleachers were emptying, and players from both teams were heading back toward the clubhouse. Liam looked over his shoulder. "I'm gonna go change out of my kit. Wait for me?"

Lucy nodded, watching him jog off to catch up with his teammates, all of them tackling each other sideways and kicking at the mud. She sat down on the grass and opened her new book—*Trainspotting*, because it seemed about time she traded in Holden Caulfield for something a bit more Scottish—and read until Liam returned, smelling like soap, with a gym bag slung over his shoulder. The rest of the crowd was long gone, and the sky was deepening, already purple at the edges.

"How do you get used to this?" she asked him, as he slung an arm around her shoulders. She shivered. "It's so gloomy."

"We Scots thrive on a little gloom," he said. "But really, you should see it in the summer. The sun comes up at like half-four and doesn't set again till nearly midnight. It's brilliant, the summers here. You'll see."

When they reached the road that bordered the rugby pitch, they waited at the bus stop, standing close together. Even after an intense match, Liam still had a restless energy to him, and Lucy watched now as he paced around on the grass.

Every once in a while, in moments like this, she found herself startled by the very fact of him. It was all so unlikely: those rugby shirts and that accent, the easy confidence and the heart-stopping smile. Sometimes, she thought she could detect a similar sense of surprise in him, too: when she declined an invitation to a party, or when she was so caught up in a book that it took her ages to notice him standing right in front of her. They were just so different, and she kept wondering if he'd realize this was a mistake at some point; if, once she stopped being the novelty, the random American, he would recognize who she really was—a nerdy bookworm, a happy loner—and move on.

But somehow, it worked. If not for their differences, they probably wouldn't have noticed each other in the first place. That there were only more differences waiting beneath the surface made it all the more interesting.

"This is taking forever," Lucy said, peering down the darkened road for the bus.

Liam shrugged. "Will we have a wee wander instead?"

She pursed her lips, but this gave way to a smile, which finally turned into a helpless laugh. "A *wee wander*?"

He pretended to look injured. "And what's wrong with that?"

"A wee wander," she repeated, still laughing.

"Not a fan of wandering?"

"It just so happens I'm a huge fan of wandering," she said. "Let's do it. This bus is the worst."

"You're not in Manhattan anymore," he reminded her, as they set off up the street. "No yellow cabs around."

"Trust me, I know."

They could have cut straight down toward the newer part of the city, avoiding the enormous hill in the center, but instead, Liam led her past Holyrood and up toward the Royal Mile, where little shops and pubs lined the cobblestone streets on the way to the castle. They stopped for fish and chips, sitting behind steamy windows where they could look out and watch the tourists pass, and when they were finished, they wound their way down toward the West End, where Lucy lived.

As they turned onto her street, where the town houses curved around a small patch of green grass, Liam cleared his throat.

"Don't suppose your parents are out..."

Lucy quickly shook her head.

"Ah," he said with a smile, coming to a stop a few feet shy of her red front door. "Then I guess I'll have to leave you here."

He reached out and placed a broad hand on her back,

pulling her closer, and even as he leaned down to kiss her, all she could think was *What's wrong with me?*

Maybe it was possible that you could take someone out of their life and drop them in the middle of another place entirely and they could seem like someone completely different. But even if that were the case, she thought, it wasn't really that *they* had changed—it was just the backdrop, the circumstances, the cast of characters. Just because you painted a house didn't mean the furniture inside was any different. It had to be the same with people. Deep down, at the very core, they'd still be the same no matter where they were, wouldn't they?

Standing there, kissing Liam in the light of a street lamp, she was beginning to believe this was true.

When they parted, finally, with a few more kisses and several promises to ring each other tomorrow, Lucy slipped inside the town house and leaned back against the door, letting out a long sigh. The house was dark, as she'd known it would be. Her parents were still in London and wouldn't be back until tomorrow.

All afternoon, she'd wondered what to do with this: the promise of an empty house. She'd spent the day watching Liam on the rugby pitch, holding his hand as they crossed through the streets of Edinburgh, joking with him over a greasy basket of chips, and then kissing him on the corner, and still—still—she hadn't been able to bring herself to invite him in.

What's wrong with me? she thought again.

He was perfect. And she was an idiot.

Her parents hadn't even thought to warn her against having people over, because for all they knew, she spent her afternoons here the same way she had in New York: walking around aimlessly, poking through bookshops, discovering new places, finding a good spot to read. She hadn't mentioned Liam to them, and she wasn't entirely sure why. For the past six weeks, she'd been half waiting for it to all fall apart, because surely two people so different couldn't last for very long. But if she was being really honest, that was only part of it. The other reason was more complicated than that.

She'd never mentioned Owen to them, either, but somehow he was there all the same, in the air, in the house, in the raised eyebrows each time the mail arrived without a postcard. They hadn't known about him, exactly, but they'd worked it out for themselves, watching those notes arrive one by one, and now that they'd stopped, she sensed a certain sympathy in their eyes.

And so she didn't tell them about Liam, she supposed, out of a weird, misplaced loyalty for Owen. Or maybe it was guilt. It was hard to tell.

When she reached over to flick on the light switch, she noticed the small pile of mail at her feet, which had been tipped through the slot. She stooped to pick it up, shuffling through the catalogs and bills on her way to the kitchen, and when she tossed the whole mess of paper down on the wooden table, a postcard slipped out of the pile.

Lucy froze, staring at the corner, where a sliver of sky

was peeking out. She knew it couldn't be from Owen—it had been a couple of months since she'd heard from him—but still, her heart was pounding like crazy. She nudged at the envelope on top of it, revealing a picture of the Golden Gate Bridge, and she felt whatever had been bubbling up inside of her suddenly deflate.

Of course, she thought. It was about the wedding. Her cousin Caitie was getting married in San Francisco the weekend before Christmas, and she and her parents were flying out to meet her brothers there in just a couple of weeks. Lucy had been looking forward to it. Not the wedding itself as much as being back in America. She'd fallen in love with Scotland in a way she hadn't expected, but that didn't mean she wasn't excited to return to the familiar: peanut butter and pretzels, cinnamon gum and root beer. Faucets that combined hot and cold water, accents that she didn't have to strain to understand, and good—or even just decent—Mexican food. They would be returning to Edinburgh just before New Year's, and she already knew that when the time came, she'd be anxious to come back, but still, she was looking forward to the trip, and to seeing her brothers especially.

She flipped the postcard over, expecting to find some sort of information about the rehearsal dinner or the bridal luncheon, but instead, she was astonished to find Owen's tiny handwriting, a few cramped words printed across the middle of the white square. She brought it closer to her face, her eyes wide and unblinking as she read.

I couldn't arrive in a new city without dropping you a line. It looks like we'll be moving here for good once the semester is over. Hopefully this one will stick, but we'll see how it goes. . . .

Hope you and Nessie are well.

P.S. We picked up a stray turtle on the way down here. I named him Bartleby. (There are a great many things he prefers not to do.)

The next morning, Lucy was waiting near the window in the front hallway when a black cab pulled up, and she watched impatiently as her parents stepped out. They'd barely made it up the steps when she opened the door, still in her pajamas.

"Hi," Mom said, clearly surprised by the greeting. The natural follow-up to this would be something like *Did you miss us?*, but they'd long ago stopped asking that, and Lucy had stopped expecting it.

"How was your trip?" she asked as they walked into the front entryway. Dad set down his bags and gave her a funny look.

"What happened?" he asked, taking off his glasses and rubbing the bridge of his nose with a weary expression. "You're reminding me way too much of your brothers right now. Did you have a party? Did something get broken?"

"No, it's not that," Lucy said, though she knew he wasn't serious. "I was just wondering about San Francisco."

"It's a large city in California," he said, and she rolled her eyes.

"No, I mean...we'll have some free time when we're there, right?"

They were heading toward the kitchen, and Lucy trailed after them.

"The wedding's up in Napa, actually," Mom said. "At a vineyard."

"Napa: a wine region north of San Francisco," Dad chimed in unhelpfully.

"We're only in the city for a night to get over our jet lag," Mom continued, setting her purse down on the counter. "Then we head up to Napa and meet up with your brothers for the wedding and Christmas." She turned around. "Why do you ask?"

But Lucy was already gone.

One night, she was thinking, as she flew up the stairs. *One night.*

13

After three months of living above a Mexican restaurant, Owen would have been happy to never see another bowl of salsa again. But here he was now, waiting for Lucy with a basket of chips in front of him and the sounds of a mariachi band drifting from the bar area, while his leg bobbed nervously beneath the table.

He'd been relieved to find that their new apartment sat above a knitting store, which meant it was mercifully free of smells of any kind, except for the faint earthy scent of Bartleby, the little box turtle they'd found in a parking lot outside Sacramento. After nearly running him over, they'd fixed him up with a shoe box full of fruit and vegetables for the rest of the drive—"the luxury suite," Dad had called it—but now he roamed free around the apartment, occasionally getting wedged beneath the ratty couch that had come with the place. The landlord didn't seem to mind this exception to the No Pets rule, nor did he care that Owen and his father couldn't sign a long-term lease.

"Week to week is fine," he'd assured them when they called in response to an online ad. "It was my mother's place. I'm just trying to collect some rent off it until I'm ready to sell."

This suited them just fine, since they weren't sure how long they might be staying. Dad swore they'd be here at least through the spring semester, so that Owen could finish high school in one place.

"I'm sure I'll find something soon," he kept promising. "I'm not worried."

Owen knew this wasn't true, but he didn't mind. He was just relieved to hear the determination in his father's voice.

The new apartment was near the marina, and from their window, they could hear the sounds of the boats bumping against the docks and the seagulls calling out to each other. Owen wondered what his friends from home would think if they could see his life now, which was so unrecognizable from what it had been in Pennsylvania. Their e-mails had mostly stopped—he knew they must have given up on him by now—but he could still picture their days as clearly as if he were there, too: the exact location of their lockers in the senior hallway, their exact lunch table in the cafeteria, their exact seats in the back row of every classroom. It was strange and a little unsettling to think how easily Owen could have been there, too, and he tried to hold on to this whenever he worried too much about their current situation. Because in spite of everything that had happened since his mother died, all the bad luck and the good, he was still happy to have seen the things they'd seen.

The last few mornings, while Dad sat at the computer, his eyes bleary as he scanned the newest job postings, Owen took off, exploring the city by foot. It was so unlike New York, all cramped together on a thin spit of island, everything crowded close like an overgrown garden. San Francisco, on the other hand, was sprawling and disjointed and colorful. It had only been a few days, but already he was falling in love with this place, just like he'd fallen for Tahoe, and so many of the other towns they'd seen along the way. And now, as he sat there waiting for Lucy, it struck him that the only one he hadn't loved— the only city that he had, in fact, been determined not to like—was New York, the place where they'd met.

He wondered if that meant something. He supposed that magic could be found anywhere, but wasn't it more likely in a Parisian café than a slum in Mumbai? He'd met Paisley on a starry night in the mountains. But with Lucy, they'd met in the stuffy elevator of an even stuffier building in the stuffiest city in the world. And yet...

He knew he shouldn't be thinking this way. He picked up his fork and twirled it absently between his fingers. But when the waitress appeared at his side, he lost his grip, and it fell to the floor with a clatter.

"Can I get you some more chips while you wait?" she asked, stooping to pick it up.

"Sorry," Owen said, flustered. He glanced at the basket in front of him, which was down to a few crumbs. He hadn't even realized he'd been eating them. "I'm okay for now."

As soon as she left, he straightened in his chair, craning his neck to look past the cactus decorations up front, wondering where she could be. In her last e-mail, she'd suggested a Mexican restaurant, since apparently there wasn't much in the way of good tacos in Edinburgh, and he'd given her directions to this place, which was just around the corner from his new apartment. He had no idea where she was staying or what time she was supposed to get in. She didn't even have a U.S. phone number anymore, so there was no way to call to see if her flight had been delayed. He sat back in his chair again and drank his whole glass of water in one gulp, then wiped his sweaty palms on his jeans.

Ever since getting her e-mail a couple of weeks ago, he'd been trying to figure out what to tell her about Paisley. The problem was, he wasn't entirely sure where they stood himself. In the days leading up to Owen's departure, they'd danced around the subject of the future; instead, she'd given him restaurant recommendations in San Francisco, and he'd asked her about her plans for Christmas. They'd talked about things like ski conditions and the new menu items at the diner. He just assumed they'd figure out the rest of it at some unspecified point later on.

But when he'd stopped by the diner on the way out of

town to say good-bye, Paisley had looked at him expectantly, as if the problems of time and distance could be solved right there, in the middle of the lunch shift, the air smelling of onions and the order for table eight growing cold on the counter.

"Well," she said eventually, seeming somehow disappointed in him. "I'm sure I'll be down to visit my dad soon. And in the meantime, I guess we'll talk."

"Sure," Owen said quickly. "We'll talk."

And he'd meant it then. Standing there, with her pale eyes focused on him, he was already thinking about calling her when they arrived. Or maybe even sooner. He'd ring her from the road. He'd text her when he got to the car. He'd be thinking about her even as he walked out the door of the diner.

But what he hadn't known then was that everything about Paisley was immediate. When you were with her, it was like being in a spotlight. It was almost blinding, that sort of brightness, and it was exactly what he'd needed all these months.

But even as they drove away, it was already beginning to fade.

In the days since he'd arrived in San Francisco, they'd mostly spoken through voice mail. It wasn't that he was avoiding her calls exactly, but he wasn't going out of his way to pick them up, either, and he suspected she was doing the same. In her absence, the urgency of what he'd felt for her, the pull of it, had simply evaporated, and each time her name appeared on his phone, he felt nothing but a vague reluctance at the thought of catching up.

If he were still in Tahoe, he knew, things would probably be different, and if he thought too hard about it, he felt a sharp stab at the memory of those blue-cold nights out by the lake and the afternoons when they drank mugs of cocoa behind the steamy windows of the diner. But their relationship had existed wholly in the moment. And he was starting to realize that moment had passed. This, it seemed, was just what happened when you left someone. They disappeared behind you like the wake of a boat.

But sitting here at this Mexican restaurant with his elbows resting on the sticky tablecloth, he was keenly aware that this had never quite happened with Lucy.

And he decided right then that there was no reason to tell her about Paisley. It wasn't like he owed her an explanation, anyway. They were only friends, he reminded himself, if they were even that.

He was still sitting there with his head bent, lost in thought, when she finally arrived. In all the noise, the relentless music and chatter, he didn't notice until she was standing right in front of him, and when he looked up through the blurry, chaotic lights of the restaurant, for a brief second he wasn't sure if it was even her. Her hair was longer than last time, and she was paler, too, the freckles on her nose more pronounced. She was watching him with a gaze a mile deep, her muddy eyes sizing him up, and neither of them said anything for what felt like a very long time.

Finally, the band stopped playing, the last note ringing out with a rattle, and she smiled at him, the moment tipping from one mood to another, from one song to the next. He scraped back his chair, standing up in a hurry, and he was already hugging her, his hands resting on her thin shoulder blades, when he realized they'd never really done this before, and without quite meaning to, he stepped back, moving away from her as if he'd been shocked. She blinked at him a few times, then offered another smile.

"It's good to see you," she said, pulling out her chair, and once she was seated, he took his as well. "Sorry I'm late."

His eyes were still caught on hers, and he opened his mouth, then closed it again. "It's okay," he said after a beat. "I just got here."

She glanced at the empty basket of chips but said nothing.

"So did you..." he began, then stopped to clear his throat. He reached for his water glass but realized it was empty. "Did you get here okay?"

"Yeah, the flight wasn't bad actually," she said, then paused and shook her head. "Wait, sorry, did you mean the restaurant?"

"Yeah. No. I mean...either one."

"Uh, yeah, it was fine," Lucy said, looking around. After

a moment, she seemed to remember that her jacket was still on, and she slipped it off her shoulders and onto the back of her chair. She was wearing a black cardigan over a purple shirt, and Owen thought of the white sundress from the elevator that day, remembered following it up the darkened hallway like some sort of apparition.

"Well," she said, smiling gamely, and he felt the full weight of it now: this stiffness between them where before there'd been such ease. Any excitement over seeing her again had deflated, sharply and suddenly, and what was left was the worst kind of awkwardness. His mind worked frantically, turning over his scrambled thoughts, searching for something to say, but there was nothing but the empty space between them.

Maybe they were never meant to have more than just one night. After all, not everything can last. Not everything is supposed to mean something.

And what other evidence did he need than this? Lucy looking around for the waitress while he played with his napkin under the table, nervously shredding it to pieces. This was the worst date of all time, and it wasn't even a date.

"So," he said finally, and she looked at him with slightly panicked eyes.

"So," she echoed, managing a smile. "How are you?"

"I'm good." He bobbed his head too hard. "Really good. How are you?"

"Great," she said. "Everything's good."

His stomach dropped so far he could just about feel it in

his toes. It was like moving through sand, this conversation, slow and plodding and full of effort. He could feel them both sinking in it. Soon they would be lost.

Lucy was biting her lip, and beneath the table, he could feel her knee jangling up and down. "You like San Francisco?" she asked, and he nodded.

"It's nice so far," he said, hating himself.

The waitress arrived to save them, at least for a few seconds. "Can I start you guys off with anything to drink?" she asked, her pen hovering above her notepad.

"Just water," Lucy said, and Owen held up two fingers. "Me too."

The waitress let out a little sigh, then headed off to get their waters, and another silence settled over the table in her wake; this one worse than the last. A woman at the next table threw her head back with laughter, and in the corner, another group erupted into cheers. There were couples on dates and a family celebrating a kid's birthday; there were people at the bar taking shots and a group of men clinking bottles of beer just behind them. Suddenly, the twangy warbling of the mariachi band felt too loud and the walls felt too close.

Across from him, Lucy leaned forward on the table, her face full of determination. "So have you been here before?" she asked, and before he could stop himself, Owen threw his head back and groaned. When he lowered his gaze again she was looking at him in surprise, and he eyed her right back. Then he stood up.

"This is the worst," he said, and this time, she smiled for real.

"It's not the best," she agreed, rising to her feet so that they were facing each other across the table, the empty basket of chips between them.

"So there's this taco truck down by the marina," he said, and her smile widened. "Any interest?" When she didn't answer right away, he raised his eyebrows. "Unless you'd prefer not to..."

She laughed. "Let's go, Bartleby," she said, and so they did.

14

It was better outside.

They were better outside.

As they walked toward the harbor, a few inches between them, Lucy could feel the horrible awkwardness beginning to melt away. They were leaving it behind, all of it: the greasy restaurant with its overpowering smells, the too-loud music, the vastness of the table between them, the stilted conversation.

Out here, they could both breathe again. And as they walked past lit restaurants and darkened bars, Lucy couldn't help glancing sideways at Owen, reassured by the sight of him: his white-blond hair, which had grown longer, curling at the ends; that loping walk of his, which made him bob like a puppet on a string. When he'd looked at her across the table in the restaurant, his eyes had been darting and nervous, but now they met hers with a brightness that matched her memory.

He lifted a long arm, pointing at a street that ran up a

steep hill. "Our place is up there," he said. "If you look out the bathroom window, you can sort of see the water."

"No better place for an ocean view."

He raised his eyebrows. "I can think of a few."

"But in the bathroom, you can sit in the tub and pretend you're a pirate," she explained, as if it were obvious, and he laughed.

"Shiver me timbers," he said, then steered them toward a square blue truck that was parked outside an Irish pub. Two men in white aprons were taking orders from a large open window that stretched across one side of it, and the striped awning above them flapped in the breezes from the nearby water. "You're going to love these. I've only been here a few days and I've already had about a million."

"I can't wait," she said as they joined the small line. "I'm completely in love with everything about Edinburgh except the food."

"Not even the haggis?" he joked, and she rolled her eyes.

"Especially not the haggis," she said. "Do you even know what's in that stuff?"

"Only the best ingredients around," he said as he dug his wallet from his pocket, his eyes on the menu. "Sheep's heart, sheep's liver, sheep's lungs . . ."

Lucy wrinkled her nose. "I didn't know about the lungs."

"It's a delicacy," he said with a grin. "A Scottish delicacy."

"I think I'll be sticking with tea and biscuits."

When it was their turn, Owen insisted on paying and

Lucy let him, even though she wasn't sure if his dad had found a job yet and guessed that money might still be tight. But there was something endearing about the way he waved her off, and now that they'd finally found a kind of hard-won rhythm again, she didn't have the heart to spoil things over a few dollars.

As they strolled down toward the harbor, they could hear the slap of the waves against the dock. A few gulls circled lazily overhead, and when they were closer, Lucy could see the tall masts of the many sailboats, which made a series of zigzags across the horizon. They found an empty bench along a path filled with bikers and joggers, and they sat on either end of it, the bag of tacos between them.

"Much better," Owen said, leaning back with a happy sigh.

"I think we're better suited to picnics, you and me."

"Apparently," he said, handing her a taco wrapped in tinfoil, which was warm against her half-numb hands. The cold here wasn't like Scotland, with its raw, battering winds, but the evening air still had a bite to it. Lucy was grateful for this. It was the middle of the night in Scotland right now, and the chilly weather was helping to keep her awake.

She hadn't slept much on the long flight, and when they'd arrived at the hotel a few hours ago, she'd been too anxious to nap. Her parents had immediately disappeared into their room across the hall, insisting they were ready to pass out, but she knew that wasn't true. Dad's phone had been glued to his ear ever since the plane landed. Even as they'd waited for their luggage, he was pacing along the serpentine perimeter of the conveyor belt, and he spent the whole limo ride into the city bent over his phone, furiously typing e-mails. Lucy had raised her eyebrows at Mom in an unspoken question, but she only shook her head.

At the hotel, they'd waved to her before ducking into their room, which was right across the hall from Lucy's. "Have fun with your friend," Dad said, and just before the door closed, she could hear the sound of his phone ringing again.

Lucy had told them she was having dinner with an old friend who'd moved to San Francisco, and it was a measure of how distracted they'd been lately that they hadn't even questioned this. They should have known as well as anyone that Lucy didn't have any friends from New York.

Still, she wasn't exactly sure why she'd lied, or why it seemed to be coming so naturally these days. Two nights ago, back in Edinburgh, she'd done the same thing to Liam when they'd gone to see a movie.

"It's a *film*," he was correcting her as they walked in.

"A movie," she persisted. "Which you see at a mooooovie theater."

He rolled his eyes. "A *cinema*," he said, then pointed to the counter. "Would you like some sweets?"

"I'd like some *candy*," she said with a grin, and he threw his hands up in defeat.

In the half-darkened theater, they talked while they

waited for the movie to start. Liam's family was going to see some relatives in Ireland over the break, and Lucy was busy peppering him with deliberately silly questions about shamrocks and rainbows, when he finally managed to get a word in edgewise.

"So what about your trip?" he asked, rattling the bag of chocolates, then offering it to her. "You must be excited to see your brothers."

"I am," she said. "It's been way too long."

"I've always wanted to go to San Francisco."

"The wedding's in Napa, actually."

"Ah," he said, glancing over at her. "So you won't get to see any of the city while you're out there?"

They'd been angled toward each other, but now Lucy turned to the screen with a shrug. "Not really," she said, and left it at that.

But throughout the movie, she found herself sneaking sideways glances at him, studying the sharp line of his jaw and his neatly trimmed hair, his steady, straightforward gaze. Deep down, she knew she was comparing him to Owen, but the differences were so obvious there hardly seemed to be a point. Besides, Liam was right here. With Owen, the details were a bit foggier. He was a voice in the dark. A presence beside her on a kitchen floor. A series of letters across the back of a postcard.

Liam was a possibility. Owen was just a memory.

So why was she still thinking about him?

Even now, sitting beside him on the bench, she couldn't

seem to keep hold of her thoughts, which were skittering around in her head like marbles. It was only when their eyes met that everything went still again, and a familiar ease settled over her. Just being with him like this again—it was almost enough to make her forget it was only temporary.

As they ate, they filled in the gaps.

From him: stories of the road trip (the cities getting smaller as the spaces between them got bigger; the cheap motels and fast food restaurants; the endless cornfields and far-flung skies; him and his dad and the ribbon of highway and a good song on the radio), and of Tahoe (the blue lake and the ring of mountains; the tiny apartment and the restaurant below; the luckless job search; the short and unremarkable stint at a school there); and, finally, of San Francisco (where things might be different).

And from her: stories of New York (the packing and the leaving and the strange mix of feelings that came along with it), and of Edinburgh (the foggy mornings and the fairy-tale castle; her father's new job and their family's new town house; the smell of stew and the early darkness; the constant presence of the sea, which was not so very different from the one laid out before them now, sprinkled with boats and the occasional bird).

As they talked, the sky went from pink to purple to navy, and the empty tinfoil husks on the bench between them had to be pinned down when the wind picked up. Lucy pulled her cold fingers into the sleeves of her jacket, listening to Owen tell the story of Bartleby, the stray turtle they'd picked up on the way here.

"I keep trying to teach him to fetch," he was saying, "or at least come when he's called, but he doesn't do a whole lot of tricks."

Lucy smiled. "He'd prefer not to."

"Exactly."

"And your dad doesn't mind having him around?"

"He's always tripping over him," Owen said with a shrug, "but it's kind of nice for it to be more than just the two of us, you know?"

Lucy swallowed hard before managing a small nod.

"Even if it *is* just a turtle."

"Turtles count," she said. "And it'll be nice for your dad to have some company next year. Have you heard from any schools yet?"

He shook his head. "It's too early."

"Where'd you end up applying?"

"Everywhere," he said with a hint of a smile, but there was something behind his eyes that didn't quite match up. "But I'm not sure I'm going."

"Why?" Lucy asked. "Because of missing so much school this year?"

"Nothing like that," he said. "I've got plenty of credits. It's just..."

She twisted her mouth. "Your dad?"

He nodded.

"But I'm sure he'd want you to go...."

"I can defer a year," he said. "Wait till we're more settled."

Lucy gave him a long look. "And he's okay with that?"

"He doesn't know," Owen said, and his voice cracked over the next words. "But how can I leave him, too?"

He looked so sad, sitting there, folded over like a comma, his eyes dark and his face pale. Lucy had no idea what to say. For her family, separation was as normal as together-ness, though if it really came down to it, and if you really needed them, she knew they would be there. Still, how could she possibly tell a boy without a mother that it was okay to walk away from his father, too?

"I don't know for sure yet," he said, before she could think of a response. "I guess there's still time to figure it out."

"Yes," she said, because it was all she could manage.

He gave her an uneven smile. "Thanks."

"For what?" she asked, surprised.

"I don't know," he said. "But just...thanks."

At some point, they'd moved closer to each other on the bench, and she realized only now that their knees were touching. Between them, someone had carved the word MAYBE into the wood in uneven letters, and she wondered if Owen saw it, too. She closed her eyes for a moment and let the word expand in her head: *maybe*. Maybe it was the cold, or maybe it was the conversation, or maybe it was something else that had pulled them so close. But here they were, angled together like this, their faces suddenly too near, and she lowered her eyes, afraid to meet his gaze. The quiet between them had gone on for too long now to pretend it was anything other than what it was. There were no more words; all that was left were two faintly beating hearts.

For a moment, as they leaned toward each other, Lucy forgot about Liam so completely it was as if he'd never existed at all, as if he hadn't kissed her hundreds of times, as if it didn't mean a thing. Her mind was muddled and blurry, wiped clean by the boy on the bench with the magnetic eyes.

But somewhere in the midst of it all—the steady tilt toward each other and the sudden flutter of anticipation— she remembered herself, and almost without meaning to, she found herself leaning back, just slightly. It was barely noticeable, only a fraction of an inch, but it was enough to shift everything from slow-motion back into the awful, mundane speed of the everyday, and just as suddenly, Owen pulled back, too.

They stared at each other. Something in his eyes had changed, and it caught her off guard. She'd been the one to stop it, but there was a look of relief on his face that made her cheeks burn, and she blinked at him, reeling from what had just happened: the nearness of him, and now, just as quickly, the distance.

"Sorry," he said, and she sat up a bit straighter. It was true that she was a little fuzzy on the etiquette involved with an almost-kiss, but it seemed to her that if she was the one who pulled away first, then she should be the one to apologize.

"No," she said, shaking her head, inching even closer to the edge of the bench. "It's my fault, I didn't—"

"I shouldn't have even been—"

"I didn't mean to—"

They were talking over each other again, and they both stopped at the same time. In another conversation, they would have been laughing about this, or at least smiling, but there was too much still hovering between them right now.

Owen raised his hands, a helpless gesture. "I should have told you earlier," he said, his words measured. "There was this girl I was seeing in Tahoe...."

"You have a girlfriend?" Lucy asked, unable to stop herself. She could feel her mouth hanging open, and she closed it abruptly.

He shook his head, then nodded, then shook his head again. "No, I mean, sort of. I don't know. It's..."

"Complicated?" Lucy asked, her voice colder than she'd intended.

"Yeah," he said. "Now that I'm down here, I'm not exactly sure where we stand. And I'd hate to do anything that would—"

"Nothing happened," Lucy said, even while she was thinking just the opposite: that everything had happened. "So you don't need to worry."

He ducked his head. "I'm really sorry."

"It doesn't matter," she said. "I have a boyfriend anyway."

"You do?" he asked, looking up sharply.

She frowned. "Is that so hard to believe?"

"No," he said, swinging his head back and forth. "Of course not. It's just—"

"We've been together pretty much since I got to Edinburgh," she said, and then, though there was no reason to continue, she added, "He's a really great guy."

"That's great," Owen said, a wounded look in his eyes. "Then I'm happy for you."

"You too," she managed to say, though she felt like crying. "What's her name?"

"Paisley," he said, and a short laugh escaped her.

"Seriously?"

He bristled. "What's wrong with that?"

"Nothing," she said lightly. "I've just never heard it before."

"Why, what's your boyfriend's name?" Owen said, practically spitting the word *boyfriend*.

Lucy hesitated, surprised by his tone, which was full of resentment. "Liam," she said quietly, and he snorted.

"Liam and Lucy?" he said. "Cute."

"There's no need to be a jerk about it."

"Does your boyfriend know you're having dinner with me?" he asked, his eyes flashing.

"Does your girlfriend?" she shot back.

"She's not my girlfriend."

"She just wouldn't want you trying to kiss other girls."

"*You* tried to kiss *me*."

"No," she said. "I was the one who stopped it."

"This is ridiculous," he said, standing abruptly. "I'm not going to sit here arguing about this."

"Fine," Lucy said, jumping up as well. Another wave of frustration washed over her, and she grabbed the foil wrappings from the tacos, pounding them into a ball, which she held in her fist. "Say hi to your girlfriend." It was a stupid, childish thing to say, but she couldn't help herself. He smirked in response, and though this should have only made her angrier, she felt suddenly deflated instead. The wind was blowing his hair so that it fell across his eyes, and he was standing with his feet planted wide, his arms crossed tightly in front of him. It was hard to tell if he was upset or jealous or both.

"Yeah, send my best to Braveheart."

"It's William Wallace," she corrected automatically, "and he's obviously not—"

"Forget it," Owen said, shoving his hands in his pockets. "I should get going."

Lucy pressed her lips together, stunned by how quickly the evening had unraveled. Finally, she shrugged. "Me too, I guess."

"Fine," he said.

"Fine," she said back.

He stared at her for what felt like a long time before finally lifting his shoulders. "Thanks for coming."

She nodded. "Thanks for the tacos."

"Yeah," he said, his voice hollow. "Have fun at the wedding."

And with that, they parted like two strangers, setting off in entirely different directions, just as they had in the past, as if it were some kind of bad habit, or maybe just a curse.

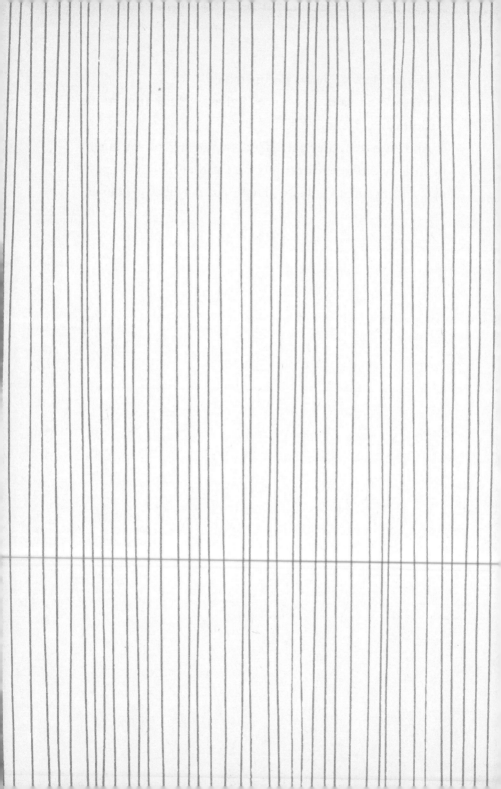

PART III

Everywhere

15

In Napa, Lucy went through the motions.

She made small talk with her relatives and admired her cousin's dress. She smiled for photos and raised her glass whenever someone toasted. She ate her cake and humored her father with a dance and drank the champagne her brothers sneaked for her, happy to have their company again, even if it was only for a short time.

When they asked, she told everyone what she loved about Edinburgh and what she missed about New York, though in neither of those two conversations did she mention the two names that would have told the real story.

When she thought of Liam, she felt her heart wrench in one direction. And when she thought of Owen, it was tugged in the other.

On their last morning in Napa, after a week of celebrations, after the wedding and Christmas, the various tours of vineyards and the many meals with relatives, Lucy stood outside the house they'd rented and watched a flock of birds moving over the fields, flecks of pepper in a salt-white sky. Without warning, they shifted direction, all coordination and grace, a winged ballet. But there was one that kept missing the cues, a little slow to turn, a little low to fly, and that was the one that held her gaze.

All that day, through the drive back to San Francisco and the hours in the airport, the long plane ride—first to New York, then to London, and then finally up to Edinburgh—Lucy kept thinking of that one little bird.

Others must have seen it, too, a flock so big it colored the dishwater sky. They must have stopped what they were doing and tipped their heads back to marvel at it, astonished by the harmony of the group, the graceful turns and the wheeling circles, all those wings beating in time.

But she couldn't stop thinking about the straggler, the missing beat, the odd one out. The single speck in the emptiest part of the sky.

She hoped that wherever he was, he'd be okay, that little bird.

In San Francisco, Owen walked.

Day after day, he crisscrossed the sprawling city. Dad stayed behind, scouring the papers and mining the Internet in search of a job, while Owen continued his odd trek, witnessing the backdrops to a thousand postcards, real or imagined. Not just the great red bridge, but other things, too: cable cars and twisty streets, Fisherman's Wharf and Chinatown, Golden Gate Park and the Haight.

The only place he didn't go—the one place he worked hard to avoid—was the little strip of grass along the marina, where a wooden bench sat looking out over the water, contemplating the possibilities with a single word: *maybe*.

If someone had asked him why all the walking, Owen wouldn't have been able to answer. The reasons were too hard to articulate, too personal to explain. He wasn't walking because there were things to see or because he had places to go. It was far simpler than that. He was walking because it was better than staying still, and because it seemed the best possible way to escape his thoughts, which crowded his head like the fog over the bay, thick as fleece and impossible to see around.

Whenever his mind drifted in Paisley's direction, he was quick to shake it clear again. But that only left room for Lucy, who was somehow much harder to cast aside. He always allowed himself to linger there for a moment, lost in that one unlikely New York night, until the memory of their recent fight startled him alert again, and he'd blink fast, then grit his teeth and hurry on.

One evening, he paused at the top of a street on his way home. The sun was already halfway gone, the light a soft winter orange. For six straight days, he'd come to this intersection and turned left, where at the top of a hill, in a tiny apartment, his father would be waiting with dinner on the table.

But tonight, on the seventh day, he found himself moving in the direction of the marina instead. For better or worse, it was the last place he'd seen her. And that was reason enough for him.

17

In Edinburgh, Lucy slept.

At first, her parents chalked it up to jet lag. But as the days wore on, they began to worry. She slept late and went to bed early, her hours matching those of the elusive winter sun, and in between, she padded around the flat in her pajamas and slippers. Whenever she showed up downstairs, Mom insisted on laying a cool hand against her forehead, but it was obvious she didn't have a fever.

"Let her sleep," she heard Dad say when she left the kitchen one day. "She's on her break. And it's nice to know where she is for once."

On New Year's Eve, there were dangerously high winds, and the street party was canceled for fear that the rides would get blown away. So instead her parents made an enormous pot of chili, and the three of them spent the evening playing board games while the wind rattled the windows of the town house.

But Lucy couldn't concentrate.

Liam would be getting back to Edinburgh the next day.

He'd e-mailed her several times over the past ten days—about his holiday in Ireland on his grandparents' farm, but also about how he couldn't wait to see her, how much he missed her, how he was thinking of her often—and she hadn't written back once. It didn't seem fair when she was suddenly so uncertain about everything.

She still had no idea what she was going to do when she saw him.

All morning, she'd been keeping an eye on her phone, assuming he'd text her when he was back in the city. But she was still in her pajamas when the doorbell rang.

From her bedroom, Lucy strained to listen to the voices downstairs, and after a moment, her father yelled up. "There's a young man named Liam here to see you," he said, raising his eyebrows as she appeared at the top of the stairs.

"Thanks," she said, shuffling down in her polka-dot pajama pants and purple NYU hoodie. Liam was standing in the open doorway, the lingering Edinburgh night sprawled out behind him, inky and cold, and he looked impossibly rugged in a woolly sweater. When he smiled up at her, she nearly tripped.

At the bottom of the stairs, he stepped forward as if to kiss her, but she held up a hand, glancing back down the hallway toward the kitchen, where she was certain her parents were lurking, and then pulled him into the library instead, shutting the glass doors behind them.

"Aha," he said, reaching for her. "Privacy."

Lucy managed a nervous laugh. "You're back."

"I am," he said, moving close so that their faces were only inches apart. "I missed you."

When he kissed her, she felt momentarily woozy, all of her resolve floating away like champagne bubbles, light and fizzy, popping only when she finally managed to pull back. For a moment, they just stared at each other, and her stomach did a little flip. It would be so easy to continue this way, to lose herself to this guy with the chiseled jaw and the easy charm. They could just keep going as if nothing had happened in California. Because it was true; nothing *had*.

But if she was being really honest with herself, she knew that wasn't entirely true. And she felt a sudden flash of anger, not toward Liam but toward Owen, who should have tried harder. He should have been the one to kiss her this time. He should have leaned forward when she leaned back, should have caught her instead of letting her go.

Standing in this room in Edinburgh, with the late-morning darkness still filling the windows, she hated Owen for being so far away, for not being *here*. And she realized that whatever else he'd done, he'd recalibrated her; because even though it had all gone horribly wrong, and even though she might never see him again, might never even speak to him, she understood something about wanting now. And here with Liam, she knew this wasn't it.

And it wasn't fair to him.

When she cleared her throat, the smile slipped from his face. There must have been something in her eyes, which were always giving her away.

"Liam," she began, and his face darkened a shade.

Behind him, the sun was only just beginning to rise.

18

In Berkeley, Owen watched the sun disappear.

For a long time it sat tangled in the leafless branches of a tree, throbbing a brilliant orange, and he stared at it through the smudged window of the coffee shop. All around him, students were pecking away at their laptops, headphones jammed into their ears, empty coffee cups strewn all around them. It was the start of a new semester, and everywhere, people were hard at work.

Owen had sent in his Berkeley application months ago, and he let his eyes rove around the room now, trying it on for size. They had an undergraduate astronomy program that meant classes in astrophysics and planetary sciences, not to mention multiple cutting-edge labs and observatories, and for a moment, he could almost see himself in this very coffee shop with a pile of books spread before him. But then he thought again of his dad, and the image went blurry. There were still too many question marks. There were still too many things to worry about.

He fixed his gaze on the door, his foot jangling beneath the table as he waited. He'd skipped his last two classes this afternoon, taking a bus to one of the BART stations downtown, then switching once more in Oakland, before finally arriving in Berkeley just as the afternoon light was fading. It would have been far quicker to take the car, but that would have meant explaining the outing to his father, which would have meant endless questions to which Owen didn't have any answers. So instead he'd told him he was playing basketball with some of his new classmates and would probably be home late. Dad, hunched over the classifieds section of the morning paper, had only waved a piece of toast at him in response.

When the bell above the door cut through the low hum of the computers and the whistle of the cappuccino maker, he looked up a bit reluctantly.

It wasn't that he didn't want to see her. It was that he'd known even when he'd first gotten her e-mail a couple of weeks ago—on January 1, as if he were a resolution, a way to start the year off right—that he would feel this way when he did.

Standing there in the doorway in a red coat with her hair in two long braids, a light went on inside him, as he'd known it would. She was beautiful, startlingly so, and she stood out brightly against the background of the coffee shop, her smile broadening at the sight of him.

She was the one who'd asked to meet. After weeks of perfunctory voice mails and the occasional text, she'd e-mailed to say that she'd be in Berkeley for a few days. He assumed she was looking at the school, but it was impossible to know for sure with her. She could have just as easily been meeting friends or attending a protest or consulting a psychic. And even if she *were* here for him, it could have just as easily been to break up with him as propose to him. With Paisley, you just never really knew.

When she was near enough to the table, Owen half stood, still unsure how to greet her. If there was an etiquette for seeing your not-quite-ex-girlfriend after six weeks of not-quite-avoiding-each-other, then he wasn't sure what it was.

"It's good to see you," she said, pulling out the chair across from him and reaching for his cup of coffee without asking. She smelled of cold air and cigarettes and pine trees, and she eyed him over the rim of the cup as she took a long sip.

"You too," he said, the words a little stiff. "What're you doing down here?"

"I've got a few different things going on," she said, then shrugged. "And it's been a while."

"That's true," Owen said, trying to think of what might come after that, but she saved him by scraping back her chair and getting to her feet.

"Need another?" she asked, waving at the chalkboard menu.

He shook his head. "I'm okay."

From across the crowded shop, he watched her laughing at

something the guy behind the counter was saying, and he waited to feel a twitch of annoyance, but there was nothing, only a weariness that made him feel sleepy, in spite of all the caffeine.

He flicked his eyes back over the window, where the sun was nearly gone, the light cold and gray.

He wondered what time it was in Edinburgh.

When Paisley returned, she set down her mug and smiled at him, but rather than pick up speed, his heart seemed to slow down. And he knew then, for sure, that what he'd chalked up to distance was actually something deeper. Because even this—being so close to her—was no longer the same. That light he'd felt when he first saw her—he understood now that it was only a lightbulb. It was quick and easy, full of electricity, but there was something artificial about it.

What he wanted was fire: heat and spark and flame.

Across the table, Paisley was saying something about the trip down, but when Owen met her eyes, something in his expression made the words fall away. Her mouth formed an *O*—the start of a question—but before she could voice it, he leaned forward.

"Paisley," he said quietly, and a look of surprise passed over her face.

Outside, it was just getting dark.

19

In Prague, Lucy walked.

This was her first trip to continental Europe. It was her first time at the opera and her first glimpse of the Charles Bridge. It was her first visit to the biggest castle in the world and her first parentally sanctioned taste of beer, served in a mug so big she had to hold it with two hands. It was her first proper puppet show, the dangling legs of the marionette dancing wildly as a street performer with kind eyes and wrinkled hands commanded it, and it was her first introduction to Kafka. They hadn't even made it out of the airport when she asked Dad for enough korunas to buy an English-language copy of *The Metamorphosis*.

She was under no great illusion about why her parents had brought her along, for the first time ever, on one of their trips. Just over a week ago, they'd broken the news to her that they'd be moving again. This time, to London.

"That job," Dad had said, examining his tie. "The one

from before? The other guy didn't work out, so it's opened up again...."

"And they offered it to you," Lucy said flatly.

"And they offered it to me."

"And you want to take it."

He coughed. "I've already taken it, actually."

She knew they expected her to be furious. Here they were, pulling her from a school only five months after they'd dropped her into it, yanking her away again less than half a year after they'd separated her from her home.

But Lucy simply couldn't muster the expected anger. Her heart was still too heavy for arguments or fireworks; instead, she just sat there feeling resigned—thinking of Liam, who hadn't been able to look at her since she'd broken up with him; of Arthur's Seat, with its views of the city; and the town house with the red door, which sat on a street shaped like a croissant—and listening as her parents strung out a long chain of promises.

"We've found a mews house in Notting Hill," Dad was saying. "Very nice little place."

"And there's a lovely school nearby," Mom told her.

"And we'll wait until spring break," said Dad, "so it won't be as disruptive."

"And to make it up to you, we were thinking maybe a little holiday was in order," Mom had said, her smile too bright. "What do you think about Prague?"

So the weekend was a three-day apology tour. But even so, this did nothing to squash Lucy's enthusiasm for the great buzzing city with its sweeping plazas and oddly shaped buildings and swaying groups of drunken tourists.

As it turned out, Prague in February meant a low gray sky and fits of stinging rain, but Lucy didn't mind that, either. All weekend, the three of them dashed from one museum or gallery to another, moving through squares filled with people and umbrellas. Her whole life, she'd been surrounded by this kind of art; she'd grown up within miles of not just the Met, but also the Guggenheim and the Whitney, the MoMA and the Frick. But they'd never gone together. Not once. Her parents' lives had always seemed to run parallel to their children's. They weren't so much a constellation, the five of them, as a series of scattered stars. There had always been something far-flung about their family, even when they were all in the same place.

Yet here they were now, meandering through the National Gallery in Prague together, spread out along a marble corridor until one of them called for the others, and they all three huddled together before a framed canvas, murmuring their thoughts.

"What did you think?" Mom asked Lucy afterward, moving over to share her umbrella as they stepped outside into the silvery rain.

"I loved it," she said, and then the words tumbled out before she had a chance to weigh them: "We should have done that more back home."

"You used to go to the Met all the time," Mom said, glancing over at her.

The rain beat on the umbrella, and Lucy spoke over the noise of it. "I meant together."

Mom paused, just briefly, but enough to fall behind. When Lucy turned back, she could see the rain making maroon polka dots across the shoulders of her red coat. After a moment, she shook her head, as if clearing water from her ear, then stepped forward to duck underneath the umbrella again. Up ahead, Dad was already pushing through the crowd, his black coat disappearing.

"There are plenty of museums in London, too," Mom said, looping an arm around Lucy's waist, and then together, they hurried to catch up, the rain falling in sheets all around them.

20

In Portland, Owen dreamed.

The rain was loud against the thin roof of the motel, and he woke with a start, the memory of his mother still with him. He felt around for the alarm clock, spinning it so that the red numbers shone in his direction. It was 5:43 AM, and the light that leaked in around the brownish curtains was pale and new.

In the next bed, his father was still sleeping, his breathing soft. Owen propped himself up on his elbows, still rattled by the dream, where his mother had been pinning plastic stars to the roof of the red Honda, which flew off one by one as they drove away from her, scattering in the wind.

Now he swung his legs off the bed and rubbed his eyes. On the floor beside him, Bartleby rustled in his shoe box. Owen stood, slipped on a pair of sneakers, and grabbed a sweatshirt, then opened the door to the hallway, pressing it closed behind him with a quiet *click*. At the end of a hall lined with dozens of identical doors, there was a small terrace, which was littered with cigarette butts. Owen stepped outside and sat down on the edge of it, so that his head was shielded from the rain even as the toes of his sneakers quickly soaked through. He didn't mind; the cool air felt nice, and the rain smelled like morning.

The terrace looked out over a huddled collection of blue trash cans, which were arranged haphazardly along the perimeter of the parking lot. But beyond that, over the tops of the trees, he could see the mountains. As the sky paled all around them, their outlines grew sharper, like a photo coming into focus. Owen leaned forward to pick at a loose thread on one of his shoes, letting out a sigh he'd been holding for what felt like days.

They hadn't been here for very long. This time, they hadn't rented an apartment. They hadn't looked for schools, either. They knew the drill now. You didn't arrive at a place and get attached. You didn't give yourself time to picture a life there, to see a future. You didn't develop routines. You didn't get to know anyone too well.

You didn't come to a full stop.

In the end, San Francisco had lasted a couple of weeks less than Tahoe. Just after New Year's, Dad had found a temp job at an office supply company in Oakland, where he mostly transferred calls and input numbers into endless spreadsheets. But when that ended a month later, there was nothing else, and before long, it was time to move on again. So they were en route to rainy Seattle, where Dad had a tenuous lead on an actual building job. But they'd decided to spend three days in Portland on the way, just in case something turned up there. Because the thought of making it all the way up to Seattle only to have the job fall through was almost too much to bear.

Dad had insisted they wait for Owen's spring break. That way, they'd have a whole week to figure things out without him missing too much school. Owen didn't have the heart to tell him that every district had a different week off, which meant the dates might not line up as well for the next school wherever they landed. But it didn't matter, anyway. They both knew he would graduate easily enough. That wasn't the point. It was more an issue of finding an actual graduation to attend.

"I don't care about that," Owen said. "The whole cap-and-gown thing, the diploma. It's not like it means anything."

"It's symbolic," Dad insisted. "It's a moment."

What he didn't say, but what they both knew, was that his mother would have loved it: the cap and gown, the walk across the stage, the rolled baton of a diploma, all of it. Owen knew she would have been in the first row. She would have been clapping the loudest.

And he had no interest in attending a ceremony that didn't include her.

That much, he knew. The rest was a bit harder to figure out right now. How could he know what the next year might hold when he didn't even know about the next week? At some point they'd find a town, and in that town, they'd find a place to live, and near that place, they'd find a school. There would be one more round of making new friends that wouldn't last, and going to classes where he already knew the answers, and it would all end with a graduation ceremony that he had no interest in attending.

But after that? It was hard to tell. Weeks from now, he'd have six answers to the six questions he'd sent out into the world in the form of college applications. An e-mail would arrive with a link to discover the news, and at the same time, six different envelopes would start to arrive at the house in Pennsylvania, which still sat snow-covered and empty, the FOR SALE sign in the front yard probably beginning to rust. One of their neighbors had been forwarding the mail whenever they landed somewhere long enough to receive it, and hopefully by then, they'd have an address that was a bit more permanent. But at the moment, Owen wasn't so sure it mattered, anyway. His future wouldn't be determined by the click of a mouse or the thickness of an envelope. It would depend on when his father got a job, and where they finally settled down; it would be decided not by things like class size and dorm rooms and cafeteria food, but by how many days passed without his dad pulling the last cigarette from the box, measured by the moment when he could listen to a particular song on the radio without his eyes going misty and his fingers going tight on the wheel.

Next year, Owen might be in Portland or Seattle, San

Francisco or San Diego. He might be with his dad in some broken-down apartment or still on the road or in a college classroom somewhere. Right here in this parking lot, the rain coming down in sheets all around him, it was impossible to know for sure.

What he did know was this: Tomorrow, they would get back into the red Honda. They'd take turns choosing a radio station and stop for burgers when they got hungry, leaving the greasy bags strewn across the floor, though they both knew it would have driven her nuts; they reveled in her invisible annoyance, as if it were a sign that she was still with them. They'd arrive in Seattle in need of a shower and some sleep, and then they'd start the same weary search for jobs and schools and houses, all the various pieces that somehow added up to a life.

But for now, Owen left the rain-soaked mountains and the cold pavement behind, moving back through the silent hallway to their room. As he tiptoed past his sleeping father—the thatch of light hair the only thing visible beneath a pile of covers—he wasn't thinking about tomorrow. He wasn't thinking about college acceptance letters or graduation or even Seattle. For once, as he kicked off his soggy sneakers and pulled the rough sheets back over him, he was just relieved to be here and now, in this bleak, colorless motel room, with only his dad and his turtle for company, a strange and slow-moving trio, a passing version of home.

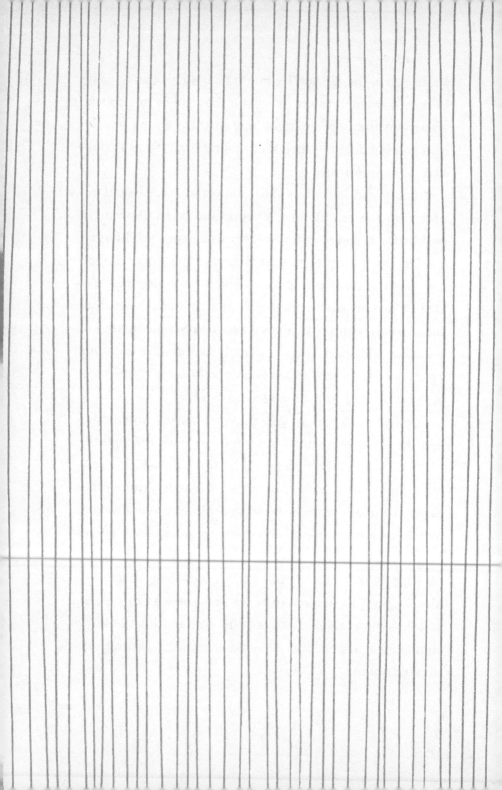

21

In Rome, Lucy read.

It was unseasonably warm for late March, and the sun was hot on her shoulders. Her parents had gone shopping, leaving her on the Spanish Steps with her book (*Julius Caesar*, because when in Rome...), and promised to be back in an hour. But Lucy was in no rush; she could have sat there all day.

When a shadow fell over her, she lifted her eyes to find a man with oily black hair smiling down at her, a basket of flowers in the crook of his arm.

"A rose for the *bella signorina*?" he asked with a heavy accent, trying to hand her one, but Lucy shook her head and returned to her book. He'd already tried to sell her the same rose earlier. In fact, in the six days they'd been in Italy—first Florence and Cinque Terre, then Siena and finally Rome, her whole spring break filled with beautiful art and astonishing architecture, staggering cliffs and seaside houses, pizza and pasta and even a little wine—she'd been offered flowers by at least two dozen people. They would leave them on your table at restaurants, try to slip them into your bag as you were walking, corner you in the piazzas, then demand a few euros. Her father had bought a couple for Lucy and her mother the very first day, and they'd tucked them in their hair, charmed by the novelty of it. But it wasn't long before they discovered that the vendors were everywhere, completely impossible to avoid, hawking not just flowers but also sunglasses and wallets, flags and pins, even small bottles of olive oil. The streets of Italy were just one giant marketplace.

Now she turned back to her book. She'd read it in school last year, and though her classmates had found it boring, Lucy was riveted by the political drama, pulled right out of Roman history. But it was different, somehow, to be reading it here, where the actual events had taken place all those hundreds of thousands of years ago. That was the thing about books, she was realizing; they could take you somewhere else entirely, it was true. But it wasn't the same thing as actually going there yourself.

A few minutes later, she was interrupted again, and she looked up, her face already set with annoyance. But she was surprised to find an old man this time, stooped and wrinkled, with a smile that revealed only a few remaining teeth.

"One for you, *bellissima*?" he said, opening a case full of simple white cards, each with a hand-sketched outline of a famous Roman site: the Colosseum, the Pantheon, the

Trevi Fountain, St. Peter's Basilica. Even the very steps where Lucy now sat.

When she shook her head, the man frowned, shoving the case forward a bit more. "For your *amore*, perhaps?" he asked, raising his gray eyebrows, but Lucy only shook her head again.

"Sorry, *grazie*," she mumbled, and with a shrug, he snapped the case shut and then shambled off to find the next potential customer.

For a long moment, Lucy just sat there, looking out over the busy square, the man's drawings still etched in her mind. Then she flipped open her book again.

They were beautiful.

But she had nowhere to send them.

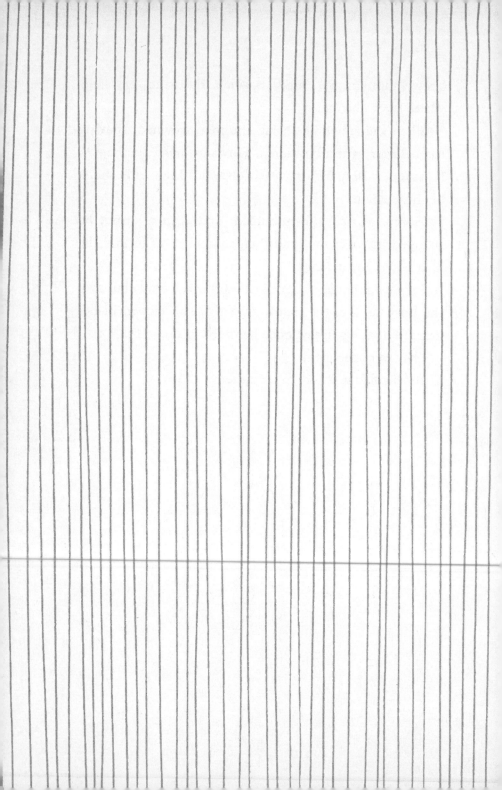

22

In Tacoma, Owen waited.

He'd been the one driving when the car had started making an awful thumping sound, metallic and insistent. His dad had drifted off to sleep about an hour earlier, but he bolted awake at the noise, looking around in bewilderment.

"Pull off," he'd croaked, pointing to the side of the highway, where there was a short gravel drive with a lookout point where tourists could take photos of Mount Rainier, the hulking rock of a mountain that dominated the horizon.

Owen had turned the wheel and was aiming in that direction when the car let out one last dying groan, rolling to a stop with the back half still on the highway. They'd had to push it the rest of the way themselves, the other cars honking as they flew by.

Now they sat together on the hood as they waited for the

tow truck, sharing a bag of pretzels and looking out at the purple mountain, which was crowned in snow.

"What happens if it's no good anymore?" Owen asked, drumming his fingers against the red paint, which was covered in a layer of dirt and grime.

"It'll be good for something."

Owen laughed. "That's optimistic of you."

"It's put in a lot of good miles," Dad said with a smile. "If we have to scrap it, we'll figure something out."

"This would be a great time to get a call about the house."

Now it was Dad's turn to laugh. He felt the pocket of his jeans for the outline of his phone, then gave it a little pat. "I'm sure it'll be any minute now."

"Asking price at *least*."

Dad nodded. "At least."

"And then we'll buy a huge place in Seattle," Owen said. "Maybe something on the water."

"Oh yeah," Dad agreed. "With at least four bedrooms."

"Bartleby can even have his own."

"He can have his own wing, if he wants."

"He'd probably prefer not to," Owen pointed out, and Dad gave a solemn nod. They were quiet for a little while. The wind rustled the trees, bringing with it the scent of pine, and a flock of birds wheeled overhead. Owen watched as they pumped their wings, moving as one, a constellation of black dots in an otherwise uninterrupted sky. As they shifted direction, he saw that one had fallen behind, and he tracked it with his eyes for a long time. He didn't realize he was holding his breath until Dad spoke again.

"You know it'll be okay, right?" he said, and Owen nodded, still watching the bird.

"Yeah," he said. "I know."

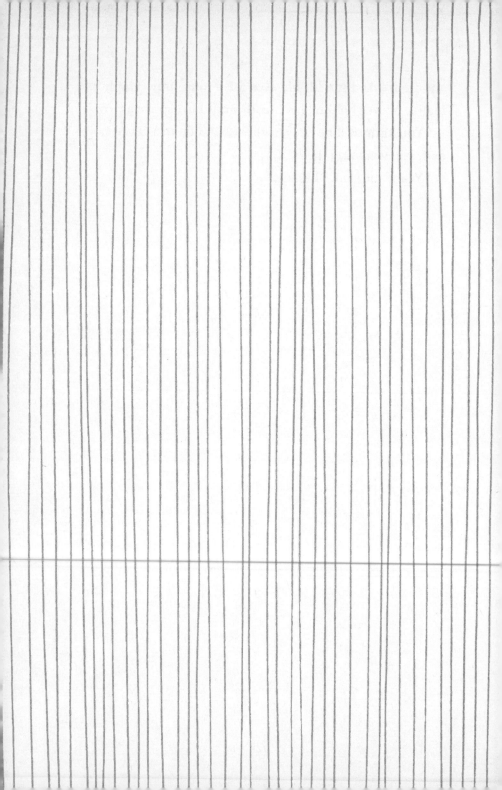

23

In London, Lucy cried.

There was absolutely nothing to cry about—at least not yet. They'd only just arrived. She hadn't seen the neighborhood or her school. She hadn't even seen the inside of the house. But still, the moment the cab had pulled up to the bright yellow door of the little brick building, which was tucked away on a nearly hidden lane, she found herself blinking back tears.

"What's wrong?" Dad asked once the cab had pulled away, as the three of them stood on the doorstep with their suitcases. The rest of their things had been shipped down while they were in Italy and would be waiting for them inside.

"She misses Scotland," Mom said, throwing him a look.

"We were barely there," he said, fumbling with the keys. "If anything, she probably misses New York."

"You can be homesick for two places at once," Mom said, sounding exasperated, but then the key finally turned, and

Dad shouldered open the yellow door, and the two of them hurried inside, half-giddy with the excitement of another new home and another new start in another new place. And not just any place, but London: which, to them, had always been home.

Lucy, however, lingered on the stoop for another minute, her eyes still damp, wondering which one was true. Maybe she was homesick for New York, or maybe it was Edinburgh. Possibly it was even both.

Or maybe—maybe—it wasn't a place at all.

In Seattle, Owen laughed.

When he saw the place where they'd soon be living, he couldn't help it. It was a little house on the edge of the city, but it looked more like a garden shed or a small barn, with weathered red wood and sagging windows.

"It's a fixer-upper," Dad said, beaming at it. There was no way to tamp down his enthusiasm. He'd gotten the job he'd come here for; he'd be part of a crew that was renovating an enormous old warehouse building downtown, turning it into hundreds of apartments at affordable prices. After using the last of their cash to fix the car, they'd spent two nights using it as a bed, sleeping in the parking lot of a Starbucks with the seats reclined. But now he'd gotten an advance on his first paycheck, and it turned out one of the guys on the crew was looking to rent this place out, which meant they'd finally have a house again. Or at least something resembling one.

"It'll be fun," Dad said, thumping Owen on the back. "We'll make it our own."

There was a small patch of lawn and a few scattered trees, a back garden and a narrow front porch, all of it huddled around the tiny box of a house. As he stood gazing up at it, Owen had the distinct feeling that whether he realized it or not, this was exactly what his father had been looking for all this time. After so many months of flight, it felt like they'd finally landed.

"It's better than the car, huh?" Dad said, looking at the house with unmistakable pride. "And a pretty far cry from that basement apartment."

Owen nodded, wondering what the stars would be like out here, remembering the way they'd burned over the darkened city that night, when he and Lucy had stood high above the basement, away from everyone and everything.

He'd been holding the shoe box under his arm like a football since they'd gotten out of the car, but now he bent to set it on the ground, letting Bartleby skitter out onto the grass. They watched together as the little turtle made his way over to the porch steps. He had a tendency to bump into things, and sure enough, as soon as he came into contact with the wood, he set his little home down right there on the flagstone and everything disappeared, his head and all four little legs zipping inside his shell. Owen had watched him do this a thousand times, but it still struck him as amazing, to be protected like that, to always be able to escape into your own small pocket of the world.

"Must be kind of nice," Dad said. "Always having your house handy like that."

"Not so different from us, really," Owen said, pointing at the car. "We've had our home with us this whole time, too."

They were both quiet for a moment, and then Dad smiled a slow smile. "Not anymore," he said, and with that, they headed inside.

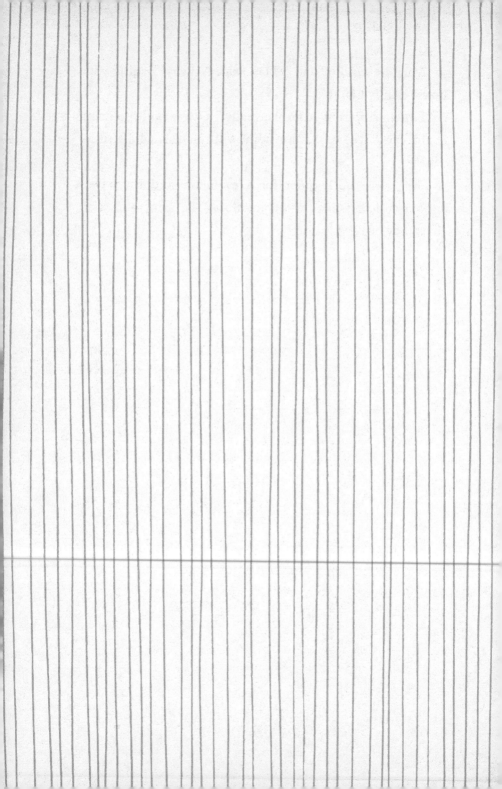

25

In the house with the yellow door, Lucy opened a newspaper.

Her eyes went right to an article about San Francisco.

"Did you know there are eleven species of sharks in the San Francisco Bay?" she asked her mother, who raised her eyebrows.

"Fascinating," she said.

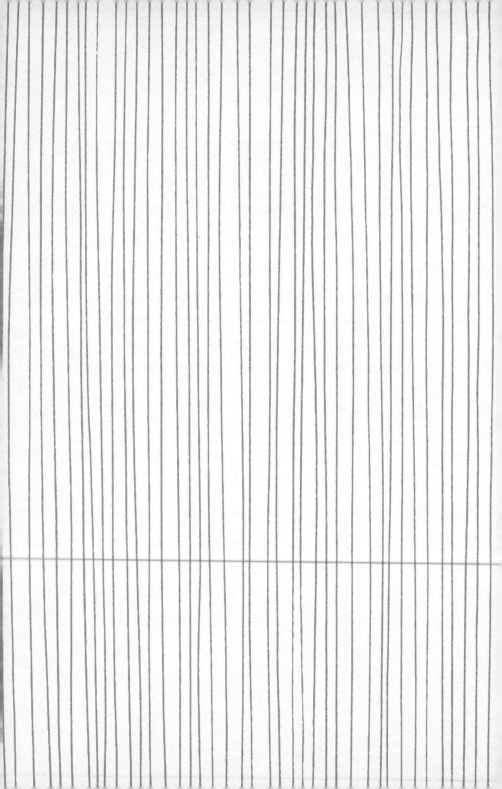

In the little red house with the peeling paint, Owen flipped through a magazine.

His eyes got caught on the word *Scotland*, and he paused.

"Did you know that the river leading out of Edinburgh is called the Firth of Forth?" he asked his dad, who gave him an odd look.

"Interesting," he said.

27

In line for the bus, Lucy daydreamed.

She was thinking of road trips and mountains and wide-open spaces.

But really, she was thinking of New York.

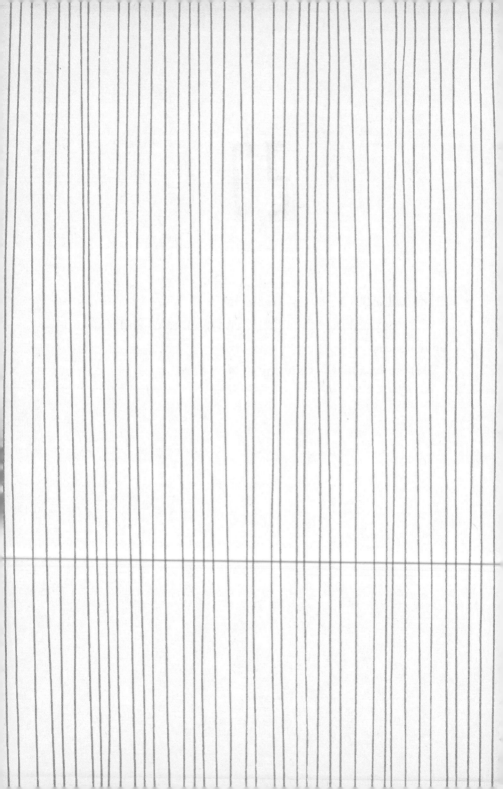

In a coffee shop, Owen's mind wandered.

He was thinking of castles and hills and cups of tea.

But really, he was thinking of that elevator.

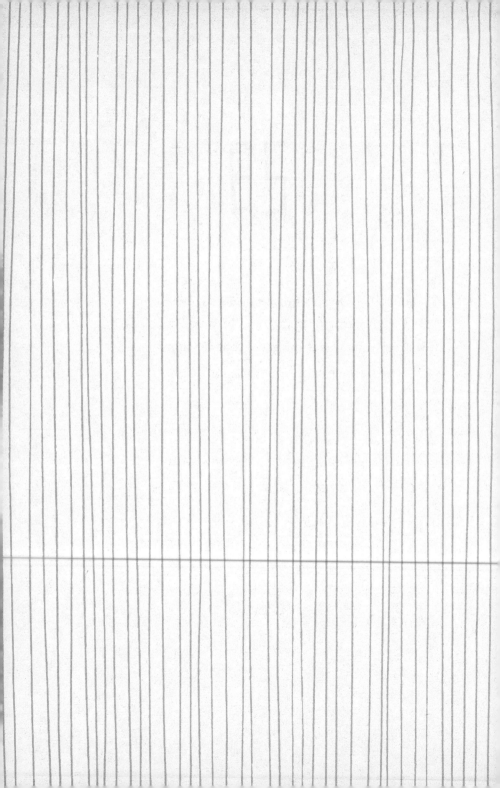

In school, Lucy sat quietly at her desk, which faced west.

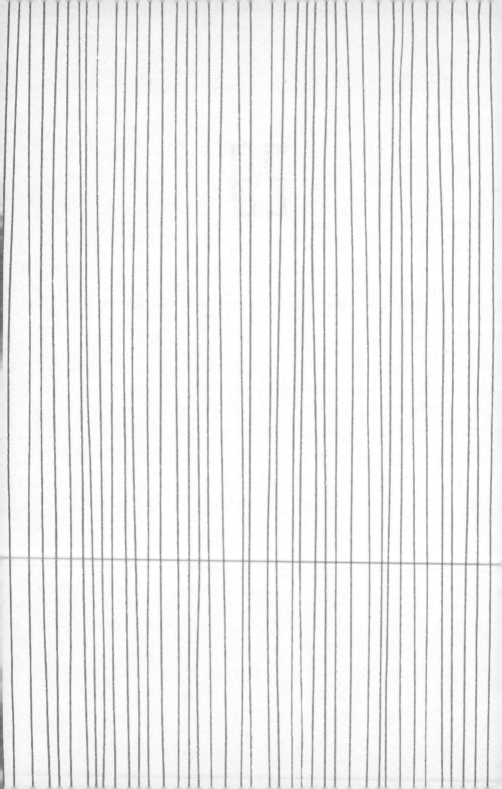

In between classes, Owen paused for a moment, his toes
pointing east.

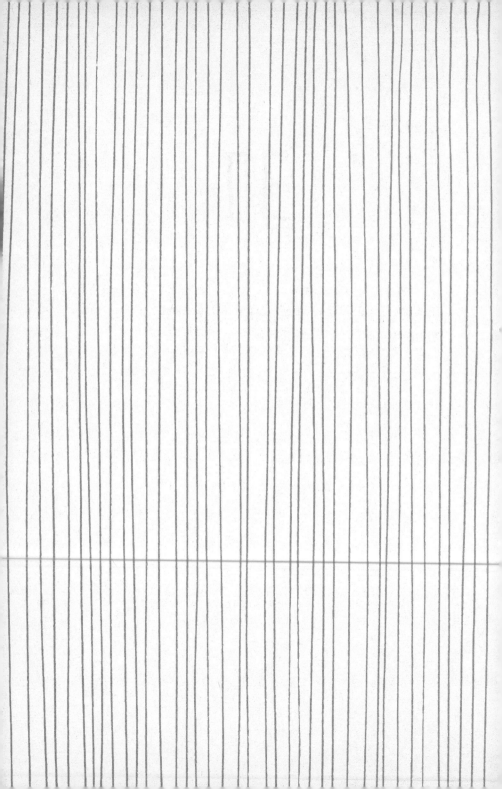

31

In bed that night, Lucy breathed in.

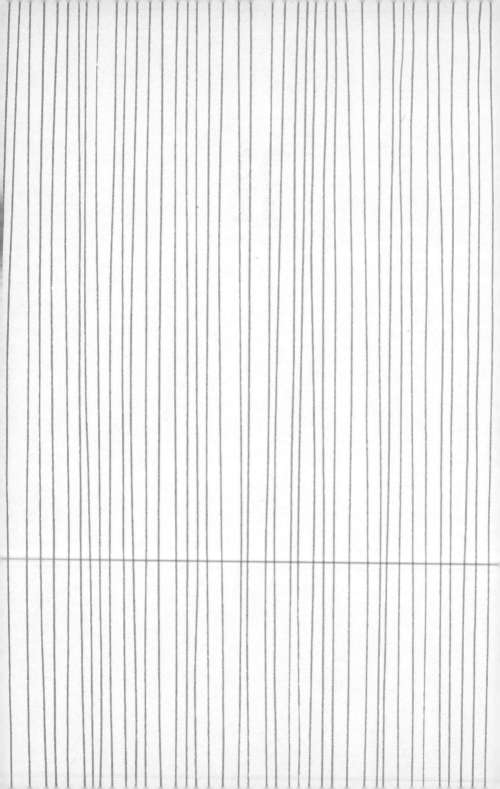

In the car that afternoon, Owen breathed out.

In London, Lucy thought of Owen.

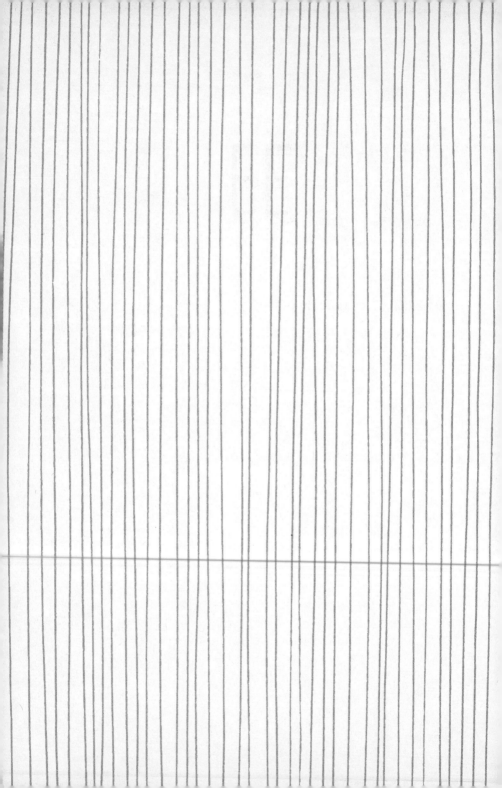

And far away in Seattle, Owen was thinking of her, too.

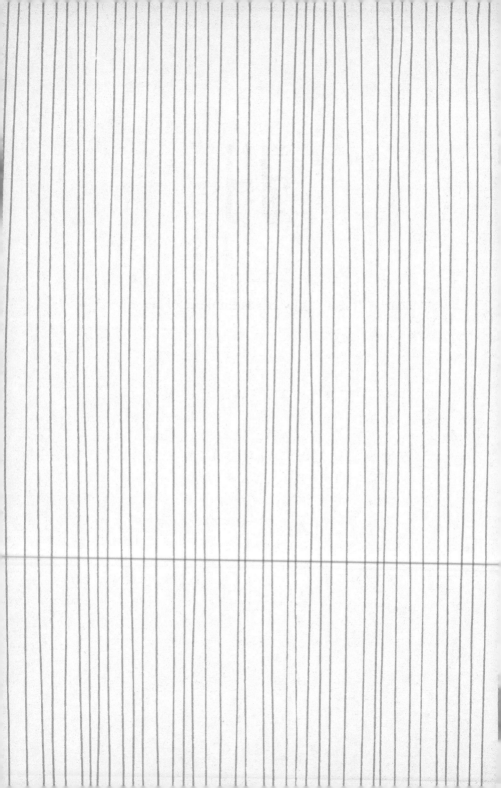

PART IV

Somewhere

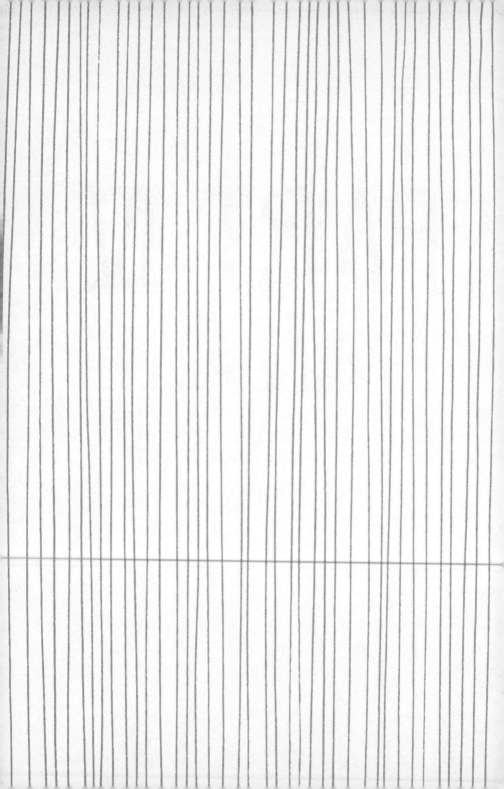

35

On a gray Saturday morning in London—which arrived on the heels of a gray Friday, and before that a gray Thursday as well—Lucy sat in the kitchen of their new house and watched her mom finish brewing a pot of tea.

"Is it like this all year?" she asked, frowning at the window, which was crowded by a low-hanging sky. It had been only two weeks since they'd gotten to town, but already Lucy had nearly forgotten what the sun felt like; everything here was raw and damp and the air still had a bite to it that felt more like winter than spring.

Mom nodded as she carried two mugs to the table. "Growing up, I never really even noticed. But after all these years away, I admit I'm finding it rather dreary." She paused to take a long sip of tea. It was just the two of them, as it usually was these days. "I was trying to convince your father that a trip someplace warm was in order, but he's too busy with work at the moment." She looked over at the oven clock. "Even on a Saturday morning, it would seem."

It was true. Dad had been working even longer hours than usual since they'd arrived in London, but Lucy didn't mind. It meant they had less time to travel without her, and that Mom was around more often. To everyone's surprise, including her own, she wasn't even bothered when they canceled their plans to be in New York for the summer. Dad couldn't get away for long enough to make the trip worth it, Mom had no real interest in returning, and, much to everyone's delight, her brothers had both managed to get internships in London, so for the first time in ages, they'd all be over here together. And that was just fine with Lucy. There were times when she missed New York—the familiarity of it, and her own deep knowledge of the place—but really, there was nothing pulling her back there anymore.

Mom was still talking about escaping the monotonous London weather. "I told him we should go to Athens for the weekend, but he swears he can't get away right now, even just for a couple of days."

"Greece," Lucy murmured, warming her hands on the mug. "Sounds nice."

"Doesn't it?"

"Not as nice as Paris, though."

Mom glanced up, her brow furrowed. "Paris?"

"I've always wanted to go," Lucy said with a shrug. "I don't know why. There's just something about it, you know?"

"I know," Mom said, watching her with a curious

expression. "I would have loved to take you. Why didn't you ever ask?"

Lucy frowned. "Ask what?"

"To come along with us."

"Because," Lucy said, grasping about for the words. She felt suddenly ill-equipped for this conversation. "Because you and Dad were always doing your own thing."

Mom's eyes softened. "We didn't want to disrupt your lives," she said. "Always pulling you and your brothers out of school just so we could travel. That would have been impractical at best, and irresponsible at worst." When she saw the look on Lucy's face, she laughed gently. "I do realize that sounds a bit hypocritical now, given our recent track record, but really, we just didn't think you'd like our kinds of trips. We weren't exactly going to Disneyland, you know."

"I know," Lucy said. "And we would have cramped your style."

"Not possible," she said, her mouth flickering briefly—the faintest hint of a smile—before she pressed her lips into a straight line, matching Lucy's more solemn expression. She reached out and patted her hand. "But darling, I wish I'd known. I wish you would have asked to come along."

"What?" Lucy said, lifting her eyes. "Just like that?"

Mom smiled in a way that made Lucy wonder whether they were still talking about the same thing. "Maybe," she said, giving her hand a squeeze. "You can't know the answer until you ask the question."

And so she did.

A week later, on another gray Saturday morning, Dad waved good-bye from the doorway as they climbed into a black taxi. At St. Pancras station, under the enormous glass dome, they boarded a train that would take them out of London and under the English Channel, only to emerge just a few hours later into the blinding sunlight of the French countryside. When they arrived at Gare du Nord and Lucy stepped off the train, her very first thought was *Finally*, which had nothing to do with the length of the trip and everything to do with all the years leading up to it.

On the train, Mom had made a list of her favorite sights in Paris, and in the cab ride to the hotel, Lucy went through with a pen and crossed out half of them.

"No museums," she said. "No tours. No lines."

Mom raised her eyebrows. "So what then?"

"Just walking."

"And eating, I hope."

Lucy grinned. "And eating."

And so they set out across the twisting streets under a mottled gray sky. Every so often, the wind shifted and the sun broke through in a dazzling column, throwing a spotlight on the city's many landmarks so that Lucy couldn't help feeling like it was a show being put on just for her.

It was impossible to take it all in as they wound their way through Pigalle and up toward Montmartre, the white dome of Sacré Coeur rising at the top of it. They wove through cobblestone streets on slanted hills, past little

254

shops selling truffles and thick loaves of bread, cafés filled with people sipping their coffee as they watched the rest of the world stroll by. At the top, they leaned against a railing and looked out over all of Paris, the Eiffel Tower winking in the sun.

Later, as they made their way over to Notre Dame, Lucy's mind wandered to Owen, as it so often did these days, and to their conversation on the roof all those months ago. On the Metro, she closed her eyes and tried to picture the brass star at the foot of the great cathedral, but all she could see was a different star: the rough chalky lines on the black surface of the roof.

When they first caught sight of the great cathedral, Lucy drew in a sharp breath and forgot to let it go. The clouds had scattered, and in the sunlight it was even more beautiful than she could have imagined, huge and imposing, yet somehow still delicate and unbelievably intricate. The large carved arches, the spiraling windows, the leering gargoyles—she tipped her head back to take it all in, her heart pounding at the scope of it.

"You'd think it wouldn't feel so big after living in New York," Mom said quietly, squinting up at it. "Not with all those skyscrapers. But this is so much grander. It still gets me every single time."

She rummaged through her bag for the camera, fussing with the settings before backing up a few steps to try to take in the whole thing all at once.

"Be right back," Lucy said, picking her way around all

the pigeons and the people, the benches and the trees, the lines for tours and the vendors selling guides, until she was standing in the thick of it, near the heavy doors at the entrance. Just a few feet away on the pavement, she spotted the worn bronze star, set inside an etched circle with the words *Point Zero* written along the edge.

If you were looking up at the church, as most people were, you might have missed it. But Lucy had known exactly where it would be. When she got there, she hesitated, but only for a moment, and then she stepped onto it slowly, as if on the edge of something unknowable: one toe first, then the other.

She wasn't sure if she'd ever stood in the exact center of anything before, but there she was, in the middle of Paris. Above her, an airplane whistled past, and in the eaves of the cathedral, a few pigeons were watching her along with the gargoyles. But they were the only ones. Nobody else was looking when she closed her eyes and made her wish.

When her mother found her, Lucy was still standing there on the star, and Mom only glanced at it and then looked away again, the significance of the spot clearly lost on her. Lucy took a small amount of pride in this, that she knew something about this city that her mother didn't. She stared down at the lines that arced around her sneakers. It was a small circle, but it was all hers.

"Sure you don't want to take a tour?" Mom asked, nodding at the line that stretched the whole length of the building, and Lucy shook her head, stepping carefully off

256

the star. Instead, they walked around the back of the building, where the spindly columns faced out over the fork in the River Seine. They crossed bridges and passed through small islands in a slow pilgrimage, and when they reached the other side, they ducked into a little bookshop with sagging shelves that smelled of paper and leather and dust, where Lucy picked out a small volume of *The Little Prince*.

Outside, there was a man selling watercolors on the bank of the river, and Mom paused to flip through them. They were small and delicately made, showing Notre Dame from all different angles and in every possible type of weather: gray skies and blue, rain and snow and sun.

"This one is lovely," Mom said to Lucy, who was standing nearby, already scanning the first page of her book. In the painting, the church glowed under a sun as powerful as the one that beat down on them now, which made everything a shade brighter than it had any right to be.

"We have that one in a magnet, too," the man said, reaching for a crate underneath his little table. "And a postcard."

Lucy froze, staring at her book.

"What do you think, Luce?" Mom asked, and there was a strained note to her voice. "Need a postcard for anyone?"

When she finally raised her eyes, Lucy was surprised to see a trace of hope in the way her mother was watching her, and all at once she understood.

She knew about Owen.

Not just the postcards but the rest of it, too. She must

have known the real reason she was going out in San Francisco that night. She must have realized why she'd muddled through the week in Napa in such a fog. She must have listened from the kitchen as Lucy said good-bye to Liam that day, and she must have understood the real reason. She must have known it all; if not the specifics, then at least the general idea of it.

And for the first time in a long time, Lucy didn't feel so alone.

The painter was still holding out a postcard, his hand wavering just slightly, and her eyes pricked with tears as she reached for it.

"You can't know the answer until you ask the question," Mom said with a smile, but Lucy was still looking at the man.

"Thank you," she said to him as she took the card, though really, the words were meant for her mother; Lucy knew she'd figure that out, too.

All the next day, as they walked along the River Seine and explored the Left Bank, Lucy thought about the postcard that was pressed between the pages of *The Little Prince*. On the train ride home that evening, her mother slept in the seat beside her while Lucy chewed on her pen, staring at the blank space on the back. It wasn't until she was home that night that she finally wrote something, the simplest and truest thing she could think to say: *Wish you were here.*

She didn't have his address in San Francisco. For all she knew, he might not even be there anymore. They could have gone back to Tahoe or somewhere else entirely by now. The logical thing would be to e-mail him, but how could she ask for his address without saying all those things that had been building up since their fight: *Hello* and *I'm sorry* and *I didn't mean it* and *I miss you* and *Why couldn't you just have kissed me?* There was something far too instant about an e-mail, and the knowledge that he could be opening it only minutes after she hit Send and then choose not to respond—or worse, choose to delete it—was almost too much to bear.

She'd rather send the postcard floating out into the world and hope for the best.

After school the next day, she sat at the kitchen counter and dialed the main number to their old building in New York. As she listened to it ring, she pictured the front desk in the lobby and felt a twinge of homesickness. She closed her eyes, waiting for someone to pick up, and when he did, she was quick to recognize the voice.

"George," she cried out, and there was a brief silence on the other end.

"Uh..."

"It's Lucy," she explained quickly. "Lucy Patterson."

"Lucy P," he said in a booming voice. "How's my girl?"

She smiled into the phone. "I'm good," she told him. "We're in London now. I miss you guys."

"We miss you, too," he said. "Not the same without you around here. Any chance you'll be back for the summer? Or what about those brothers of yours?"

"I don't think so," she told him. "Looks like we're all going to be over here, actually."

"Well, that'll be nice," he said. "Not often all five of you are in the same place."

Lucy smiled. "I know," she said. "It's crazy, right?"

"So, what," George said, "are you just calling to catch up on some of the gossip around here? Because I've got some great stories...."

"I'm sure you do," she said, laughing. "But I think my dad would have a heart attack over the phone bill if you told me even half of them. I'm actually calling because I have a favor to ask. You don't happen to have a forwarding address for the Buckleys, do you?"

There was a brief pause. "That super?"

She nodded, though he couldn't see her. "Yup."

"I'm not even going to ask," he said. "Talk about gossip...."

"C'mon, George."

"Okay, okay," he said, and there was typing in the background. "It's in Pennsylvania."

Lucy blinked. "Really? I guess they haven't sold the house yet."

"I don't know. But it's all I've got. You want it?"

"Yeah," she said. "Just let me grab a pen."

As she searched through the drawer beneath the phone,

she thought about the other possibility. That the house had been sold, and they just hadn't updated the building with their new information. After all, it had been more than six months since they'd left, and it was doubtful they were getting much mail there anymore. She glanced at the postcard on the counter, suddenly deflated. Maybe it would never find its way to Owen, who could be anywhere by now. Maybe it wasn't even worth trying.

But on the other end of the phone, George was clearing his throat. "Ready?" he asked, just as Lucy's fingers brushed against a pencil. She took a deep breath and positioned it above the paper.

"Ready," she said.

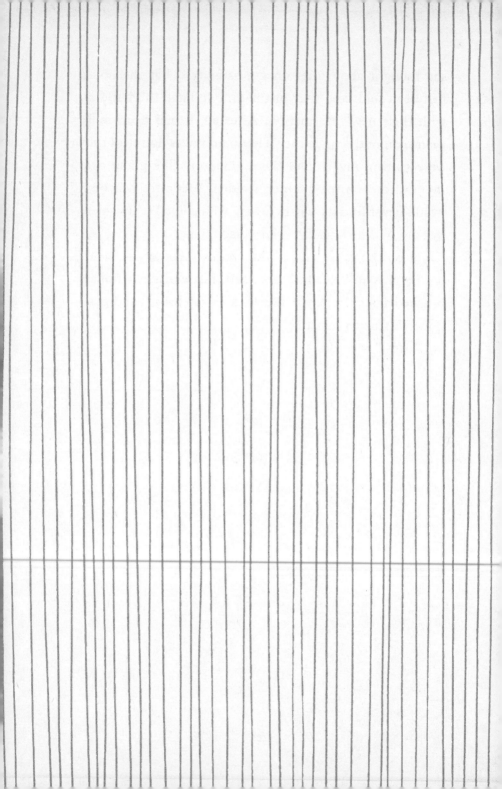

36

No car ride is ever truly silent. There's always something—the soft *swish* of the windshield wipers, the rumble of the tires, the hum of the engine—to break it up. But here now, somewhere in the middle of Pennsylvania, with his dad at the wheel of a too-small rental car, there was a quiet between them that was as absolute as Owen had ever experienced.

On the trip out west, and then again on the way up the coast from San Francisco to Seattle, there'd been times when they'd switched off the radio, letting whoever wasn't driving have a chance to sleep. Other times, they'd driven for long stretches without talking, simply watching the road disappear beneath the car. But those had been comfortable silences, punctuated by stray thoughts and occasional laughter, easily set aside with the clearing of a throat.

This, however, was different. It was a brittle quiet, sharp around the edges, and the stiffness of it had settled into every corner of the tiny car, making Owen shift uncomfortably in his seat. Back at the rental place, he'd offered to drive. He knew Dad hadn't slept on the plane—a crowded red-eye from Seattle to Philadelphia—and he was slumped against the counter, rubbing at his bleary eyes. But he'd shaken his head.

"It's fine," he said, his voice gruff. "I've got it."

As they drove out of the airport, Owen was thinking about the oddness of this trip. It was meant to be a good thing. When they'd learned that the house had finally sold, they'd toasted with mugs of apple juice. Afterward, in the backyard of their new home in Seattle, they'd circled the yard together, making plans and pointing out all the things they'd do to the place once they had money again.

But there's no such thing as a completely fresh start. Everything new arrives on the heels of something old, and every beginning comes at the cost of an ending. It wasn't just that they'd have to close up the Pennsylvania house, to sign the papers and collect their things; they'd also have to face their ghosts and say their good-byes. They'd have to look the past—the one they'd been running from all these months—right in the eye.

And Owen wasn't so sure they were ready for that.

"We should stop on the way," Dad had announced on the plane, just after they'd landed. All around them, people had shot to their feet, gathering their bags from the overhead bins, but Owen and his father remained seated. "Before we go to the house."

"Stop where?" Owen asked, but as soon as he said it, he knew. "Oh. Right. Yeah."

They'd last visited his mother's grave on their way out of New York, the two of them standing with bent heads and folded hands and blank eyes. There hadn't been any tears. They were saving those, each of them, for the moments when it felt like she was truly with them, which wasn't there on the windswept hill, on a chilly September day, where there was only the rough headstone and the clipped grass and the vast emptiness of a sprawling cemetery.

But today they would go back. It was supposed to be their first and only stop on the way to the house, but when a gas station loomed up ahead, hugging the highway on the right, Dad wrenched the wheel in its direction without explanation. Owen craned his neck to check the gauge, which of course showed that the tank was completely full; they couldn't have been twelve miles out of the airport. Instead of pulling up to one of the pumps, Dad parked the car in front of the mini-mart, then stepped out without a word.

Owen sat up a bit straighter in his seat, watching his father disappear inside, and a few minutes later, Dad emerged with a bouquet of flowers wrapped in cellophane. He set them carefully in the backseat, the car door *ding*-ing, and then climbed back in and started the engine. Neither of them said a word as they eased back out onto the highway.

As they drew closer, the sights becoming familiar again,

the car was still filled with a palpable dread, but it had at least started to feel as if they were in this together, which of course they were. At a stoplight, Dad even gave him a grim smile. It was part apology and part acknowledgment; it was all he had to offer at the moment, and Owen could tell it cost him a lot.

They turned in at the gated entrance to the cemetery, which stretched across a series of gentle hills, all of them dashed with gray headstones like an elaborate message in Morse code. It was 10:24 AM on a Wednesday, and the place was mostly empty. Owen was grateful for that. The first time they'd come, it had been for the funeral, and they'd both been raw with grief. The second time, just two months later, there was a numbness to the visit. Now there were months and months and miles and miles behind them, and Owen wasn't sure how to feel. After parking the car, they followed a narrow path through some of the older gravestones, and while his mouth was dry and his hands were damp, his careful heart did nothing but beat in time with his careful footsteps.

When they arrived, they both stopped a few feet short of her headstone, which was simple, her name written in block letters across the top. Owen looked at it for a long time, waiting for his lump of a heart to do some sort of trick, something appropriate to the moment: He waited for it to leap or bound or skip or sink; he waited for it to be extraordinarily heavy or unexpectedly light; he waited for it to seize up or slow down. But it just kept ticking the way it always did, the way it was meant to, as well-behaved and predictable as its owner.

Dad was standing a few feet away, still gripping the bouquet. "Do you think she'd be okay with it?" he asked after some time had passed, and Owen looked over sharply. It had been nearly an hour since either of them had spoken. "We could have stayed, you know. We could have just gotten over ourselves and lived in the house. I'd have found a job eventually, I'm sure. But taking off like that..." He shrugged his thin shoulders. "I think she wouldn't have minded the New York part, if that had worked, but I'm not sure about the rest of it."

"She'd have been fine with it," Owen said quietly. "She loved the years you were on the road."

Dad's frown deepened. "Yeah, but we were adults."

"Barely."

"We were having an adventure."

"So are we," Owen said with a little smile.

"I've had you in four different schools this year. She would've hated that. She would've wanted you to have a normal senior year."

"None of this is normal," Owen said, his eyes on the grave. "Or maybe all of it is. It's kind of hard to tell anymore."

They stood there for a long time. A couple of squirrels darted past, using the gravestones in their game of hide-and-seek, and when the wind picked up, rustling the cellophane on the bouquet, Dad glanced down, surprised to find it still in his arms. He took a step forward and laid it on the stone, then backpedaled until he was at Owen's side.

"Let's go," he said, and though his voice was soft, Owen could still hear the unspoken word at the end of it: *home*.

It was a short drive, not nearly long enough to recover from their last stop and prepare themselves for the next. When they pulled onto their old street, Owen could see Dad's fingers tense on the wheel, and as the house came into sight, he was overcome by a wave of sadness more powerful than anything he'd felt at the cemetery. Even from here, he could already tell: It was the same house; it just wasn't their home anymore.

Maybe it had started the moment she died, or maybe it was when they left. But now, as they parked out front and Owen stepped out of the car, he could see that the transition was complete. This house that they'd all loved, the house his parents had always dreamed of—with its green siding and white trim and wraparound porch—had been left empty for too long. One of their neighbors had been checking in on it from time to time, and there had been a few scattered showings with the real estate agent, but for the most part, it had simply sat here through the months without them, through a Halloween without trick-or-treaters, a Thanksgiving without the smell of turkey, a Christmas without the uneven lights Dad always put up around the windows.

When they opened the door, they were suddenly like

strangers, like neighbors, like visitors. The house was cold, the air gone out of the place, and as they moved through it, Owen realized that in spite of all the stuff—the furniture and the utensils and the curtains, the picture frames and the bedding and the books—the real measures of their lives here were now well and truly gone.

On the kitchen table, there was a sloping pile of mail. It was a mess of catalogs and bills and envelopes, most of it probably junk, but Owen also knew that his college letters would be in there, too. If he'd wanted to, he could have checked online already; the schools had sent him long chains of user names and passwords, instructions with dates and times, but Owen hadn't been in a rush. Soon enough, his shapeless future would start to mold itself into something more concrete. In the meantime, he was in no hurry.

Over the past months, their neighbor—an elderly man who used to bring them fresh-cut flowers from his garden every spring—had been forwarding batches of mail each time they settled somewhere long enough to let him know. But when they found out the house had sold, Dad called and said he could stop. They'd be there soon to collect the rest themselves.

And now here they were.

Dad walked over to the pile, trailing his fingers across the top, and Owen could see that he was glad for the distraction, for something to focus on before the walls of the house could close in around them.

"Big moment," he said quietly, and Owen felt a brief urge to laugh. Standing in their old house, just after a visit to his mother's grave, he thought this seemed like the smallest moment possible.

"I guess," he managed, and Dad nudged the pile.

"Should we go fishing?"

"Only if you think we'll catch something."

"I have a pretty good feeling," he said, tossing a catalog aside as he started to go through the stack. The first envelope he pulled out was large and rectangular, and it had the UC Berkeley emblem in the corner. When Dad held it up in the square of light from the window, Owen could see the dust motes floating around it. "Looks promising," Dad said, sliding it across the table. "Let's see what else we've got."

Before long, there were six envelopes stacked neatly between them, all of them roughly the same size and thickness. They stared at them for a few moments, and Owen blinked a few times.

"Well," he said finally.

Dad grinned. "Well."

For other kids his age, Owen knew this was a big deal. The arrival of a thick envelope, the unveiling of the acceptance letter, the jumping up and down, the anticipation about what the next year would bring. But though he tried to summon some kind of joy, that lightness you were supposed to feel at moments like these, his stubborn heart refused to budge.

Solemnly, he slid a finger under the flap of each envelope, and one by one he wrestled the papers out to find the same answer each time: *yes, yes, yes*. First Berkeley, then UCLA, then Portland and San Diego and Santa Barbara. With each one, he passed the letter over to his father, but it wasn't until he got to the University of Washington that he realized Dad was crying, his blond head bent over the pile.

Owen paused, stiffening, waiting for him to say it: *She should have been here* or *She would have loved this* or *She would have been so proud*. But instead, Dad looked up with a blurry smile.

"Six for six," he said, shaking his head. "Where the hell did you come from, anyway?"

Owen grinned, looking around the kitchen. "From right here, actually."

"Well, as much as I miss this place," Dad said, "I'm glad we won't be so far apart next year." He gestured at the pile. "Same time zone, no matter what."

There was a hitch in Owen's chest. "No matter what," he said.

"And it'll be nice to head into graduation knowing you've got some options."

Owen lowered his gaze. "Dad."

"No, I mean it," he said, leaning forward on the table. "You know how many kids will be standing up there onstage in a total panic? And you've got all these choices." He glanced at the letters and shook his head. "All six. *Six*."

"I know," Owen said. "I'm just not sure...."

"She would have been so proud," he said finally, inevitably, standing up and placing a large palm on Owen's shoulder. Then he leaned down and kissed the top of his head. "And so am I."

There was nothing for Owen to do but nod. "Thanks."

As Dad walked out of the kitchen to begin taking stock of the rest of the house, Owen sat and listened to his footsteps on the echoing floorboards. Out the window, a cloud drifted by, snuffing out the sun, and the room went abruptly dim. On the wall, the familiar clock ticked its familiar rhythm, and when Owen took a deep breath, he almost expected the faint scent of cigarette smoke.

But of course, there was nothing.

He reached for the stack of acceptance letters, shuffling them into a neat pile. Then he set them aside and grabbed the rest of the mail. As he sorted through old Christmas and birthday cards, bills and coupons and glossy magazines, he couldn't help wondering whether his friends—if you could even still call them that—had gotten their letters, too. Both of them lived in this neighborhood, and it was strange to think that at this very moment, they were only blocks away, with no idea that Owen was nearby.

Last year, they'd hardly talked about college, and Owen knew he was the only one with dreams of getting out of Pennsylvania. But even if they ended up staying closer to home, Casey and Josh would still likely be splitting up, too, each going their separate ways, and it struck Owen now as inevitable, this distance between them. It would have happened anyway. He just happened to leave a year early. Even if nothing had changed at all, everything would still be about to; even if he'd stayed, they'd still be getting ready to say good-bye. They'd each go off to college, losing themselves in their new lives, seeing each other only at Thanksgiving or Christmas or during the summer. And then it would all go back to normal the way it always did with lifelong friends. As if no time had passed at all.

The point wasn't the distance. It was the homecoming.

He turned over a catalog in his hands, staring at the photograph on the front: a mother and father and their young son. The perfect family. When he looked up again, he realized he wasn't ready to venture any farther into the house just yet. He didn't want to think about college or graduation, his mother or his father, Seattle or Pennsylvania or anywhere in between.

Instead, he reached for his phone. He would call his friends, and they would go for pizza at their favorite place, and he'd tell them about all of it: New York and Chicago, the endless roads through Iowa and Nebraska, the snow in Lake Tahoe, the diner where he'd worked, the months in San Francisco and their new house in Seattle.

He dialed Casey's number first, and as the phone began to ring in his hand, he sifted absently through the mail, raking over the pile. He was nearly to the bottom when he spotted it: a postcard of Paris. Without thinking, he snapped the phone shut, hanging up before anyone could answer, and then he sat there staring at it in the fading light of the kitchen: the cathedral at the very center of the city.

Even before he flipped it over to find the note, he was thinking the very same thing: that he wished more than anything that she was here, too. And just like that, his heart—that dead thing inside of him—came to life again.

37

Lucy's first instinct, when the elevator jolted to a stop, was to laugh.

Even before the floor had quit vibrating beneath their feet, hovering midway between the third and fourth floors of the Liberty department store, her three fellow travelers—an old man in a sweater vest and a young mother with her son, who couldn't have been older than three—were giving her strange looks, as if she'd already cracked under the pressure of the situation, just four seconds in.

"The lift is stuck," the little boy pointed out, tilting his head back to take in the ornate wooden carvings along the ceiling. The lights were still on, and when the woman hit the red button, a crackling voice was quick to come over the speaker.

"Are you in need of assistance?" someone asked in a clipped English accent.

"It's stuck," the boy said with more force this time. He accompanied this with a little stamp of his foot.

"We seem to have stopped," his mother said, her mouth close to the speaker.

"Right," said the voice. "We're looking into it. Be back with you straightaway."

Lucy was still shaking her head, unable to get rid of the smile on her face. The woman gave her a look as if to suggest she wasn't taking this quite seriously enough, but she was quickly distracted by her son, who had started to cry, great heaving sobs that made his shoulders rise and fall. It built to such a pitch in the small space that the old man actually clapped his hands over his ears.

"Would anyone like a mint?" Lucy asked, digging through her bag, and the man glanced over at her, lowering his hands again.

"You're prepared," he said, and she smiled.

"Not my first rodeo," she told him, still amused by the unlikeliness of the situation. Only a few minutes ago, she'd been trailing her mother through the fourth floor of the airy store, running her fingers absently over the endless bolts of brightly colored fabrics. But she'd soon grown bored, and when she spotted a directory that advertised a haberdashery on the third floor, she decided she had to see it. She knew there would only be hats, and she'd probably be far more interested in the travel accessories and notebooks found farther down, but how often did you get to visit a haberdashery? There were stairs across the store, but the elevator was right there, and she'd stepped in without thinking about it.

And now here she was—stuck once again.

Only this time, it all seemed sort of funny. The old man was tapping his fingers against the wooden panels, and the woman was fanning herself with her hand, though it wasn't particularly hot—was, in fact, practically cold compared to the last elevator Lucy had been stuck inside—and the little boy was hiccupping now, fat tears still rolling down his rosy cheeks. It was all just so unlikely, that she should find herself in this situation twice in such a short amount of time, and the only person she wanted to tell—the only person who would really appreciate it—was Owen.

It had been two weeks since she'd sent the postcard, and she hadn't heard back. Not that she'd expected to; even if he wasn't still angry after their argument in San Francisco, and even if he wasn't still with Paisley, it had been sent off to a place where he hadn't lived in several months. And it struck her now—with a kind of jarring obviousness—that a postcard was just about the stupidest possible form of communication. There were so many things that could go wrong, so many ways it could have gotten lost, so many opportunities for it to go astray. It was almost as if she hadn't *wanted* it to reach him. Suddenly, dropping that postcard in the mail seemed about as useful as throwing a paper airplane out of a window. It was a coward's move, a way of doing something without really doing much of anything.

Beside her, the old man raised his wiry eyebrows to the

ceiling and then thumped a hand to his chest, a hollow sound that seemed to vibrate in the crowded space.

Lucy looked at him with alarm. "Are you okay?"

"Heart problems," he muttered.

"Maybe you should sit down," Lucy suggested, trying not to sound panicky, but he shook his head.

"Not mine," he said. "My wife's."

Lucy exchanged a look with the other woman, who only shrugged.

"I snuck off to buy her some perfume," he explained, his eyes swimming. "She's downstairs looking at fabrics. She'll be worried when she can't find me, and her heart..."

Lucy put a hand on his shoulder. "She'll be fine," she said, surprised by the emotion in her voice. "I'm sure they'll have us out soon."

There was a lump in her throat as she watched him fidget with the buttons on his vest, and it struck her as the truest form of kindness, the most basic sort of love: to be worried about the one who was worrying about you.

Only seven minutes had passed, but they were slow minutes, long and unhurried. She thought of Owen again, and how quickly he'd made the time pass when they'd been stuck. Without him, it felt like something was missing.

She should have been braver. She should have e-mailed him. It wouldn't have mattered if he didn't write back; that wasn't the point. The old man worrying about his wife didn't know if she was worried about him, too. He wasn't thinking about himself at all. He was too busy loving her simply because she was out there somewhere.

The little boy banged a fist against the wall, and they all paused to listen for a moment, but there was no response.

"Come on," Lucy muttered, glaring at the speaker. She shifted from one foot to the other, jangly and on edge, then sighed and squeezed her eyes shut. The minute she stepped out of this elevator, she knew that any sense of urgency would drain away. But right now, in a wood-paneled box with three strangers who were not Owen, she wanted nothing more than to reach him somehow.

The last time, when they'd been in this together, the opening of the doors had felt like the breaking of some spell. But this time, as the elevator cranked to life again, moving downward in a motion that felt sudden after eight long minutes of being suspended, there was only relief. Lucy's eyes flickered open and she blinked a few times, meeting the gaze of the old man, which was suddenly peaceful: He was on his way home.

She envied him that.

On the ground floor, the doors opened with two short *ding*s, and there was a small knot of people waiting for them: the store manager with his patterned tie, a maintenance man in a khaki shirt, an elderly woman with a halo of white hair, who rushed to embrace the old man, and finally Lucy's mother, who shook her head from side to side with a slow smile.

"Let's try not to make this too much of a habit," she said, slinging an arm over Lucy's shoulders. "You okay?"

Lucy nodded absently as her mother launched into her side of the saga, how she'd been looking for Lucy when she saw the maintenance man hurry past with the manager, and she'd had an inkling her daughter might be involved. So she'd dropped the fabric she was thinking about buying, then followed them down to the ground floor to wait.

"I think you should seriously consider using the stairs from now on," she was saying. "You don't seem to have the best luck in this area."

Normally, Lucy would have made a joke here. She would have been reveling in the hard-won attention of her mother, so rare before and now—still sort of unbelievably—so normal. She didn't know if it was her father's new job or the fact that they were in a new country, or maybe it was just that they all missed her brothers, who were so far away, but whatever the reason, they were suddenly a family again: eating dinners together, traveling on weekends, going to museums, joking and laughing and being there. Maybe they'd only needed a change of scenery. Or maybe they'd needed to leave home in order to find it.

But right now, Lucy was too distracted to enjoy their newfound complicity. She was busy collecting the right words, which were too many to fit on a postcard, too heavy for such a slim piece of cardboard. She carried them with her as they walked out the wooden doors of the building and through the winding streets of the West End to Oxford

Circus, where they caught the Central Line to Notting Hill Gate and emerged from the tube stop beneath a steely London sky, then wove up Portobello Road past buildings painted the color of Easter eggs and stalls selling everything imaginable, all the way to the little brick mews house tucked like a jewel in the center of this city she'd so quickly grown to love.

As she walked upstairs, the words multiplied with each step—there was suddenly so much to say!—and she realized she'd been carrying them with her even longer than that, at least since San Francisco, but maybe even since Edinburgh or New York, and she hurried up the last few steps, ready to set them down, one by one, across a blank screen, to say the honest thing, the truest words she could find: that even though she'd been the one stuck inside that elevator, all she'd been able to think about was him walking around outside of it; that it wasn't her heart she was worrying about—it was his.

But when she flipped open her computer, she was pulled up short by the sight of his name, and it was her own heart that once again needed rescuing.

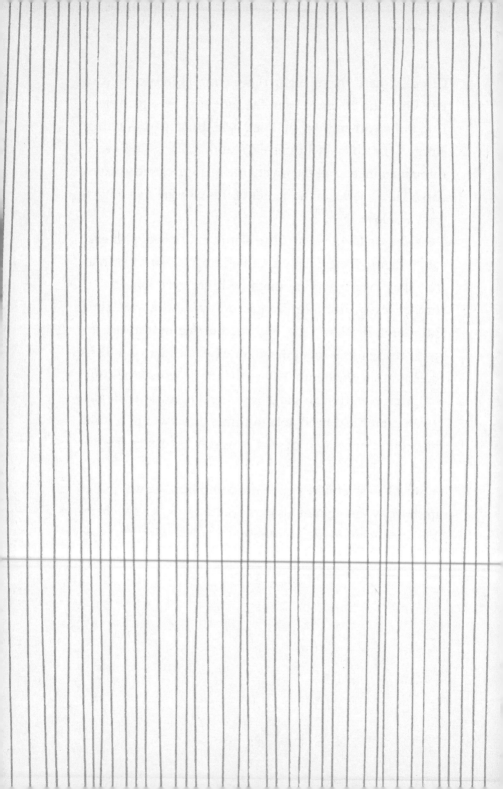

For a long time after he sent the e-mail, Owen just sat there, trying to decide whether or not to panic.

The house was quiet. It was Saturday, but Dad had been eager to get back to work after their trip. He'd set out this morning with a look of great contentment, clearly thrilled at the prospect of spending a day with a hammer in hand after a week of bubble wrap and cardboard boxes and duct tape.

"There's very little in this world that can't be cured by bashing in some nails," he used to say, and Owen knew he needed that more than ever today, after too much time spent clearing away the last reminders of their previous life.

He'd left earlier than usual after putting in a load of laundry, and now Owen could hear the thumping of the washing machine downstairs, which was an encouraging sign. For months, they'd been living in temporary spaces like a couple of teenagers; there was always toothpaste in the sink and crumbs in the kitchen and a layer of grime over pretty much every appliance. But seeing the old house in Pennsylvania must have jolted something in him. After getting back from the airport last night, Owen had watched his father tear around the house, picking up dirty socks and scrubbing at the grout around the faucets. It wasn't quite up to Mom's standards yet, but it was getting closer.

Now Owen sat listening as the wash cycle ended and the machine beeped, the sound carrying upstairs. Out the window, a car slid past, and a few birds called back and forth, but otherwise there was nothing: just Owen, alone in his room, staring at his computer screen and trying to figure out what he'd been thinking.

There was no logical explanation for the e-mail he'd just sent, and he was suddenly remembering why, until now, he'd always stuck to postcards. With those, there was still time to change your mind: just after putting the pen down, or on the way to the mailbox, or at any point in between. But there was nothing to be done about the e-mail. With one click, it had gone flying across the miles, straight to Lucy's computer, and there was no getting it back.

He closed his eyes and rubbed at his forehead as the rain started up outside. It always seemed to be half raining here, something between a mist and drizzle, so that it felt like the sky was spitting at you. Owen watched for a few minutes, his thoughts wiped clean by the weather, then he stood up, grabbed his rain jacket, and headed outside.

At the corner, he caught a bus, watching the rain make patterns on the windows, and when he stepped off about twenty minutes later, the sun was trying its best to emerge, trimming the clouds in gold.

The fish market was crowded, as it had been that first weekend when he'd come here with his dad, the two of them standing at the edge as they took it all in: the slap of fish on paper, the people shouting their orders, the guy playing harmonica off to one side. There were fish flying through the air as vendors in stained aprons tossed them as casually as you would a baseball, and the smell of it made his eyes burn, but Owen had loved it right away, just as he'd loved this city from the moment they'd arrived. It wasn't exactly home—not yet—but when they flew in last night, he'd looked out the window of the plane at the orange lights of the city, bounded by water and mountains, and he'd felt something deep within him settle.

For the first time in all their travels, he thought he could see a future here.

He'd told his friends that just a few days ago, over an enormous pizza, and they'd asked him about the ferries and the fish market and the university, and when he was done, they told him about their plans for next year, skipping like a record over the other things, the holes in his life that had caused holes in their friendship, before they stopped talking altogether and simply played video games until it got too late and they parted with promises to stay in better touch.

"It's all you," Josh teased him. "You're the weak link here."

"It's my phone," Owen had said with a grin. "It's completely worthless. I'll have to send you a postcard instead."

They both laughed; they couldn't have possibly known he was serious.

Now he left the chaos of the market behind, heading toward the water, and as he walked, he thought back to what Lucy had said about New York, how the only way to truly know the place was to see it from the ground up. When the gray waters of Puget Sound came into sight, dotted with ferries, he found himself thinking about the marina in San Francisco and the path along the Hudson River in New York, and how in all of these very different places, this was something that rarely changed: the same blue-gray water, the same rise and fall of the waves, the same smells of salt and fish.

He wondered if the harbor in Edinburgh was the same, too. He hoped it was.

The rain picked up again, and Owen pulled at his hood.

He needed to figure out what to do about the e-mail.

The problem, of course, wasn't so much what he'd written; it was what he was going to do about her response.

He didn't regret what he'd said. After finding her postcard from Paris, he'd carried it with him all week, tucked in his back pocket like a good-luck charm, something to buoy him whenever he felt he was sinking under the weight of the task at hand: the dismantling of all of their memories. And by the time he'd gotten back to Seattle last night, he'd written and rewritten the e-mail in his mind enough times to know it by heart.

He apologized for what happened in San Francisco and explained that he'd ended things with Paisley and admitted that he thought of Lucy all the time even though they hadn't been in touch.

I miss you, he'd written at the end. *And I wish you were here, too.*

That was when he should have hit Send.

But for some reason, he found himself writing one last line: *By the way, I'm not sure if you're still planning to be in New York for the summer, but I'll actually be there the first week of June, so let me know and maybe we could meet up....*

And that, right there, was the problem.

Because not only did Owen have no plans whatsoever to be in New York City the first week of June, he also had no money and no way of getting there.

And no idea what he'd do if—against all odds—she actually wanted to see him.

There were so many things to worry about: the chance that she might be angry with him, the odds that she was still with Liam, the sheer ridiculousness of the suggestion, and most of all, the possibility that she might say yes.

But deep down, he knew that his biggest worry wasn't any of these things.

It was much worse.

His biggest worry was that she'd say no.

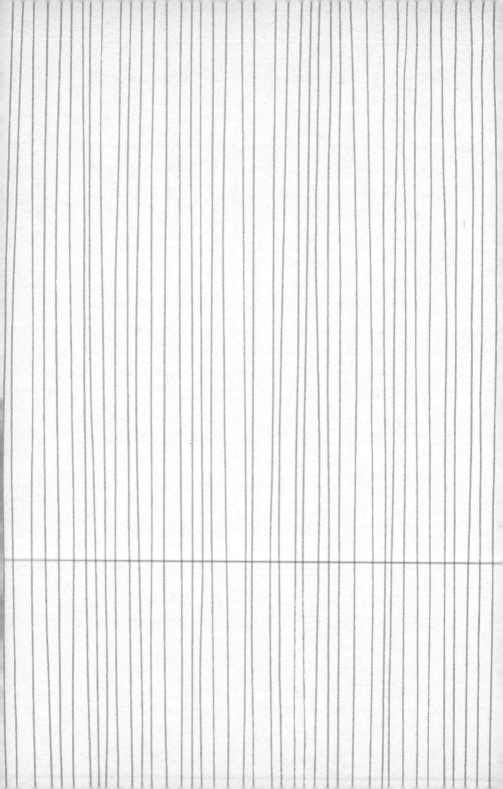

39

Lucy stared at the computer for a long time before lifting her fingers to the keyboard, and with a pounding heart, she punched at three different letters, one at a time, watching nervously as they appeared across the screen:

Yes.

PART V

Home

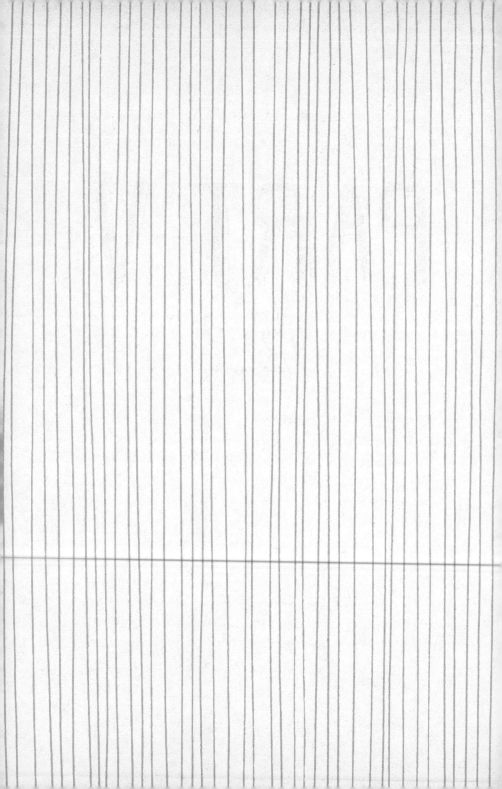

At first, she'd planned to tell him the truth.

But the truth was so much less appealing.

The truth meant sitting by herself in London that first week of June, imagining Owen in New York: walking through Central Park, waiting in line at the ice-cream shop, watching the sailboats glide up the Hudson. The truth meant doing nothing. It meant missing out. And most of all, it meant not getting to see him again.

And so, instead, she'd said yes.

Then she panicked.

Earlier in the year, when they were still in Edinburgh, they'd planned to go back to New York for the beginning of the summer. But that had all changed with Dad's new job in London, where he was working too many hours to escape even for a long weekend, much less an entire month. For a while, Lucy and Mom had still talked about going on their own, since it seemed likely that the boys would be there, but now that they both had summer internships in London, there was little reason to go.

"Summers are too hot in New York anyway," Mom had said. "You'll like London a lot better."

Lucy thought this was probably true. So far, she loved everything about this city: the street markets and the colorful buildings, the twisting lanes and expansive parks and the way most everyone sounded like a version of her mother. She even liked her classmates at school, who were not just from England or even America but from all over the world: India and South Africa and Australia and Dubai. In New York, she'd stood apart, and in Edinburgh, she'd stood out; but here, she just stood alongside everyone else, and there was a comfort in that, in fitting in for once.

She liked the weather here, too, which was always gray and damp, never too cold and never too warm, so she had no doubt that she'd enjoy the London summer. But even so, as her mother complained about all those years they'd suffered through the high temperatures in New York, Lucy had been jolted by the memory of that night on the roof, where she and Owen had lain beneath a stagnant sky, sticky with heat and grinning at every limp breeze that managed to reach them, and for a moment, she found herself wishing they'd go back.

But there was no reason to make the trip.

Until yesterday, when she got Owen's e-mail and decided that in this case, anyway, the lie was a lot more exciting than the truth.

And so she'd written back: *I'll be there. What's the plan?*

It had taken him a full day to respond, and she spent the hours in between with a knot in her stomach, stunned by the possibility of it. It wasn't that she thought she'd never see him again, because she had more faith in the world than that. But they'd done so much zigging and zagging over the past months, had missed so many chances and squandered so much time, that it seemed hard to believe they might just get another shot at this.

She knew it might not turn out well. It might end up like San Francisco again. It could be a complete and total disaster: They might argue or be overly polite; they might be awkward or nervous or both; they might realize they were better from a distance, better as friends or pen pals or nothing at all.

But they had to see each other again to find out.

When he finally responded late the following night, Lucy was lying in bed, staring at her phone and attempting to calculate the hours between San Francisco and London. As soon as she saw his name appear at the top of the screen, she sat up to read his note, which was a measly seven words.

The lobby at noon on June 7.

The light from the screen seemed to pulse in the dark room, giving the ceiling a whitish glow. She stared at the note for a long time, amused by its matter-of-fact tone, then typed her reply—*Not the top of the Empire State Building?*—and hit Send before she could think better of it.

Once again, she sat in the dark, awaiting his response, hoping he knew she was only kidding. They were accustomed to corresponding by postcard, where there was endless time between letters rather than endless space on a screen, and they hadn't adjusted their style just yet.

Finally, after what felt like a very long time, a new e-mail arrived.

How about the Statue of Liberty at midnight? it read, and she laughed, picturing him at his computer, leaning back in his chair with a crooked grin as he waited for her reply. She propped a few pillows behind her, sitting up again.

Or better yet, she wrote, *a rowboat in Central Park at dusk.*

A taxi on Broadway at sunrise.

A horse-drawn carriage at the Plaza at high noon.

Colonel Mustard with the rope in the study, he wrote, and she laughed again, the sound loud in the quiet house.

After that, it was easy again. For hours, they wrote back and forth, a conversation punctuated by short periods of waiting, where Lucy held her breath and kept watch over her phone, resenting the constraints of technology, the limits of distance.

All night, they wrote to each other, an endless volley of thoughts and worries and memories, the information pinging this way and that across the globe. She told him about breaking up with Liam, and he told her more about what had happened with Paisley. He apologized again for what happened in San Francisco, and she apologized right back. As the night crept toward morning, Lucy's fingers flew across the screen, and she had to reach for the tangled wire of her charger to keep the light from going out, to keep the flame of conversation from dying as they joked and teased and reassured each other, as they talked all night from opposite ends of the world.

Why did we never do this before? she typed eventually, as her eyelids grew heavy and the screen started to swim in front of her.

We wanted to support the local postal service? he replied. *We're old-fashioned? We couldn't ever figure out the time difference?*

Or we're just idiots.

Or that, he wrote. *But at least we're idiots together.*

Later, when they'd said almost everything else, the only thing left was good-bye.

See you soon, Bartleby, she wrote.

Can't wait, Colonel Mustard.

As she set her phone on the bedside table, she realized there was only one thing she hadn't told him: that she didn't actually have any plans to be in New York.

But it didn't matter. As she drifted off to sleep, fuzzy-headed and heavy-limbed and unreasonably happy, she knew that she'd find a way to get there.

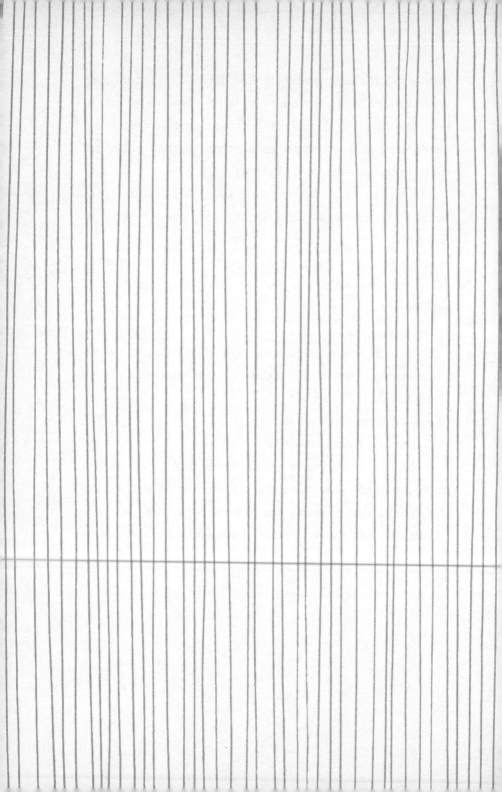

41

Until the Day of a Hundred E-mails, Owen wasn't completely sure he'd follow through with it. There was still time to back out, to say that his trip was canceled or that his plans had changed. But last night, after so many hours and e-mails had flown by, the rain stopped and a gray dusk settled over Seattle and he finally came up for air, blinking and disoriented and grinning like an idiot, and he'd known for sure then that he would be going to New York.

He wanted to see her.

It was as simple and as complicated as that.

The next morning was Sunday, which meant that Dad was off work, and Owen woke to the smell of pancakes. It had been a long time since his father had cooked anything for breakfast, but ever since they returned from Pennsylvania, they'd resumed the Sunday-morning tradition. When he was little, Owen remembered getting his pancakes in the shape of a mouse, while Mom's were always slightly crooked hearts. These days, they were mostly just circles, but it wasn't the shape that mattered; it was that they were there at all. Owen knew it was a small thing, but it felt big; it felt like they'd traveled a very long way just to make it here, to this kitchen with the bubbling batter and the smell of syrup.

As he slid into his seat, Dad waved the spatula in greeting. "Sleep well?" he asked, and Owen nodded distractedly. He had a question to ask, and he was busy trying to figure out the best way to do that. But Dad was in too good a mood to notice. He slid a plate of warm pancakes in front of Owen with a grin. "For my favorite son."

"Your only son appreciates it," Owen said, reaching for the syrup. As Dad moved around the tiny kitchen— turning off the griddle and putting the butter back in the fridge, all while humming a little tune under his breath— Owen chewed slowly, still making calculations.

He didn't have any savings—not anymore. There wasn't exactly a lot to begin with, but when money was tight on the drive, Owen had started paying for things himself. Not anything big, just the odd tank of gas or some groceries when it was his turn to run into the store. And then in Tahoe, he'd done the same with his dishwashing money, and anything he'd managed to scrape together since. He'd never mentioned it to his dad, who had still been too distraught at that point to notice much of anything, but it felt good to help, especially as the expenses stacked up and the weeks stretched on.

But now, suddenly, this had become a problem. Owen

had looked up flights online, and they weren't as bad as he thought, a few hundred dollars maybe, but that was still a few hundred dollars more than he had. Upstairs, tucked in one of his drawers, was the key to the roof of their old building, which meant he didn't need a place to stay. If worse came to worse, he could easily sleep up there for a couple of nights; it was warm enough, and he was pretty sure nobody would notice. So it was really just the plane ticket and a few other essentials, but he had a plan that would cover those, and he had two whole weeks to do it. He just needed to work up the nerve to ask.

"So," he said as his father finally took a seat across from him. "The site's coming along?"

"Yeah," he said, beaming. "It's coming up fast. And the foreman told me yesterday that they've got another job lined up right after, and he wants me on the crew."

"That's great," Owen said, watching him take a long swig of orange juice. "So do they . . . have enough help?"

"Help?" Dad asked, without looking up from his breakfast.

"Yeah, you know . . . workers."

"Plenty," he said with a nod, then frowned, his fork left hanging a few inches from his mouth. "How come?"

"I just thought, if they ever needed an extra pair of hands or anything, maybe I could—"

Dad laughed a short bark of a laugh. "You?"

"Yeah," said Owen, feeling his face go warm. "I mean, I've been helping around the house, and I really like it. . . ."

This was only half-true, and they both knew it. In the six weeks that they'd been here, the house had come a long way, but it was mostly due to Dad's work. He'd put in new windows and repaired the front steps, painted the porch and the wood trim around the door, installed a new sink, and refinished the hardwood floors. Owen always trailed along after him, handing over tools and completing small tasks when instructed, but he lacked the skill for this kind of work. More often than not, he spilled the paint or missed the nail. He just wasn't very comfortable with a hammer or a drill—unlike Dad, who should have come home from the construction site exhausted every day but instead returned with a brand of energy Owen hadn't seen in him since before the accident, switching out his tool belt with genuine enthusiasm.

He was watching him now across the table with one eyebrow raised. "You hate that kind of stuff," he said finally, and Owen shrugged.

"It would just be nice to have some extra money."

"Story of our lives, huh?" Dad said with a smile, but when he saw Owen's expression, his mouth straightened again. "Look, we're doing okay now, so if you're worried about college—"

"I'm not," he said, and for once he meant it. Over the past few weeks, he'd been researching student loans and scholarships, had been making plans without quite admitting to himself that he was doing it. And he'd made his decision. "Actually, I checked," he said, "and UW has really great financial assistance."

Dad stared at him. "Does that mean...?"

"Yeah," Owen said with a grin. "University of Washington."

"So you'll be...?"

"Right across town."

Dad smacked the table, making the plates wobble. "Well, that's great news," he said, beaming, but then his smile fell and he leaned forward with a worried expression. "But you're not just doing it because of me, are you? Because you can go anywhere, you know. I'll be fine. And I'll come visit."

"It's not for you," Owen said, picking up his fork. "It's for your pancakes."

Dad laughed. "But really."

"Really," Owen said, meeting his eye. "I like it here."

"Me too." He rubbed at his chin, looking off toward the window. "And I was thinking...between the job and finally selling the house, we've got some room to breathe, and now with this, it seems only fitting that you get some sort of graduation present...."

"Dad..." Owen began, his voice strained, but it didn't stop him.

"And I know what you did," he said, his eyes bright. "With your savings. On the trip. And I'm proud of you for that, too. So I'd like to give you a little something for—I don't know. To have some fun with, I guess, or to get you started, you know?"

Owen lowered his eyes and stabbed at his pancake. "Dad, I can't."

"You don't even know how much it is yet, so you can't say it's too much," he said with a broad smile. "I was thinking that a couple hundred bucks should do it, but then I remembered that these are special circumstances, and for a guy who went 6 and 0 with college applications, I think five hundred would probably be more fitting."

For a brief moment, Owen actually considered doing it—going through with graduation, just to get the money. He could already imagine walking up Broadway, turning the corner into the lobby of the building, finding Lucy there by the elevators where they'd first met. It was almost worth it, just to see her.

But that wasn't him. He just wasn't built that way. And he still couldn't imagine walking across a stage to receive his diploma without his mother out there in the audience.

Besides, it was no accident that he'd suggested June 7 to Lucy.

June 7 was graduation day.

It took him a long time to meet his father's gaze. "Thank you," he said quietly. "Really. But I can't...."

Dad tilted his head to one side, clearly confused. The conversation had started with Owen needing money, and now here he was refusing it. "Why not?"

"Because I'm not graduating." Owen shook his head.

"I mean—I am, technically. But I'm not going to the ceremony."

"Why not?" he asked. "It's such a big deal."

"Not to me," Owen told him. "Not anymore."

Dad's eyes went soft behind his glasses as he finally understood. "Ah," he said, blinking a few times. Outside, the sun emerged from behind the clouds, filling the room with an orangey light, and they sat there as the pancakes went cold on their plates and the clock on the wall—the one from their kitchen back home—marched ahead.

Eventually, Dad shrugged. "Well, who cares about a stupid cap and gown, anyway?"

"Thanks," Owen said gratefully.

"Besides, she would have hated it," he said. "All that pomp and ceremony."

"Circumstance. Pomp and circumstance."

"Whatever," he said. "It's the pomp that's the real problem."

Owen laughed. "She would have loved it."

"Yeah," he agreed. "She would have. But she'd have been proud of you either way. Just like I am."

To Owen's surprise, Dad scraped back his chair then and walked over to one of the drawers beneath the toaster. He paused there for a moment, his shoulders rising and falling, before turning around and holding out a pale blue box.

"Sorry it's not wrapped," he said. "I was going to wait till graduation, but now..."

Owen reached for it, turning it around to where a plastic window showed a jumble of glow-in-the-dark stars. He stared at it, gripping the edges of the box so hard that the edges bent under his fingers.

"I tried to pry the old ones off the ceiling back home," Dad said, returning to his seat. "But they were stuck on pretty tight. I guess whoever lives there next is going to fall asleep under them, too."

There was a lump in Owen's throat. "That's kind of cool."

"Anyway, I'm sure no self-respecting astronomy major goes to sleep under fake stars," Dad said, gesturing at the box, "but you can always put them up here, for whenever you come home."

"Thank you," he said, the words a little wobbly. "I love them."

They were both quiet for a moment, lost in their own separate memories, but then Owen remembered where this had all started, and he cleared his throat.

"Dad?"

His father looked up. "Yeah?"

"This is great," he said, rattling the box. "Really. And I don't want to sound greedy, but the thing is . . . I could still use that money. Or at least some of it."

"For what?" he asked with a frown, and Owen coughed into his hand.

"It's just . . ."

"What?"

306

He sighed. "There's this girl...."

To his astonishment, Dad began to laugh. He took off his glasses and rubbed his eyes, his shoulders shaking.

"What?" Owen asked, confused. "What's so funny?"

"Nothing," he said. "I've just been wondering when you'd get around to telling me about her."

He stared at him, unable to hide his surprise. "You knew?"

"Of course I knew."

"I thought you were too busy...."

"Being sad?"

Owen gave him a rueful grin. "Well...yeah."

"You know what made me less sad?"

"What?"

"Seeing you happy," he told him. "And for a while there, it seemed like those postcards were the only things that did the trick."

Owen wasn't sure what to say, but before he could find the words, Dad leaned forward in his seat, reaching into his back pocket for his cracked leather wallet, which he tossed onto the table. It landed heavily beside the bottle of syrup and they both stared at it for a moment. Then Dad raised his glass of orange juice in a toast.

"Happy graduation," he said. "Now go get her."

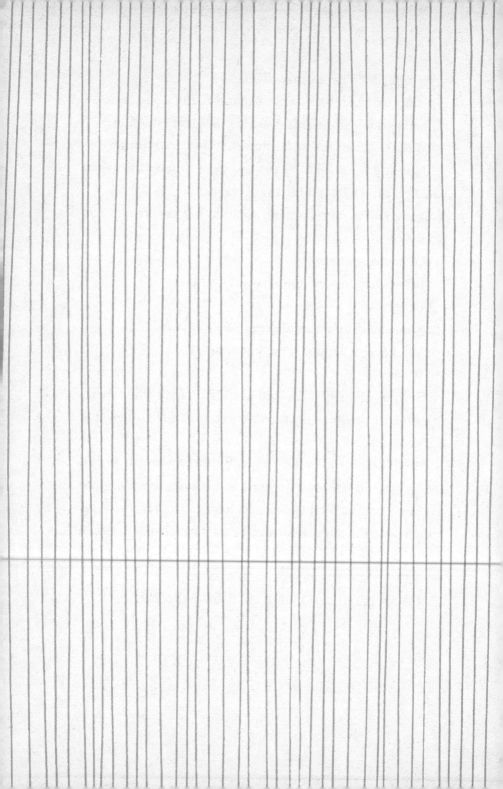

Lucy woke in the last hour of the flight, blinking into the gray haze of the quiet airplane. Beside her, the window shade was open a few inches, and she yawned as she looked out at the steep banks of clouds moving past like dreamy mountain ranges. On the screen in front of her, a timer ticked down the minutes until they reached New York. It wouldn't be long.

For sixteen years, Lucy had hardly ventured off the island of Manhattan, and now, eight months and five countries later, she was finally returning. She reached for the bag at her feet, pulling out her old copy of *The Catcher in the Rye*—her security blanket, her teddy bear—but instead of opening it, she just held it in her lap, gripping the edges.

Soon, she would be seeing the apartment where she grew up, the building she'd lived in her whole life, and the neighborhood she'd known so well, but it didn't feel the way she thought it would. It didn't feel like going home.

A part of her would always love New York, but she'd

loved Edinburgh, too, and now London. And if you were to set her down in Paris or Rome or Prague or any of the other places they'd visited, she was certain she'd find a way to fall in love with those, too.

All these years, she'd imagined her parents were out there in the world trying to take in as much as possible: photos and stories and memories, check marks on a list of countries and pins on a globe. But what she hadn't understood until now was that they'd left pieces of themselves in all those places, too. They'd made a little home for themselves wherever they went, and now Lucy would do the same.

But first, there was New York. The little cartoon airplane on the screen inched out across the blue of the map and toward the green, and Lucy ran a finger along the cracked spine of the book in her lap, closing her eyes.

At first, she'd tried telling her parents that she'd simply changed her mind about going back for the summer.

"Not for the whole time," she said one afternoon as they strolled through Kensington Gardens, enjoying the rare sunshine and the even rarer appearance of Dad in daylight hours. "I was just thinking it would actually be kind of nice to visit, you know?"

Along the edge of the pond, a trio of ducks sat honking at everyone who passed by, and Dad watched them intently, his mouth turned down at the edges.

"Wish I could go back for a visit," he said, squinting at the water.

But Mom only raised her eyebrows. "What kind of visit?"

"I don't know," Lucy said. "Maybe just to see some sights...or some friends."

At this, Mom stopped short, her hands on her hips. "Some friends?"

Lucy nodded.

"In New York?" she asked, then turned to Dad without bothering to wait for an answer. "Are you buying this?"

He glanced over at her with a blank look. "What?"

"Mom," Lucy said with a groan. "It would only be for a few days."

"And you'd be there all by yourself?"

Lucy dropped her gaze. "Yeah," she said to the gravel path.

"Nope," Mom said. "No way."

Dad looked from one to the other as if this were some kind of sporting event where he didn't quite understand the rules. "I think Lucy's perfectly capable of being there on her own," he said. "It's not like she hasn't done it before."

"Yes," Mom said in a measured tone, "but this time, there's a boy in the picture."

Lucy let out a strangled noise.

"A boy?" Dad said, as if the concept had never occurred to him. "What boy?"

"He's in town that first week of June," Lucy admitted, ignoring him as she turned back to Mom. "He thinks I'll be there already, because I told him that a million years ago, and he wants to meet up...."

Mom was watching her with an unreadable expression. "And you really want to see him."

Lucy nodded miserably. "And I really want to see him."

Dad shook his head. "What boy?"

There was a long pause while Mom seemed to consider this, and then—finally, amazingly—her face softened.

"*What boy?*" Dad had asked again.

Now Lucy's seat shook as Mom leaned over the top of it from the row behind her. "Hi," she said. "Sleep well?"

She swiveled to look at her. "Did you?"

"No," Mom said, but her eyes were shining. "I'm too excited."

"Really?"

"Really," she said with a grin. "It seems that distance does indeed make the heart grow fonder."

"I think that's absence."

Mom shrugged. "Either way."

Lucy turned back to the window, where the plane had broken free of the clouds, and the blue-gray ocean swept out beneath them. When she pressed her cheek to the glass, she could see ahead to where it met the land, stopping abruptly at the edge of New York. "Not a whole lot of distance now."

"That's okay," Mom said, sitting back down, so that she spoke through the space between seats, her voice close to

Lucy's ear. "Someone once told me it's best to see a city from the ground up."

They left the water behind, the scene below becoming a grid of grayish buildings, and made a wide sweeping turn as they moved inland, the plane tipping leisurely to one side so that Lucy could see the rivers that cut through the land like veins.

As the ground rushed up at them, she remembered her father's advice about calling the car company as soon as they landed, and she sat forward, reaching for her bag. In her wallet, there was a business card with the number, which her dad had carried around in his own wallet for years. It was fuzzy at the corners and bent across the middle, but he'd handed it to her with pride.

"This is what we always used to get home to you after every trip," he said. "Now that you've become something of a traveler, too, I'm officially passing the baton." He pulled her into a hug and kissed her on the forehead. "Say hi to New York for me."

As she slid the card carefully from the folds of her wallet, she felt the lump at the bottom of the change purse. Over the past months, she'd become so used to the shape of it that she'd nearly forgotten what it was, but now she pulled it out, twisting the cigarette in her fingers. It was a little bit flattened now, crushed by the months spent tucked beneath all those heavy British coins, but it was still mostly intact, and she studied it, remembering how she'd found it the morning after the blackout. She brought it to her nose and inhaled deeply, thinking that it smelled a bit like Owen, and then—before the flight attendant could remind her that there was no smoking on board the plane—she wedged it back inside her wallet, her chest suddenly light.

Out the window, she could see that they were circling over Brooklyn now, but in the distance, the spiky outline of Manhattan rose up in an arrangement of towering buildings and valleys made out of vast green parks, all of it bordered by two rivers like a pair of cupped hands. And as they dropped lower in the sky, she could see the outlines of roads and parking lots and backyards, all of them fanning out around the heart of the city, where people were busy going on with their lives, walking and eating and laughing and working, and somewhere below, in the middle of it all, there was Owen: nothing but a yellow dot from above, waiting just for her.

There was traffic on the way in from the airport. Owen leaned against the window of the bus as it inched toward the Lincoln Tunnel, watching the long chain of cars spitting clouds of exhaust into the afternoon heat. Above him, beyond the tunnel and across the Hudson River, the city seemed to shimmer. From where he sat behind the smudged glass, it looked almost like a mirage, the kind of place where you could forever draw closer without ever actually reaching it.

But Owen knew he'd get there eventually. And he had plenty of time. He wasn't meeting Lucy until noon tomorrow, which meant he had the rest of the day to prepare. His dad had given him enough money for a cheap hotel room, but Owen planned to spend the night up on the roof anyway; if there was ever a place that had felt like home in the city, that was it, and there was nowhere else he'd rather be tonight.

The plan was simple. When he arrived at Port Authority,

he'd take the subway up to Seventy-Second Street and see if the back door to the building was open. Sometimes, if you caught the maintenance guys at the right time, it was easy to slip in that way, and Owen had often gone that route just to avoid the uncomfortable splendor of the lobby. If it happened to be locked, he planned to walk in through the front door, say hello to whichever doorman was on duty, then walk straight over to the elevator like he belonged there, though it was obvious he never had. If anyone asked where he was going, he'd give Lucy's name, which wasn't a lie, since he'd be there to see her the next day, and then he'd head straight up to the roof.

In the morning, he'd go around the corner to the gym that was always offering free trials, where he'd take a shower, change into clean clothes, then buy some flowers on the way back and wait for her in the lobby.

His head felt light as he thought about it, and in the cramped space of the bus, his knee jangled against the back of the seat in front of him. He'd been like this ever since Dad dropped him off at the airport this morning, giving him a bear hug and wishing him luck. On the flight, he'd been so rattled that he spilled his orange juice, drenching not only himself but the lady beside him. He still smelled faintly of sour citrus.

It wasn't that he was nervous to see Lucy. It was more that he didn't know what this was to her, and there was something scary in that. Just because he knew what *he* wanted now didn't mean that she did, too. And just

316

because he'd made up an excuse to fly all the way across the country didn't mean that she was equally excited.

That first time, during the blackout, they'd met as strangers. Then in San Francisco, they'd met as friends, eager to find out whether the strange magnetic pull they felt toward each other was real or an illusion.

But this time, Owen wasn't sure what to think.

When there was nothing but space between you, everything felt like a leap.

As the bus began to ease into the Lincoln Tunnel, the phrase came to him all at once, pulled from a memory like an echo: *It is what it is.*

He smiled as he remembered Lucy's objection to the words, but he realized now that she was wrong. It was true that things could always change. But it was also true that some things remained as they were, and this was one of them: nine months ago, he'd met a girl in an elevator, and she'd been on his mind ever since.

All around him, the other passengers were blinking into the deep black of the tunnel, but not Owen. He knew exactly what he wanted, and he could see it just as clearly in the dark.

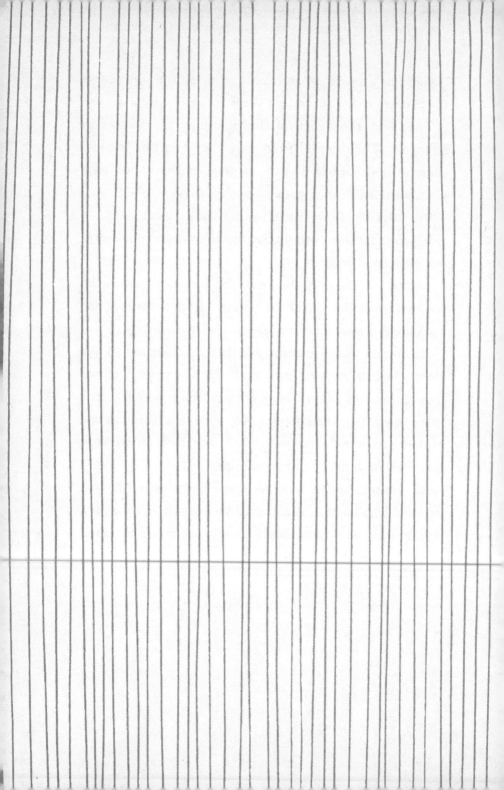

They stood in the quiet of the apartment, the last of the day's light coming through the windows at a slant, and neither spoke. Finally, Lucy dropped her bag, and the sound of it seemed to echo for a long time.

"It looks the same," she said, not sure whether she meant that as a good thing or a bad thing. The place had a hushed quality to it, left on its own all this time with only the occasional cleaning lady for company. She kept half expecting to hear her brothers laughing in the next room, or the sound of her father's voice as the front door creaked open. "It doesn't *feel* the same, though."

"It's just been so long," her mother said, trailing a hand along the back of the couch as she walked over to the window. "Too long."

Lucy glanced at her, where she was silhouetted against the orange sky, the sun burning itself down in the reflections behind her. "It's been forever," she said, and Mom looked over her shoulder.

"Not quite," she said with a smile. "Maybe just half a forever."

Once they'd walked through the apartment from end to end—poking their heads in the bathrooms and laughing at the things they'd left behind, surveying bedrooms and rummaging through the cabinets like tourists in their own home, picking it over for memories and souvenirs, marveling at the sheer oddity of being back after so long—Lucy announced that she was going out.

"You're welcome to come..." she said, but she trailed off in a way that made Mom laugh.

"Go," she said. "I know you're just going to wander endlessly, and my feet will only get tired." She paused, glancing out the window, where the sky had gone from pink to gray. "Just be careful, okay? It's been a while since we've been in the big, bad city."

Lucy smiled. "It's not so bad."

"Where do you go, anyway?" she asked. "When you walk?"

"Nowhere," she said with a shrug, then changed her mind. "Everywhere," she corrected, and they left it at that.

In the hallway, she punched the button for the elevator, already trying to decide where to go first—Riverside Park or Central Park, uptown or downtown—but when the doors opened with that familiar *ding* and she stepped inside, she found herself stalled there. Her hand was inches from the button that would take her to the lobby, but instead—without even thinking about it—she sent the car moving up, the ground lifting beneath her feet, and she raised her chin and watched the dial go from the twenty-fourth floor to the twenty-fifth and on and on until the doors opened onto the little hallway that formed an entrance to the roof.

She had no idea why she had come. Tomorrow, she would see Owen. In less than twenty-four hours, they would be together. It wasn't long to wait. But still, when she'd thought of him over the past months, this had been the backdrop, unfamiliar and slightly magical, and now she couldn't stop herself from wanting to see it again.

He'd told her once that the door was left open sometimes, and she'd been amazed at this, astonished that she could have lived her whole life in a building and never known such a place existed.

Now she held her breath as she twisted the metal knob of the door, and when it turned, she used her shoulder to open it the rest of the way, then grabbed a nearby brick to use as a doorstop, propping it open a few inches so it wouldn't lock behind her.

When she turned around, she felt her lungs expand, happy for no other reason than to be alone up here beneath a sky like a chalkboard, the night still new and unwritten. The city was spread before her, all twinkling lights and staggering scale, and with the breeze on her face and the distant fog of noise below, it took her a moment to register the click of the door falling shut somewhere behind her. She spun around, her thoughts wild as her thumping heart—expecting to find herself stranded up here, cursing herself for not wedging the brick better—but then she saw the figure by the door, and all this melted away.

"You're early," he said, but it didn't feel that way to Lucy.

To her, it felt like it had been forever.

45

It was hard to tell exactly how it had happened or who had moved first, but suddenly there they were: standing only inches apart in the middle of the inky-black roof, the air between them electric. Owen opened his mouth to say something, to explain his presence here, to make some sort of a joke, but then he changed his mind, because he was tired of talking, at least for the moment, done passing words between them. All he wanted to do right now was kiss her.

And so—at last—he did.

When he moved closer, her eyes flickered with surprise before falling shut, and he closed his, too, so that as their lips met and their hands found each other's, it was once again just the two of them in the dark, a blackness complete but for the sparks behind his eyelids, which were so bright they might as well have been stars.

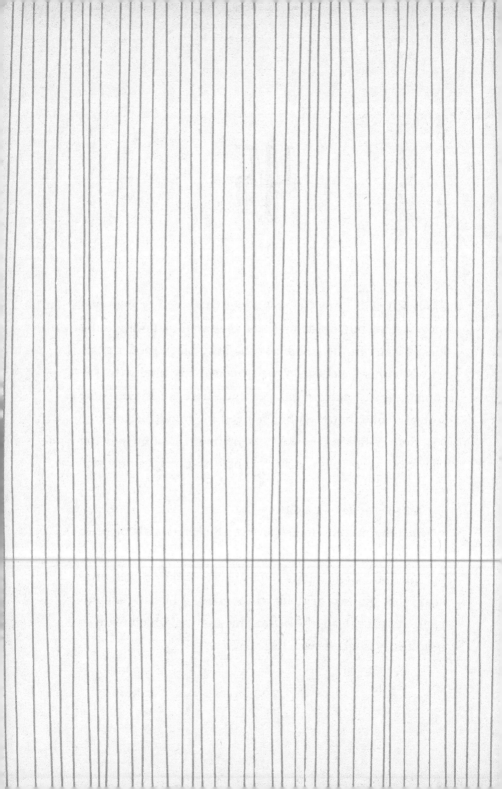

46

"No seriously," he said, pulling away after what felt like no time at all. "You're early. I had all these plans. We were going to meet in the lobby and then have a picnic in the park, and then we were gonna get ice cream at that place—the one from the blackout—and come up here to eat it, and then—"

Lucy, still inches from his face, leaned back with a smile. "Well, we're already up here, so . . ."

"But there was going to be ice cream."

"I don't care about ice cream."

"And a picnic."

"Owen," she said, laughing.

"And we were going to lie on our backs and stare at the sky and look for stars."

"There are no stars," she pointed out, "but we can certainly stare at the sky."

He gave her a helpless look. "But I had all these plans. . . ."

"It's okay," she said, taking his hand again. "This is better."

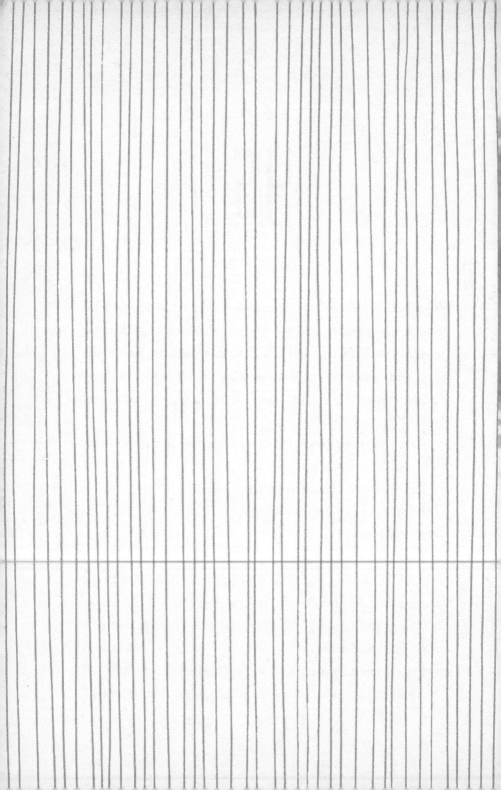

47

They sat together against the ledge, their knees touching.

"So do you come up here a lot?" he asked, and Lucy glanced over at him, her face difficult to read. She seemed to be weighing something, and it took her a moment to decide on an answer.

"Actually," she said, "I just got in this morning."

Owen stared at her. "I thought you were..."

"No," she said. "Our plans changed."

"So you're just here—"

"For a couple of days," she said, ducking her head. "To see you."

He smiled. "Really?"

She nodded, wincing already, and he understood why; he knew better than anyone how it sounded, realized how crazy it was to fly halfway around the world to see a person you hardly knew. But he also knew exactly what to say to make her feel better.

"Me too," he said, moving close so that there was only the rustle of clothing and limbs and beating hearts as he looped an arm over her shoulder. "I only came to see you."

"So," she said later, after the sky had gone fully dark and the birds had all gone to bed and the lights of the city made the whole world glow. "What else don't I know about you?"

He looked thoughtful. "I can juggle."

"No, I meant—wait, you can?"

"Yup. And I also hate peanut butter."

"Who hates peanut butter?"

"People with refined palates," he said. "And I know some good card tricks. And jokes."

"Like what?"

He considered this a moment. "Why did the scarecrow win the Nobel Prize?"

"Why?" she asked, wrinkling her nose.

"For being outstanding in his field."

In spite of herself, Lucy laughed, but Owen's face had gone serious again.

"And I decided to go to college next year."

At this, she sat up. "Really?"

"Really," he said with a smile. "University of Washington."

"That's perfect," she said. "Your dad must be really happy."

"He is," he said. "We both are."

"Okay, then," she said, shaking her head. "So there's apparently a *lot* I don't know about you. But I was actually talking about the smoking thing."

Beside her, Owen stiffened. "What smoking thing?"

"The morning after the blackout," Lucy explained, "there was a cigarette on the kitchen floor. I'd totally forgotten about it, but I found it again on the plane, and—"

His face had gone ashen. "You still have it?"

"Yeah," she said, a little embarrassed. "I guess it was sort of like a souvenir. . . ."

"So you kept it," he said, watching her intently.

She nodded. "It's downstairs in my wallet."

To her surprise, a look of genuine relief passed over his face. "Thank you."

"Sure," she said, frowning. "But what's the deal? You've been waiting for a smoke all this time?"

"Something like that," he said, his eyes shining, and she realized just how much there was she didn't know about him. He was like one of her novels, still unfinished and best understood in the right place and at the right time.

She couldn't wait to read the rest.

Later, they lay on their backs, their shoulders pressed together, laughing up at the charcoal sky. There were tears running down the side of Owen's face.

"Wait," he said, trying to catch his breath, the whole thing inexplicably hilarious. "You live in *London* now?"

"Yeah," she said, curling into him, giggling uncontrollably. "And you live in *Seattle*?"

"Yeah," he said. "What's so funny about that?"

"Nothing," she said. "What's so funny about London?"

"Nothing," he said, and just like that, they began to laugh again.

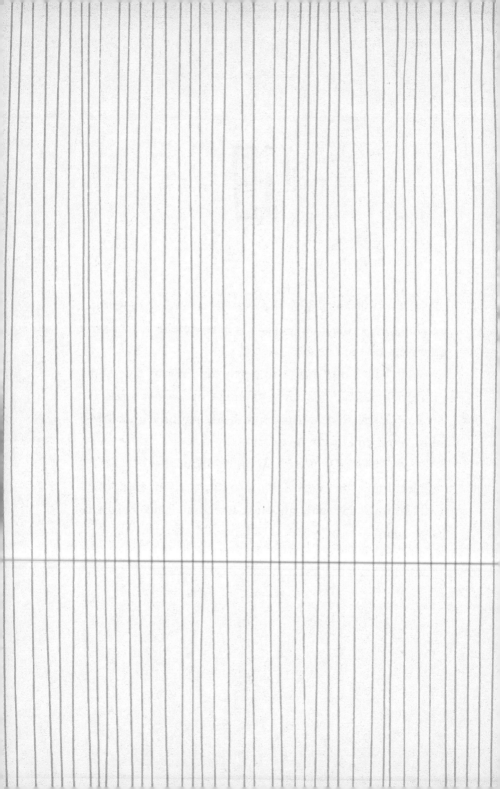

"Right there," he said even later, pointing up.

"Really?"

"Yeah, I see one."

She squinted. "Where?"

"You don't see it?" he said, using his hands to trace something across the night sky, which was fixed tight as a lid over the simmering city. "It's right there."

"That doesn't help," she said, propping herself up on her elbows.

"It's—I think—it might be—" He paused dramatically. "Yup, it's the Big Dipper."

She gave him a dubious look.

"No, really," he said, grabbing her hand and using it to draw shapes across the middle of all the uninterrupted black. "There's the tail, and there's the cup. It's a cup, right?"

"I'm pretty sure it's a ladle," she told him. "But you're the science guy."

"A cup, then," he said, moving her hand to the left and making three dots. "And there's Orion's belt."

"You're crazy," she said. "There's nothing."

"What happened to all that relentless optimism?" he said. "Aren't you supposed to be the positive one?"

"Right," she said, looking up again. "Okay."

He was studying her closely. "Anything?"

"I think, maybe...yup, I see one."

"Where?"

She took his hand and guided it toward the highest part of the sky. "Right there," she said. "It's a big one. And it's really bright...."

When he spoke, there was laughter in his voice. "That's the moon."

"Is it?"

"It is," he confirmed, and she smiled.

"Even better."

51

"There's something else you don't know," he said later. Her head was resting on his chest, and he was running a hand through her hair.

"What's that?" she asked, stifling a yawn.

"You don't know this yet," he whispered, his mouth close to her ear, "but we're going to have an amazing week. We're gonna walk across the Brooklyn Bridge and go see the Statue of Liberty and wander around Times Square like a couple of tourists." He paused. "Or a couple of pigeons."

There was a smile in her voice. "And we'll get you an *I ♥ NY* T-shirt."

"The T-shirt is optional," he said, which made her laugh.

"And then what?" she asked, though this time the words were quieter, smaller; they were heavy with things unspoken: questions without answers and promises without assurances.

Owen wanted to say this: *And then we'll be together forever.* Or this: *And then we'll live happily ever after.*

But he couldn't. Instead, he fixed his eyes on the empty sky, feeling his once heavy heart go floating off like a balloon.

"And then we'll have to go home," he said eventually, because it was the truth, and after everything they'd been through, it was the only thing he could give her.

They were both silent for a long time. She twisted at a piece of his T-shirt, then let it go and laid her palm flat against his chest, right over his heart, and he could suddenly feel it again: the steady thump of it drowning out all his other thoughts. It was more drumbeat than countdown, more metronome than ticking clock, and he felt himself carried forward with each muffled beat, as if hope were a rhythm, a song he'd only just discovered.

He tucked a loose strand of hair behind her ear, then leaned forward and kissed the top of her head. "But it'll be okay," he promised. "We'll keep writing. And we'll figure out a way to see each other again."

"You think so?"

"I do," he said, the words thick in his throat. "We'll make it happen. Maybe I'll come to London. Or you can come to Seattle. Or we'll meet up somewhere else entirely."

"Okay," she said after a moment. "Let's make it somewhere exciting then. Like Saint Petersburg. Or Athens. Or New Zealand."

"Or Alaska," he suggested. "We could wander around the tundra."

"Like a couple of penguins."

"Exactly," he said with a laugh.

"Or maybe Buenos Aires."

He nodded. "Or Paris, so you can show me the exact center of the city."

"And you can make a wish, too."

"What was yours?" he asked. "To go back again someday?"

"Not exactly."

"What then?"

She lifted her head to look at him. "To come back here someday."

He smiled. "The only problem is, I think we're about fifteen yards off," he said, pointing at the spot where they'd sat the last time, where he'd made a star appear in the unlikeliest of places. "I'm pretty sure the exact center of the world is just over there."

"I don't know," she said, and he could see that she was smiling, too. "I think this might be it."

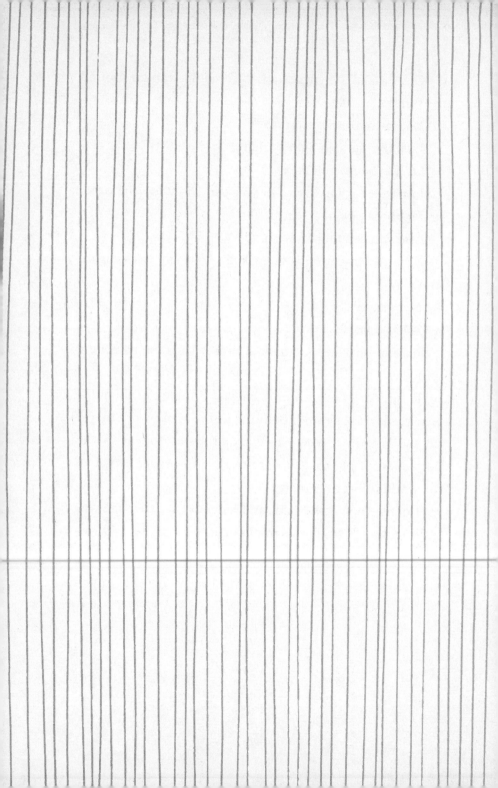

ACKNOWLEDGMENTS

This book would not have happened without the guidance, encouragement, and support of so many people, including Jennifer Joel, Elizabeth Bewley, Farrin Jacobs, Megan Tingley, Frankie Gray, Stephanie Thwaites, Sophie Harris, Binky Urban, Hallie Patterson, Sam Eades, Libby McGuire, Jennifer Hershey, Josie Freedman, Liz Casal, Pam Gruber, Clay Ezell, and Jenni Hamill. I'm also very grateful to my pal Owen Atkins for allowing me to borrow his name, and to my family: Mom, Dad, Kelly, and Errol. Cheers to all of you.

Turn the page for a sneak peek
at Jennifer E. Smith's new book,
*Hello, Goodbye,
and Everything
in Between.*

Prologue

When Aidan opens the door, Clare rises onto her tiptoes to kiss him, and for a moment, it feels like any other night.

"Hi," she says, once she's stepped back again, and he smiles.

"Hi."

They stare at each other for a few long seconds, neither quite sure how to begin.

"So," Clare says eventually.

Aidan attempts a smile. "So."

"I guess this is it."

He nods. "I guess it is."

"The last night," she says, and he tilts his head at her.

"You know it doesn't have to be."

"Aidan..."

"I know, I know," he says, holding up his hands. "But you can't really blame me, right? I've still got a little bit of time left to change your mind."

"Only twelve hours," she says, glancing at her watch. "I can't believe that's all we have left."

"And that's only if we don't sleep."

"We're definitely not wasting any time on sleep," she tells him, pulling a folded piece of notebook paper from the pocket of her dress. "We have way too much to do."

Aidan raises an eyebrow. "That better not be a list of reasons why we should break up...."

"It's not," she says as she hands it over to him, watching as he scans the page with a bemused expression. "I just figured maybe we could use a plan."

"And this is it?"

She nods. "This is it."

"Okay," he says, taking a deep breath. "Then I guess we should get going."

Together, they start to walk in the direction of the car, but halfway there, Clare stops short, suddenly and unaccountably nervous, her heart drumming hard in her chest. She looks over at Aidan with slightly panicked eyes. "This is kind of crazy, isn't it?"

"What?" he asks.

"That we leave tomorrow," she says, her voice rising a little. "That after all this time, we only have twelve hours left. I mean...we're finally here, you know? At the end of the road."

"Or," he reminds her, "the beginning."

Clare doesn't say anything; she wants desperately to believe him, but standing here on the edge of something so big, it seems impossible.

"Trust me," Aidan says, reaching for her hand. "A lot can happen in twelve hours."

Stop #1

The High School

6:24 PM

In the car, Aidan pauses before turning the key in the ignition, and for a brief second, Clare lets herself imagine that they're on their way out to dinner or a movie, or anywhere, really, even just the kind of aimless, purposeless drive that's been the only thing on the agenda so many times before. Their nights always seem to begin in this way: the two of them sitting in Aidan's dusty Volvo, trying to decide what to do.

But tonight is different.

It's not a beginning at all. Tonight is an ending.

Aidan's hand is still hovering over the keys, and Clare glances down at the piece of notebook paper on her lap. During the short walk over to the Gallaghers' house—a walk she's made about a thousand times in the past two years—she folded and refolded the page so many times that it's already soft and wrinkled.

"Maybe we should just take off or something," Aidan says, looking at her sideways. "Just keep driving till we hit Canada."

"Canada, huh?" Clare says, raising her eyebrows. "Are we going on the lam?"

He shrugs. "Fine. Maybe just Wisconsin then."

She reaches over, resting a hand on the back of his neck, where his reddish hair is newly trimmed, cut close in a way that makes him look older somehow. "I'm leaving first thing in the morning," she says gently. "The car's already packed. And your flight's at noon."

"I know," he says, but he won't look at her. His eyes are fixed on the closed door of the garage. "That's my point. Let's skip it all."

"College?" she says with a smile, letting her hand drop.

"Yeah," he says, nodding now. "Who needs it? Let's run away together instead. Just for a year or so. We'll start a new life. In the country. Or better yet, a deserted island."

"You *would* look nice in a hula skirt."

"I'm serious," he says, though she knows he's not. He's just desperate and sad, nervous and excited, wildly unsure of everything as they barrel toward the invisible line that will separate their lives into a before and an after. Same as her.

"Aidan," she says quietly, and this time, his eyes find hers. "This is happening. Tomorrow. No matter what."

"I know," he admits.

"Which is why we have to figure out what to do about it."

"Right, but—"

"Nope," she says, cutting him off. She holds up the piece of paper. "No more talking. We've been talking all summer, and it's gotten us nowhere. We've just been going around in circles: Stay together, break up, stay together, break up...."

"Stay together," Aidan finishes, grinning a little.

Clare laughs. "The point is that we're hopeless. So no more talking. For now, let's just drive, okay?"

He leans forward, reaching for the keys, and then turns over the engine.

"Okay," he says.

Their first stop isn't far away, and they drive in silence, all the familiar sights of the town slipping by outside the window: the bridge over the ravine, the road lined with pine trees, the gazebo in the park. Clare tries to absorb each one of them as they whip past, because by the time she returns at Thanksgiving, she knows she might be someone entirely different, and she suspects that—because of that—all this might look different, too. And something about that scares her. So one by one, she tries to pin them all in place: each tree, each road, each house.

This is how it all started this morning, when she woke up in a panic about how many goodbyes she still had to say. Not just the people: Aidan, of course; and her best friend, Stella; Aidan's sister, Riley; and his pal, Scotty; plus the handful of their other friends who are still around.

But there was also the town itself. All the landmarks that had been the background to her childhood. She couldn't leave without going to the village green one more time, or getting one last slice of pizza at their favorite spot. She couldn't possibly take off without one more trip to the beach, one final party, one last drive past the high school.

And so she made a list. But it didn't take long for her to realize that most of the things that meant something to her were inextricably tied to Aidan. This place was a ghost town of sorts, littered with milestones and memories from their nearly two-year relationship.

So it had turned into something else, this night: a nostalgia tour, a journey into the past, a walk down memory lane. It would be a way for her to say goodbye to this town where she'd lived her whole life, and maybe—somehow— to Aidan, too.

She can't help shivering a little at the thought of this, and she presses the button on the car door, closing her window.

Aidan glances over. "Too windy?" he asks, rolling up his own window, and she nods. But it's more than that. It's the same icy dread that fills her each time she starts to imagine it; not just the goodbye, but everything that's to come afterward: the hurt that will surely trail them to opposite coasts, so strong that she can already feel it even now, when he's only inches away.

The truth is, she's still waiting for her heart to get on board with the decision her head has made. But she's running out of time.

When they reach the long drive leading up to the high school, Aidan frowns. "So tell me," he says as they pull up to the front of the sprawling building and into one of the empty parking spots. "Why exactly are we here?"

It's early evening on a Friday in the middle of August, and the school sits hushed and empty. Though she spent four years here, Clare's already having trouble remembering the feel of the place when it's full of students, everyone spilling out the wooden doors and onto the front lawn. It's only been two months, but somehow, all that seems like a very long time ago.

"Because," she says, turning to Aidan, "it's the first stop on the list."

"I know *that*," he says. "But how come?"

"It's where we met," she explains as she gets out of the car. "And the idea is to start at the beginning."

"So this is a *chronological* scavenger hunt then."

"It's not a scavenger hunt at all. Think of it more like a refresher course."

"A refresher course in what?"

She smiles at him over the top of the car. "Us."

"So kind of like our greatest hits," he says, twirling the keys on his finger as he walks around to her, and for a moment, it's like none of the rest of it happened. Just now, just for this second, he's not the person she knows best in the world, but the new kid again, the one who'd shown up on the very first day of junior year, all red hair and freckles and ridiculous height, appearing out of nowhere and turning her inside out.

The slanted light is at his back, forcing Clare to squint as she studies him for a few long seconds. "Did I ever tell you," she says, "that I used to be late to English every single day, just so I could bump into you on your way to Pre-calc?"

"Well, now I feel kind of bad," Aidan says, his eyes creasing at the corners. "If I'd known *that*, I would've tried to be more punctual."

"It wouldn't have mattered," she says, remembering the way he used to come loping around the corner, his books tucked under his arm like a football, always missing the bell, at first because he'd get lost, and later because he'd always manage to lose track of time. "I would've waited all day. I probably would've waited forever."

She's not serious, of course, but there's something wistful in his smile.

"Yeah?" he says.

She shrugs. "Yeah."

"I wish you still would," he says, though not spitefully; he says it quietly, evenly, a simple truth, an earnest request.

But it still leaves a mark.

"You have to stop doing that," Clare says. "Stop being the romantic one."

Aidan looks surprised. "What?"

"It's not fair," she says. "I hate that you get to be the good guy here. It's not like I *want* to break up with you. It kills me just thinking about it, but I'm trying to be practical. Starting tomorrow, we're gonna be a million miles away from each other, and it doesn't make sense to do this any other way. So you have to stop."

"Stop...being romantic?" Aidan asks, looking amused.

"Yes."

"Have you ever thought that maybe you need to stop being so practical?"

Clare sighs. "One of us has to be."

"The one who planned a romantic scavenger hunt for our last night?" he says, looping an arm around her shoulders and giving her a little squeeze.

She rolls her eyes. "It's not a scavenger hunt."

"Well, whatever it is, I think it's suspiciously romantic for someone so annoyingly practical," he says, drawing her closer. Her head only comes up to his chest, so she has to tip her chin up to look at him. When she does, he leans down to kiss her, and even though they've kissed a thousand times before—have kissed, even, in this very parking lot—it still makes her stomach go wobbly, and she's seized by a sudden worry over how few of these they have left.

Together, they walk up the front steps of the school, and Clare tugs on the handle of the big wooden door, but it refuses to budge. She knocks a few times, in case there might be a security guard inside, but nobody answers.

"It's still a couple weeks till classes start," Aidan points out. "I'm sure nobody's here on a Friday night."

"I thought maybe there'd be summer school or something...."

"Let's just skip to whatever's next."

Clare shakes her head, not sure how to explain that this is the whole point of the night. To fit two whole years into one final evening; to dump all the pieces out of the box and then put them back together again in the right order so that they can see the whole thing spread out before them.

And so that they can say goodbye.

But to do that, they need to start at the beginning.

"No," she says, looking up at the stone building. "There has to be a way in. It's the first place we saw each other...."

Aidan smiles. "Mr. Coady's Earth Science class."

"Exactly," she says. "Not that you remember."

"Of course I do."

"You do not. At least not that first day."

"Oh, come on," Aidan says, laughing. "How could anyone not remember *you*?"

"Impossible," she agrees, though she knows that's not true. Clare's been called a lot of things—smart and funny, driven and talented—but memorable certainly isn't one of them. The most important things about her—the ones she's most proud of—are apparent only once you get to know her. At first glance, she's almost entirely unremarkable: brown hair and brown eyes, average height and ordinary looks. Mostly, she just blends in, which has always been fine with her: You could do a lot worse in high school. But that meant that before Aidan, no boy had ever really noticed her before.

That first day, he'd sat down in the desk right behind hers. The teacher was handing out geodes to pass around the room, and when it was her turn with one of them, Clare cupped it in her hands. It looked like a regular old rock on the outside, but inside, it was full of glittering purple crystals. When she turned to pass it to the new kid, he kept his eyes on the stone. But later—after he'd finally noticed her, after they'd both realized that this was the start of something—she would come back to that moment again and again. Because that's how she felt when she was with him—like she'd been a rock her whole life, ordinary and dull, and it wasn't until she met him that something cracked open inside her, and just like that, she began to shine.

"We have to get inside," she says now, feeling oddly desperate.

Aidan gives her a strange look. "Does it really matter?"

"Yes," she says, rattling the door handle once more, though it's clearly useless. "We have to start this thing right."

She knows he doesn't understand why this is so important to her, and she's not sure she could tell him even if she tried. It's just that the clock is ticking down fast toward tomorrow, when everything will change. And this—this plan for their last night together—was supposed to be the one thing she could control.

All summer, Clare has been poring over class descriptions and campus maps and messages from her new roommate, trying to get a clearer picture of what her life will soon look like. But as much as she's read, as much as she's tried to find out, it's impossible to imagine the details. And it's the not knowing that's the hardest part.

There's so much of it, too. She doesn't know whether she'll be able to balance Intro to Psychology with History of Japan, or whether she'll find someone to sit with in the dining hall during those first few crucial days, when loose collections of strangers start to solidify into groups of friends like hardening cement.

She doesn't know whether she'll get along with her

roommate, a girl from New York City named Beatrice St. James, who seems to only want to talk about what bands she's been seeing this summer, and who—Clare suspects—will end up wallpapering their room with concert posters.

She doesn't know whether it's a mistake to leave her winter coat behind until Thanksgiving break, whether she'll find it unbearable to share a bathroom with twenty other people, whether girls from the East Coast will dress differently than the girls here in Chicago. She doesn't know whether she'll stand out or blend in, sink or swim, feel homesick or independent, happy or miserable.

And mostly, she doesn't know if she'll be able to survive all this without having Aidan on the other end of the phone.

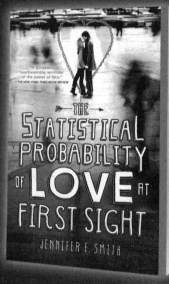